W9-ACV-283

Acclaim for
OWEN SHEERS's
I SAW A MAN

"An extended examination of grief, responsibility, guilt and redemption. . . . The suspense is almost physically frustrating. . . . Sheers knows when to let the line out and when to reel it in."   —*The New York Times*

"Gripping and stylish. . . . Sheers's narrative is one of finely tuned suspense that erupts into visceral drama. . . . But this is also a novel driven by ideas. . . . Bold and satisfying."
—*Daily Mail* (UK)

"Taut as a thriller, but resonant with motifs of intimacy and distance, guilt and redemption, and the nature of stories and storytelling. . . . It twists and turns and plays its cards close to its chest, showing its full hand only in the final pages, when we are forced to reassess everything that has gone before."
—*The Guardian* (UK)

"Deeply poignant. . . . A profound meditation on memory and mourning, Sheers's novel captures the 'unbearably fragile' nature of joy."   —*The Observer* (UK)

"Sheers's thriller is driven as much by subtle ideas as suspense. . . . Psychologically astute."   —*The Independent* (UK)

"A genuinely gripping piece of storytelling." —*Financial Times*

"Extraordinarily tense and powerful, and beautifully written."
—*The Mail on Sunday* (UK)

"A powerful moral thriller. . . . Sheers skillfully drip-feeds the reader his characters' secrets and lies, including a remarkable sequence leading up to the book's central, shocking moment of revelation. *I Saw a Man*'s ending is similarly bravura, elegantly throwing into new light much of what has gone before."

—*Literary Review*

"Manages to capture the rhythms, and fragility, of love and family; Sheers is quietly moving on the timeless topic of grief. . . . Sheers really does pull off the oft-trumpeted blending of the personal and political." —*Independent on Sunday* (UK)

"Paul Auster meets Ian McEwan—a great success."

—*NDR Kultur* (Germany)

"Quite simply the most stylish thriller I've read: always intelligent, beautifully made." —Claire Lowdon,
Times Literary Supplement (Book of the Year)

OWEN SHEERS
I SAW A MAN

Owen Sheers is an author, poet, and playwright. His first novel, *Resistance*, was translated into ten languages and adapted into a film. *The Dust Diaries*, his Zimbabwean nonfiction narrative, was shortlisted for the Royal Society of Literature Onaadtje Prize and won the Welsh Book of the Year. His awards for poetry and drama include the Somerset Maugham Award for *Skirrid Hill*; the Amnesty International Freedom of Expression Award for his play *The Two Worlds of Charlie F.*; and the Hay Festival Medal for Poetry and Welsh Book of the Year for *Pink Mist*, which was also a *Guardian* and *Observer* top ten of the year theater selection. *I Saw A Man* was shortlisted for the Prix Femina Étranger. He has been a New York Public Library Cullman Fellow and is currently Professor in Creativity at Swansea University. He lives in Wales with his wife and daughter.

ALSO BY OWEN SHEERS

FICTION
Resistance
White Ravens
The Gospel of Us

NONFICTION
The Dust Diaries
Calon

POETRY
The Blue Book
Skirrid Hill
Pink Mist
A Poet's Guide to Britain (editor)

PLAYS
The Passion
The Two Worlds of Charlie F.
Mametz

I SAW A MAN

OWEN SHEERS

A NOVEL

 ANCHOR CANADA

This book is a work of fiction. Names, characters, businesses, organizations, places, events, and incidents either are the product of the author's imagination or are used fictitiously. Any resemblance to actual persons, living or dead, is entirely coincidental.

Copyright © 2015 Owen Sheers
Anchor Canada edition published 2016

All rights reserved. The use of any part of this publication, reproduced, transmitted in any form or by any means electronic, mechanical, photocopying, recording or otherwise, or stored in a retrieval system without the prior written consent of the publisher—or in the case of photocopying or other reprographic copying, license from the Canadian Copyright Licensing agency—is an infringement of the copyright law.

Anchor Canada is a registered trademark.

Library and Archives Canada Cataloguing in Publication

Sheers, Owen, 1974-, author
    I saw a man / Owen Sheers.

ISBN 978-0-385-68364-7 (pbk.)

    I. Title.

PR6069.H3966I2 2016   823'.92   C2014-907469-7

Book design by Maria Carella
Cover design by Faber
Cover images © PhotosbyAndy / Shutterstock

Printed and bound in the USA

Published in Canada by Anchor Canada,
A division of Random House of Canada Limited,
A Penguin Random House Company

www.penguinrandomhouse.ca

10 9 8 7 6 5 4 3 2 1

Penguin
Random House
ANCHOR CANADA

FOR SAMANTHA

Yesterday, upon the stair,
I saw a man who wasn't there.
He wasn't there again today,
I wish, I wish he'd go away

—from a version of "Antigonish"
by William Hughes Mearns

CHAPTER
ONE

THE EVENT THAT changed all of their lives happened on a Saturday afternoon in June, just minutes after Michael Turner—thinking the Nelsons' house was empty—stepped through their back door. Although it was early in the month, London was blistered under a heat wave. All along South Hill Drive windows hung open, the cars parked on either side hot to the touch, their seams ticking in the sun. A morning breeze had ebbed, leaving the sycamores lining the street motionless. The oaks and beeches on the surrounding Heath were also still. The heat wave was only a week old, but already the taller grass beyond the shade of these trees was bleaching blond.

Michael had found the Nelsons' back door unlocked and ajar. Resting his forearm against its frame, he'd leant in to the gap and called out for his neighbours.

"Josh? Samantha?"

There was no reply. The house absorbed his voice without an echo. He looked down at his old pair of deck shoes, their soles thick with freshly watered soil. He'd been gardening since lunchtime and had come straight over to the Nelsons' without washing. His knees, showing under his shorts, were also smudged with dirt.

Hooking the heel of his left shoe under the toe of his right,

Michael pulled it off. As he did the same with the other, he listened for signs of life inside the house. Again, there was nothing. He looked at his watch—it was twenty past three. He had a fencing lesson on the other side of the Heath at four. It would take him at least half an hour to walk there. He went to push the door wider, but on seeing the soil on his hands, nudged it open with his elbow instead, then stepped inside.

The kitchen was cool and dark, and Michael had to pause for a moment to allow the sunlight to dissolve from his vision. Behind him his neighbours' garden sloped away between a pear tree and a shrunken herbaceous border. The parched lawn tapered to a wooden fence shot through with reeds. Beyond this fence a weeping willow bowed to one of the ponds on the Heath. In the last month these ponds had grown a skin of green duckweed, surprising in its brightness. Just a few minutes earlier, while resting on his heels, Michael had watched a coot as she'd cut her way through it on the far side, her nun's head pumping her forward, a cover of chicks crisscrossing over her wake.

Standing in the kitchen, Michael listened once more. He'd never known Josh and Samantha to leave their house unlocked and not be home. He knew Samantha was away with her sister, Martha, for the weekend. But Josh and the girls, he'd thought, had stayed. The house, though, was silent. The only sounds Michael could hear were from the Heath at his back: a dog barking, the chatter of distant picnics, the splash of a diver from the swimming pond beyond the walkway. Closer, in a nearby garden, he heard a sprinkler begin chopping at the afternoon. Such was the stillness of the house that from where he stood in the kitchen these sounds already had the texture of memory, as if he'd crossed a threshold in time, not of a home.

Perhaps Josh had left a note? Michael went to the fridge to look. It was a broad-shouldered American model in brushed steel, an icemaker embedded in its door. A desk's worth of papers jostled for position across its surface, pinned under a collection of Rothko fridge magnets. Michael scanned the takeaway menus, shopping lists, school notes, but none of them gave any clue as to where Josh might be. He turned from the fridge and looked around the rest of the room, hoping to find something that might explain why the back door was open but no one at home.

Like the rest of their house, Samantha and Josh's kitchen was solid and generous. At its centre the slatted shadow of a venetian blind fell across an island work surface. Around this were an oven, two hobs and a chef's array of utensils. On the other side of a breakfast bar, potted plants fringed a sagging sofa and two armchairs in the conservatory, ochre blinds drawn over its glass. Back within the kitchen itself, an oval dining table occupied the far end of the room, and there, hanging above it, were the Nelsons.

The portrait was in black-and-white, a studio shot taken when Rachel was still a toddler and Lucy a baby. The two children, wearing matching white dresses, sat on their parents' laps. Samantha laughed down at her daughters, her eyes averted from the camera. Josh, however, smiled directly into its lens, his jaw more angular than that of the man Michael knew now. His hair, too, was darker, cut in the same boyish style he still wore, but without the dustings of grey spreading at his temples.

Michael met the gaze of this younger Josh for a moment. He wondered if he should call him and let him know about the open back door. But his phone was in his flat, and Michael didn't know either Josh or Samantha's numbers. And perhaps he shouldn't worry them, anyway? From what he could tell there were no signs of disturbance. The kitchen looked just as it always did.

Michael had known the Nelsons for only seven months by then, but their friendship, once made, had been quick to gather momentum. Over the last few weeks it had felt as if he'd eaten at their table more often than at his own next door. The path that led from their lawn through a break in the hedge to the communal garden of his own block of flats had been indiscernible when he'd first moved in. But now there was already the faint tracing of a track, worn by his feet when he dropped by in the evenings and those of Samantha and the girls when they called for him on the weekends. As a family, the Nelsons had become a settling presence in his life, a vital ballast against all that had gone before. Which is why Michael could be so sure the kitchen hadn't been searched or disturbed. It was the room in which he'd spent the most time with them, where they'd eaten and drunk and where so much of his recent healing had happened. The room where for the first time since he'd lost Caroline he'd learnt, with the help of Josh and Samantha, to remember not just her absence, but also her.

Looking past the family portrait, Michael glanced over the chairs and sideboards in the conservatory. He should probably check the rest of the house, too. This is what he told himself as he went over to the phone and browsed the Post-it notes scattered around its handset. Samantha and Josh wouldn't want him to leave without doing so. But he'd have to be quick. He'd come round only to retrieve a screwdriver he'd lent Josh a few nights before. He needed it to fix a blade for his lesson. Once he'd found it and had checked the other rooms, he'd be gone.

Michael looked at his watch again. It was already almost twenty-five past three. If anything looked amiss he could always call Josh as he walked to his lesson over the Heath. Wherever he was, Michael figured, he and the girls couldn't be too far from the house. Turning from the phone and its scribbled notes, Michael walked towards the door leading into the hallway. As he crossed the kitchen, its terra-cotta tiles cool against his feet, his damp socks left a trail of moist footprints, slow-shrinking behind him as if a wind were covering his tracks.

CHAPTER
TWO

IT WAS JOSH whom Michael had first met, on the same night he'd moved onto South Hill Drive seven months earlier. Michael had never thought he'd live in London again. But when his wife, Caroline, hadn't returned from what should have been a two-week job in Pakistan, he'd eventually decided to sell their cottage in Wales and move back to the capital.

Coed y Bryn was an old Welsh longhouse, a low-ceilinged cottage and barn built into an isolated hillside outside Chepstow. The nearest other building was a rural chapel, used only for weddings and funerals. Woods and sky filled the views from its windows. It was not, Michael was told by his friends, a place to be alone. With Caroline gone, they'd said, he needed people, distraction. Eventually one of her work colleagues, Peter, had offered him a flat to rent in a fifties block overlooking Hampstead Heath. When Peter sent through the details, Michael didn't open the email for days. But then one night, after another long day on his own, he'd uncorked a bottle of red and sat down with his laptop beside the fire. Opening his browser, he'd clicked on Peter's message and looked through its attachments.

The first photograph was of a pair of wide windows, their frames filled with trees and the undulations of the Heath. As an autumn wind buffeted the back of the cottage, the fire crackling beside him, Michael scrolled through the other images—a broad street of Georgian town houses, occasionally interrupted by modern blocks; two sparsely furnished bedrooms; a living area, the carpet stained and worn; an outdated galley kitchen in magnolia and pine.

It was a flat of many lives. Many people had stood at those windows and lain on those beds. With Caroline gone, Michael needed to start again. But he also did not want to start again. So he'd replied to Peter and said yes. Partly because the flat looked more like a holding pattern than a new beginning. But also because he knew Peter was only doing what Caroline had asked of him. Trying to take care of her husband, to help. Michael hoped perhaps once he was settled back in London, Peter might feel less diligent about his duty; that, having housed Michael, he might feel able to leave him alone.

—

When Michael and Caroline had moved from London to Wales they'd hired the removal company's largest lorry to bring their combined belongings to Coed y Bryn. They'd both led independent, largely single lives into their thirties and although neither had been rooted for long, both had been keepers rather than leavers. Michael's books and belongings were scattered in storage lockers and friends' spare rooms on both sides of the Atlantic, while the detritus of his teenage years was still in the attic of his late parents' house in Cornwall. Caroline, despite her nomadic lifestyle, had fostered a magpie's attraction for artefacts, shoes, and furniture. Between them, through a decade's succession of apartments and flats, they'd accumulated enough belongings to fill a house twice the size of the cottage.

The addresses that had led Caroline to Coed y Bryn were a paper trail of the regions she'd covered as a foreign correspondent for a U.S. satellite station. Since leaving university she'd had homes on several continents. Often they were no more than places to pass through. A series of studios, company flats, rooms in shared houses in Cape Town, Nairobi, Sydney, Berlin, and Beirut. In 2001, still in her twenties, she'd been embedded with an Uzbek division of the Northern Alliance as they'd fought their way towards Kabul. In 2003 she'd celebrated her thirtieth birthday with a bottle of Jack Daniel's and an American marine in the back of an armoured car on the outskirts of Baghdad. Until she met Michael, her life had been a sequence of erratic excitements. Airports relaxed her, as if transit was her natural domain. Arrivals and departures were her strongest memories, bracketing, as they did, the chapters of her life. For Caroline, giving herself to the rhythm of events was a kind of freedom. Being sent on a story at short notice, having no say in where she went, or when. And it was familiar, too. Born in Cape Town, brought up in Melbourne, university in Boston. She'd always been the newcomer, the outsider, her belongings left in storage while she moved on again.

As Caroline grew into her job through her twenties she began to pride herself on her ability for assimilation, on her detachment from attachment. When she changed planes on a grey day in Amsterdam her tanned skin spoke of rocky deserts, souks, and bazaars. In clubs and bars men sensed her transience like a pheromone. She would soon be gone. This is what she tried to communicate in the directness of her stare, which somehow gave her petite frame presence. She rarely wore makeup and her blonde hair was seldom as sleekly groomed as that of the other women perched along a hotel bar. Sometimes, if she'd just landed, a hint of stale sweat lingered on her clothes.

But still they came to her. Men who worked in offices, whose bodies remained structured by suits, even when they no longer wore them. In cafés, crowded pubs, sometimes even on the street, they came to her, recognising her brevity, as if she were a comet they knew would trace their nights only once in a lifetime.

She witnessed the aftermath of horrors. She saw what humans could do to one another. She lost friends. In Bosnia, Afghanistan, Lebanon, Sri Lanka, Iraq. One night in Kabul the body of her interpreter was found eyeless and tongueless on a sofa in his home. She grieved, and her family worried. But for Caroline these deaths, although felt, were another passing through. They and the grief in their wake were the price of life. She took them, like all the other leavings and lost friendships, in her stride.

She was not always happy. As she edged into her thirties she recognised she was becoming cursory; how depths—of time, connection—had a tendency to unnerve her. But she was comfortable. Life, she felt, was an instrument, and the trick was to find the tune you could play on it. In this respect she considered herself lucky. She'd found her tune early, and she was playing it well.

And then, one day, waking alone in a hotel room in Dubai, she'd felt differently. As if the same chain of experiences that had taught her the price of life had finally, on that morning, revealed its value, too. It was a lesson of omission. A learning from what she didn't know, not from what she did. Her aunt had died the week before and she hadn't travelled back to Australia for the funeral. Her mother had said it was fine, that everyone would understand. Caroline was never sure if it was this phone call that had been the catalyst. At the time she'd have said it wasn't. But whatever the impetus, she'd wanted it to stop, to play a different tune. She'd wanted to wake up and know, straightaway, where she was. She'd wanted to be wanted, to be missed and needed, not merely understood.

When she returned to Beirut from Dubai, Caroline applied for a transfer to the London office. London was on the other side of the world from her family in Melbourne, but she didn't want home. And she didn't want America, either. She wanted something older than both, so she opted for London. Her scattered acquaintances—cameramen, photojournalists, editors, reporters— all passed through the city at some point on their travels. And there, on London's doorstep, was the rest of Europe too, as a fall-back, a safety net for when the impulse rose in her, as she knew it would, and she needed to leave and arrive again.

In contrast to Caroline's movements across the globe, all Michael's previous addresses, except for his childhood home and one apartment in Manhattan, had been in London. Having left Cornwall to study in the capital, he'd stayed on after graduation, joining the *Evening Standard* as an intern. Over the next five years of jobbing journalism—diary pieces, reviews, news features, and comment—Michael had steadily increased his word length and salary until, in his late twenties, fearing the ossification he'd detected in some of his older colleagues, he'd left the *Standard* and moved to Manhattan. He'd arrived in the city holding a journalist's visa and equipped with a list of British editors who'd agreed to use him as a stringer, feeding their publications' appetites for all things New York. Which is exactly what Michael did. But he hadn't moved to America to follow the same path he'd been cutting in Britain. The distance he'd flown from London to New York had been about attempting another journey, too: from being a journalist, which he'd called himself ever since university, towards becoming an author.

Michael's first book, *BrotherHoods,* was the story of Nico and Raoul, two Dominican brothers from Inwood. A close portrait of their lives and world, the book was a narrative of thwarted ambition, of failure. For Michael it was the consequence of one, too. All through his first year in America, as he'd written reports on parties, observational pieces about the Super Bowl, travel articles on the Hudson Valley painters, Michael had harboured aspirations of becoming a novelist. But fiction had continued to elude him. For reasons he never fathomed, regardless of how many hours he spent at his desk, or in how many cafés he made notes, his imagination kept falling short at the border of the invented. The prose of the writers he admired—Salter, Balzac, Fitzgerald, Atwood—remained unattainable to him. He could register their effect when he read them, he could see how their novels and stories worked, how their moving parts fitted together. But like the engineer skilled at dismantling a plane's engine, and yet unable to make it fly, Michael found his own words remained stubbornly grounded on the page.

Michael had been convinced that New York would unlock the novel he'd failed to write in London. The Hudson gleaming magnesium of a morning; the taillight rivers on Lexington and Third; the city's scale, at once intimate and grand. Manhattan already felt like a novel to him, as if all he'd have to do was take dictation from its streets. But he'd been wrong, which is why halfway through his second year of living in the city, in the wake of his failure with fiction, Michael started splicing the taste of it into his journalism instead.

He began on his own doorstep, telling the story of Ali, the Armenian deli owner on the corner of his block, from his early-morning washing of the sidewalk to his midnight serving of condoms and chewing gum to coked-up SoHo models. When this piece was taken by *The Atlantic,* the editor asked him for another. So Michael moved his attention across the street to Marilia, the black mother of six who'd volunteered at the school crossing every morning and evening for the last twenty years. Through Marilia he'd gained an introduction into the school itself, where he'd found his next subject in its harrowed headmaster, shadowing him as he juggled the timetable, staff shortages, gun detection, and the demands of downtown parents.

In researching these early stories, Michael found his Englishness opened doors for him. Not in institutions, but in people. There was, in all his subjects, an assumption of his integrity, drawn, he supposed, from associations with the BBC and films by Merchant Ivory. Combined with his natural manner—a calm patience laced with pressing curiosity—this cultural assumption allowed Michael to get close quickly. The people he interviewed trusted him, and in return he took their trust seriously, listening, recording, and taking notes as they talked; trying, as best as he could, to see the city through their eyes and feel it through their skin.

With every story he took on, from the Central Park millionaire to the street-sleeper in the Bronx, Michael's technique was immersive. His initial approach was time: the willingness to spend it, to be there and observe at even the most mundane of events until, despite his height and his accent, people began to forget his presence. He took to cutting hundreds of strips of white card, slender enough to fit into the inside pocket of his jacket. These, he found, were less obtrusive than a notebook and somehow less threatening, too, as if what he wrote on them wasn't being recorded but merely jotted down and would, like any other scrap of paper, not be around for long.

When, after months of such research, Michael felt he'd seen and heard enough—and it was always a feeling more than a knowing, a sense at the edges of his vision—he would leave his subjects' lives as suddenly as he'd entered them. Taking their stories to his desk in his SoHo apartment, he'd immerse himself again, this time borrowing a novelistic style to disappear himself not just from his subjects' lives, but also from the paragraphs he wrote about them. Even though he'd been there at their sides when the events he described happened—when the health inspector had seen a rat, when a kid attacked his maths teacher, when the millionaire's dog was put down—in the finished published piece, Michael was never there. Just the characters remained, living their lives in third person through the hours of the city as if through the pages of a novel.

His style became the antithesis of Gonzo journalism, an eradication of the writer in the writing. A disappearing act of saturation that was informed by the immersive nature of his research, but unfettered, too, by direct experience. So although he hadn't been with them, Michael still described Ali waking in bed, Marilia singing in the shower, or the way the millionaire picked up his coffee at a morning meeting in Brazil. Such moments, although unseen by Michael, were written from what he'd learnt about his subjects at other times, in other places, upon not just what he knew was true, but also what he knew to *be* true. And this is what he'd hoped to achieve in those early New York stories: to find a way of using the freedoms of descriptive fiction to make the real lives he wrote about even more real.

By the time Michael met Nico and Raoul he'd already begun looking for a subject through which to extend his writing from the pages of a magazine to the pages of a book. His desire to be an author hadn't ebbed when he turned his back on a novel. With a clutch of respected pieces under his belt, and a cast of characters rendered through his immersive style, he was ready to try again.

It was a policeman who'd put Michael in touch with Nico and Raoul. They were chatting outside the subway entrance on Broadway and 201st, a couple of take-out coffees steaming in their hands. It was February and smudged banks of snow still bordered the street. A flat winter light fell upon the storefronts. Men and women commuted to work in padded coats, wearing gloves and hats made for the mountains.

Michael had travelled up to Inwood Hill Park that morning to see the site where Dutch traders first bought Manhattan, trading it from the Lenape Indians for a bag of trinkets worth twenty-four dollars. He'd only recently got to know the area north of Washington Heights, but its rawness had already got under his skin. The street theatre he'd discovered up there in the blocks off Inwood, Dyckman, and Broadway seemed more varied than that a hundred blocks south, more explicitly immigrant in its nature. Dominican men played dominoes outside O'Grady's, The Gael Bar, The Old Brigade Pub, their walls still painted with shamrocks and IRA flags. Dark-windowed Yukons throbbed with Reggaeton at the stoplights. Puerto Rican drag queens drank cocktails in the salsa clubs, youths in thug nighties to their knees catcalling them from the corners. Farther off, in the park itself, rangy black kids surged between the hoops of basketball courts while Italian grandfathers watched Little League baseball, the hollow punts of a Mexican soccer game filtering up from the field below.

Up there, above 200th, as he'd wandered the streets, Michael had felt he was within touching distance of Manhattan's original desire. That whatever had driven those Dutch traders could still be tasted in the air, and unlike farther south in the city, where origin had been diluted by money, the island's history of immigrant fuel was still on display. Each community he saw up there—the Dominicans, the Mexicans, the Irish, the African—seemed like the rings of a tree to him, ethnic watermarks of the island's growth and change.

Michael had got talking to the policeman at a coffee stand on the edge of the park. As they'd stirred in their sugars he'd asked him if he'd seen much change in the neighbourhood. The cop had laughed, shaking his head. "Oh, man," he'd said. "Like you wouldn't believe. Always changin' up here." They'd carried on talking as they'd strolled back towards his position at the subway entrance, Michael asking him if they got much trouble in the area. The cop had shrugged. "Some," he'd said. "Mostly drugs, domestics." Then, blowing on his coffee and stamping his feet, he'd told Michael about "a couple of punks," two Dominican brothers who'd walked the length of Arden at four in the morning the night before, smashing the roadside window of every car. They'd left the street thick with alarm sirens, shirtless men shouting down at the sidewalks from tall apartment blocks swirling with car lights.

As Michael had listened to the policeman describe the scene, he'd known immediately that he wanted to meet these boys, to find out who they were and why they'd landed on such a dramatic gesture of vandalism. He could already sense the hinterland behind the act, the stories emanating either side of the moment. He asked the policeman if he could meet them, these brothers. The cop raised his eyebrows, then sucked in the air through his teeth. He was Latino, broad-faced, with a full moustache. Michael pulled a fifty from his wallet and folded it twice. The policeman looked at it for a moment, then took it, shrugging again as he slipped it into his pocket, as if to say who was he to change the order of things? The following morning, in the office of their caseworker, Michael came eye-to-eye for the first time with the mistrusting stares of Nico and Raoul.

For the next three years, sometimes as often as four times a week, Michael rode the A train north, immersing himself in the lives of the brothers. He began spending days at a time in the neighbourhood, staying at a guesthouse overlooking the wooded slopes of the park. From his top-floor bedroom he witnessed three autumns burnish its trees, among which the island's original Lenape inhabitants had once made their cave dwellings. After a year of regularly checking him in, the owner supplied Michael with a desk, an old pine table notched and scarred with the cuttings of a kitchen knife. As he wrote up his notes in that room over those three falls, he witnessed the beginnings of gentrification take root in the area. Temporary Sunday market stalls evolved into permanent secondhand bookstores and cafés. Real estate offices moved in to occupy the premises of launderettes and cobblers. Young white couples began painting the exteriors of boarded-up houses. The bright colours of baby buggies and infant slings began dotting the pathways of the park on midweek afternoons.

—

At first, Michael's ignorance of the brothers' world in the streets and blocks west of this park was in his favour. He was an oddity: a tall English guy with a preppy haircut and an accent like from one of those British sitcoms. Handy to have around for a word to a social worker, or to touch for money. At times he was like a child to them, eager to learn, to harvest what they knew. But gradually, over the months and then the years, the scales of knowledge began to tip. After the apprenticeship of his magazine stories Michael had become adept at fitting himself to the lives of others. He never blended as such, but he did begin to stick. Among Nico and Raoul's friends an appreciation for his stubbornness began to grow, and with it an acknowledgement that at least he wanted to listen, at least he wanted to try and see things from their point of view. In the goldfish bowl of Inwood's street life he even began to be sought after, for advice or confidence. When Nico's girlfriend got pregnant, Michael knew before he did. When Raoul ran for a rival dealer, he made Michael swear he'd never tell his brother. But his learning of their world was not always helpful. The police pressured him to give them leads, while the growing currency of his knowledge began to unnerve some of the older boys. Michael in the dark was one thing. Michael knowing too much was another thing altogether.

The A train Michael took from SoHo up to Inwood followed the route of a Lenape hunting path that once traced the length of Manhattan's forests and hills. One morning, as if he'd sensed a regeneration of that route's purpose in Michael's visits, Nico had called him on what he was doing. They were hanging out at their aunt's apartment at the time, a studio high in the projects on Tenth Avenue.

"*El tronco*'s a hunter, bro, I tellin' you," Nico said from the couch, speaking to Raoul but holding Michael's eye. "Ain't you, Mikey?" he continued, flicking a toothpick at him. "A lootin' *puta*. Ain't that you? Jus' divin' on us wrecks up here."

Michael laughed it off at the time, but for a few seconds he'd felt the air tighten between them. Not so much because of the threat in Nico's voice, but because they all knew, whether intentionally or not, what he'd said was true.

—

Five years after first meeting Nico and Raoul in their caseworker's office, Michael published *BrotherHoods*. He'd hoped the book would help the brothers, but it didn't. HBO bought their life rights, for $25,000 each. They said they wanted to make a series. That they wanted to use their characters to build a long-running franchise. Box sets, advertisements on the sides of city buses. But nothing came of it. For a brief period the two of them basked in their newfound notoriety. But in the end the attention, the money, fanned their troubles more than doused them. As the book became the talked-of publication in Manhattan, Nico, its central character, began a sentence upstate for unlawful possession of a firearm. Raoul, in trouble with a dealer and without his brother's protection, went to stay with a cousin in a one-bed in Pennsylvania. At the same time as they left the city, readers across Manhattan were being introduced to them. On subway trains, park benches, under duvets by the light of bedside lamps. Throughout New York and beyond—in Vermont, San Francisco, across the whole country— students on college lawns, commuters on trains, middle-aged couples on sofas were all embarking on the small tragedies of the brothers' lives.

Within weeks of publication Michael was receiving requests for interviews and to appear on talk shows. *The New York Times,* which had once run his pieces, now ran a profile on him instead. While he was researching and writing the book he'd neglected his personal life. Although he'd begun a couple of relationships, none of them had withstood the intensity of his research, nor his split existence at each end of the island. Increasingly his thoughts had been taken up with the brothers, and then with the writing of the book, with their lives in its pages. For five years he'd lived not just alongside Nico and Raoul, but also often through them, his own life becoming a shell of routine and observation. Now, though, on the other side of the book's publication, women suddenly seemed available to him. He was thirty-five and single, and had been anointed by New York success. He started seeing his publicist. Then there'd been a Dominican journalist. Her interview with him had been challenging, even aggressive. But afterwards she'd invited him to dinner and they'd soon become a couple. When that had eventually ended, in the weeks following a reading at Columbia, Michael had gone home with not one but two of the students who'd been in the audience.

He was aware of the clichés he was living, of how predictable it looked. But, he told himself, he wasn't harming anyone, and wasn't this, perhaps, part of what he'd earned during those three years of riding the A train the length of the island and then another two sitting alone at his desk? But above all Michael had known it wouldn't last, and that's why he'd given himself so willingly to his unlikely present, half expecting every day to wake and find it already transfigured into his past.

For Nico and Raoul, *BrotherHoods* and its author became another disappointment in their lives, confirmation, as they'd always suspected, that the world was set against them. Michael tried to keep in touch with them, but with the appearance of the book their already diverging paths accelerated. While Nico served his time upstate and Raoul sat out his self-imposed exile in Pennsylvania, Michael's publisher sent him on a national book tour. In a series of events across the country, despite his uneasiness in front of an audience, Michael began to discover a public persona—a diffident, dry humour that journalists and publicists billed as "British." On the underlying issues of the book, though, he was never anything other than serious. The title, he'd explain to smatterings of readers in Ohio and Carolina, and then again to capacity auditoriums in Los Angeles and Austin, referred to us all. Not just to Nico and Raoul and the territories over which they and their peers fought, but also to the cheek-by-jowl neighbourhoods of Manhattan, of America, the world. Look about you, he'd told them. These people and their stories are happening under your nose. Their story is our story. No man, woman, or child is an island. Yes, the book was about two young Dominican men in Inwood, but it was also, through them, about us all, about our ability to live close, and yet so far from one another.

The audiences had nodded, applauded, and afterwards asked for Michael's signature on the title page of the book. When the paperback was published he donated a percentage of his royalties to education projects in Inwood and Washington Heights. But still, every time he said his sentence about neighbourhoods, about living close and far, he knew he himself was moving further away from the brothers who'd first lent him their lives. As he'd moved across the country on his tour, from hotel to airport to university, so Nico and Raoul had moved, too. Nico from cell to refectory to exercise yard and back to his cell again. Raoul from his cousin's bedsit in Pennsylvania to another in Albany, to the room of a girl he'd met on the street, to the couch of her friend. Within just a few months the years Michael had shared with the brothers had become undone, unravelled by the publication of his story about their time together.

—

The last time Michael had heard Nico's voice was on a collect call from his correctional facility upstate. Michael was finally moving back to London. His mother, widowed three years previously, was ill. *BrotherHoods* was due to be published in Britain. It was time for him to leave New York. If he stayed any longer he was worried it would never let him go. Although he'd found his voice in the city, and his story, to remain would have felt like treading water. New York had been about transition. Now that transition had been made, he wanted to move on, which, for a reason he couldn't quite fathom, meant moving back.

When the phone rang Michael had been on his knees among packing boxes and bubble wrap scattered across the floor of his Sullivan Street apartment. He'd accepted the call, but before Nico came on the line he'd flicked the phone to answering machine. He'd already spoken to Nico twice that week and he couldn't take another stilted, awkward conversation. Not now, as he was preparing to leave. So instead he'd just listened, standing in his half-empty apartment, a fire truck's siren insistent on Sixth, as the voice of a man he'd once known as a boy filled his living room.

"Hey, Mikey?" Nico said. He sounded lost in a large space. His voice deep, but somehow shallow, too. "It's me, Nico. You there? Man, it's Nico, pick up."

Michael heard the clang of a door, the crackle and fuzzy speech of a guard's radio.

For a second or two Nico breathed on the line, deliberate and slow. "Huh, well," he'd said eventually. "*Hasta luego,* bro. Take it easy, yeah?"

The line went dead. The message light began to blink. Michael watched it pulse for a moment, then, sliding his keys off the kitchen table, left the apartment. He pushed through the lobby doors downstairs and crossed the street into the spring light of the morning and walked north towards Washington Square. The higher windows of the buildings were catching the sun, making them flash in the corner of his eye. As he crossed over Prince a cooling breeze ushered a scent of cinnamon and bagels down the street. Michael walked faster into it, as if he were trying to outpace the memory of Nico's voice behind him, or discover some kind of a promise in the sweetness ahead.

CHAPTER
THREE

THEY MET JUST three weeks after Caroline moved to London. A mutual friend was screening a film at the Frontline in Paddington, a social club for correspondents, journalists, and filmmakers. As the documentary played in a darkened room on the top floor, the windowpanes crackling with spring rain, images of Harare, Bulawayo, and the Zimbabwean veldt appeared on the screen. The film was about Mugabe's operation Murambatsvina, "throw out the rubbish," a forced clearance of urban slum dwellings that had left 700,000 Zimbabweans homeless in winter. Caroline watched as a grandmother in a red bobble hat, overlooked by policemen, heaved a sledgehammer against the crumbling breezeblocks of her home.

Something about the juxtaposition of the rain against the windows and the film on the screen made Caroline nervous. The shower against the glass, the wash of tyres in the street below, the acacia and jacaranda trees silhouetted against a southern sun. She'd lived in Nairobi and Cape Town, and had worked all over Africa. She hated what she was watching on the screen, but she knew she loved it, too. Already, just three weeks after arriving in London, she could feel the pull of those images, an umbilical desire to be a part of it. But then, in immediate response, she felt an equally strong urge to resist. To stay. Whatever had been the catalyst for what she'd felt that morning in Dubai, the residue of it was still a counterweight within her, an instinctive force she didn't understand but to which she felt compelled to listen.

Caroline first caught sight of Michael sitting a few rows ahead of her, his profile partly lit by the screen. As the film played she studied what she could of him. His fair hair was swept back from his forehead and the collar of his shirt was askew, the label showing. When he turned to say something to the person next to him she saw the suggestion of a break to his nose. It lent him, she thought, an interest beyond good looks. He seemed familiar but it was only later, when she saw his face in the full light of the bar, that she remembered where she'd seen him before: on the back cover of one of the books she'd packed into her hand luggage three weeks earlier.

The only people Caroline knew at the screening had already left, so taking a last swig from her bottle of beer, she approached Michael. He was talking to an older man, a grey-haired reporter with a beaten manner who'd made his name filing stories from the front lines of Vietnam. Caroline didn't wait for a break in their conversation.

"'All they got is the facts,'" she said as she squeezed between them, putting the empty bottle on the bar. She looked up at Michael. "'But what about everything else?' Good line, that," she continued, holding his eye. "True, too."

Michael looked down at the woman who'd interrupted them. At first he had no idea what she was talking about. When he did, he couldn't tell if she was serious or taking the piss. She was smiling up at him, but her face betrayed nothing.

"Thanks," he said. "But it wasn't mine. I just wrote it down."

She cast a glance at the rest of the bar. "Join the club," she said. "Think anyone here's ever told their own story? And anyway, isn't that the important bit?"

Michael looked over to his friend. "Think that's true, Bill?" But Bill had already turned away and was talking to someone else.

"Caroline," she said, holding out her hand.

"Michael," he replied. Her grip was small but firm. As she pushed herself onto the stool Bill had vacated, Michael noticed the slimness of her thighs. She wore jeans, biker boots, and an oversized jumper. Its neckline was broad and fell loose from one shoulder. There was, Michael could tell, a heat to her tanned skin. When she looked at him again he saw her brown eyes were flecked with gold. A few weeks later, lying in bed together, he'd call those eyes her "fool's gold," bait for men like him. But for now he just returned the forthrightness of their gaze.

"I really did like it," Caroline said. "That line. And the rest of the book, too."

"Are you a writer?" he asked her.

"No," she said. She looked out at the bar again, as if weighing the crowd. Michael waited for her to elaborate, but she didn't.

"Do you want to get something to eat?" she said, turning back to him. "There's too many swinging dicks in here to hear yourself think."

He couldn't place her accent. Her words began in Europe but then migrated, like a swallow, mid-sentence to Africa.

Michael laughed, and as he did Caroline thought she might want to sleep with this man whose book she'd once half-read on a plane, and who she'd now discovered in a bar in London.

A woman behind them raised her voice, shouting over a balding man shaking his head.

"But that's nothing!" the woman said, gesticulating with a half-full glass of wine. "I mean, were you in Somalia?"

"Jesus!" Caroline said, wincing away from her. As she did, she heard Michael in her ear.

"Even those who haven't got one," he said, "are at it." Which is when, she told him one morning over breakfast a month after they were married, she'd been sure.

———

They found shelter from the rain in a Lebanese restaurant near the Tube, where they ordered food but left much of it untouched. Instead they got drunk on two bottles of rosé from the Beqaa Valley, where, Caroline told Michael, she'd once spent a week trying to film hashish growers during the civil war.

By the time they left, the kitchen was clattering with the sounds of cleaning, the waiters turning chairs over the tables. Outside, the rain had stopped. As they walked to the Tube, the wet pavement reflected the street's neon signs. Slipping her arm around Michael's waist, Caroline tucked the tips of her fingers into his jeans. He put his arm about her shoulder and in reply she rested her head against his chest. For a few paces they walked like this in silence. But then Caroline felt Michael take a deep breath under her cheek, and she knew what was coming. He had a girlfriend, he told her. She was still in New York, staying there for her job. But they'd decided to try and make it work. To try and stay together.

As soon as Michael heard himself say it he knew the situation sounded hopeless. Caroline, too, recognised the familiar notes of a dying relationship. But she still listened to him as he apologised and qualified, only ducking from under his arm as they reached the entrance to the station and he stopped talking. She backed away from him, her hands held up in mock surrender.

"In that case, Mr. Writer," she said, "I'll get a cab." Turning on her heel, she walked towards the kerb, already raising her arm to hail a taxi. "Thanks for dinner, though," she called over her shoulder. "It was fun."

"Yeah, it was," Michael replied. "Look——" he started, but she was already out of earshot, on tiptoe, flagging down a cab.

Michael watched as Caroline climbed inside the taxi. With her hand on the door, she called across the pavement to him again.

"Let me know when it's over," she said, before closing it and leaning forward to give the driver her address.

As the cab edged into the traffic Michael didn't wave, and nor did Caroline, but neither did they take their eyes off each other. For as long as they could, Caroline framed in the cab's rear window and Michael from the pavement, they watched as she became just another car on the road, and he became just another man on the street, his tall body silhouetted against the illuminated entrance to the Tube.

—

In the months following their meeting, Michael and Caroline's friends often agreed it was timing, more than anything else, that had brought them together. Few thought them compatible, and no one mentioned love. But whatever had happened that night, at least they all recognised it was mutual, and that rather than heady or rash, the climate of their meeting had been surprisingly calm, like a return more than a beginning, a recollection coming clear.

The next time they saw each other was for dinner in Covent Garden. Caroline, who Michael had last seen climbing into that cab wearing her jeans, boots, and a jumper, arrived at the restaurant in a floor-length grey coat over a tightly fitting black dress and high heels. She'd straightened her hair and was wearing makeup. As she left her coat at the desk and walked towards him Michael saw the eyes of other diners catch on her as she passed. Caroline, he realised, was a woman who, if she chose to, could provoke this kind of reaction on a daily basis. As he stood to meet her it was the fact that she didn't, as much as her attractiveness, that excited him. When he pulled out her chair for her Michael felt as if he'd somehow won a suitors' competition that had been running, without his knowledge, for years.

As far as Caroline was concerned, she'd already decided she wanted Michael. Not just because of what else she wanted in her life, and not because she was attracted to the subtlety of his humour and his looks, both of which had grown on her gradually, like a secret she'd been let in on. She'd found these qualities in previous relationships, and had learnt they were insufficient, in the end, to hold her attention. But what she'd never encountered before was Michael's stillness, his capacity to hold the world lightly without appearing aloof or frivolous. She wasn't aware of it over that dinner, and perhaps she never came to appreciate it over their brief marriage, but it was a manner born more of place than of character. Had she ever travelled to Cornwall and visited the coastal villages and towns where Michael was brought up—Gorran Haven, Saint Mawes, Mevagissey—she'd have met other men possessed of a similar quality. Fishermen, farmers, storekeepers. In all of them she'd have been able to trace that same wary ease with the world, an outlook bred through generations of coastal families by the giving and taking of the sea. It just happened that rather than stay close to the landscape that had shaped him, Michael had left for London, where a resonance of that coast remained with him. In later years he'd even go so far as to wonder if it hadn't been the Cornish sea with which Caroline had fallen in love. As if what she'd sensed making her whole wasn't as much himself as the place he was from, unseen to her yet known through its echo in him.

They slept together for the first time that night, in the flat Caroline was renting in Farringdon. As her small hands explored under his shirt Michael unzipped her dress and pushed it off her shoulders. Her body was taut, spare, her underwear surprisingly ordinary. But she was not. He'd stayed and the next morning she'd woken him with her hands again, guiding him inside her from behind as they lay half-dazed with sleep, sunlight washing through the sheet she'd hung as a curtain.

It was several weeks later that their sex became a conduit for something else. It was another night marked by rain. Michael had already given Caroline a set of keys to his flat by Hammersmith Bridge, but he was working late at the library that day, so rather than have her come round he'd agreed to meet her the following morning instead. As he'd cycled home a storm that had been threatening all day finally broke. By the time he reached his flat London was polished under rain, the Thames either side of the bridge pock-marked by the deluge. Wheeling his bike into the hallway, he'd stripped off his coat, shoes, and socks, then gone through into the kitchen. As he did he'd noticed the message light was blinking on the phone. Hardly anyone used his landline anymore, so as he pressed play he'd half expected to hear Nico's voice following him from across the Atlantic.

But it wasn't Nico.

"Hello, Michael."

She sounded as if she were sitting there in the kitchen, raising her head from a book to welcome him home. He could tell she was smiling.

"Guess who's upstairs? Want to come and join me?"

He'd found her in the bathroom, its steamed air scented with amber, the water drawn to the rim and tea lights balanced around the sink. She was sitting up in the bath, her knees against her breasts like a shy girl. Her shoulders and arms were sheened in the heat and the mirror above her was an oval of mist.

She'd watched him undress, the faintest of smiles playing across her mouth. As he stepped into the bath goose bumps broke out on his arms and legs. Slowly, he'd sunk into its warmth. Neither of them spoke. As he went farther, submerging his shoulders and head, she'd lifted herself to give him room, revealing her breasts, rising slick above the water. When he rose again he drew her towards him, sending splashes swilling over the bath's rim. Which is when she finally spoke. "What took you so long?" she said, speaking into his neck. "A girl could get bored up here all alone."

Afterwards they'd stumbled into the bedroom, wrapped in half-undone towels and each other's limbs, their wet bodies imprinting patterns of their embrace across the duvet and pillows. Drugged by the warmth of the bath, they'd moved slowly, as if they'd just woken. Caroline's hair was damp, and felt as heavy as velvet when

Michael wrapped it about his knuckles. She'd turned over so he could enter her from behind, her back, hips, and arse making the shape of a cello as she rose onto the heels of her palms and pushed herself against him. But she wanted to see him as well as feel him, so, pulling away, she'd turned round and drawn him on top of her. The friction of their bodies released the amber perfume of the bath oils still on their skin. Michael travelled steadily inside her, inching himself deeper until she held his full length and he came, powerfully and suddenly.

For a moment they'd lain in the wake of his climax, the full weight of his body pressing her into the bed, their hearts working against each other. But then, before he began ebbing from her, Caroline rolled Michael onto his back and sat astride him. From that position, with his hands cupping her breasts, she'd looked down at him, her hair swinging about her face, obscuring then revealing her fool's-gold eyes as they held his. Grinding her hips with a heightening tempo, she'd pushed herself down against the firmness of his stomach. As she'd worked faster and harder her head began to rise until, showing him the full tautness of her throat, she, too, came, crying out over the sounds of the rain-loud city beyond their window.

When Michael woke the next morning it had been as simple as a single thought repeating in his mind, a voice belonging to both his past and his future self. "I don't want this to stop." But with it came a fear he hadn't experienced so purely since childhood. It was the trepidation of happiness, a spreading sensation in his chest provoked by a joy so palpable that by its very nature it was unbearably fragile, too—beaten thin in its expansion, ephemeral before the certainties of life, death.

As Caroline showered, she, too, became aware of a shift in her perception. In previous relationships her single life had been a whispering promise she'd had to keep at bay. But now that whisper had faded to silence, and she realised where once she'd only ever wanted herself, now she wanted Michael too. As she'd lain on top of him the previous night, both of them breathing like sprinters, distant cars sounding over the bridge, she'd felt a subtle conception somewhere deep within her. Not of a child, but of what, if she allowed it, could happen next. Because this was no longer about sex or feeling wanted or new experience. And this is what she told Michael over their breakfast that morning. That it wasn't about infatuation or abating loneliness. It was about something else now, but whatever it was, she could speak of it only in terms of what it wasn't because she'd never felt it before. But, she said, pouring them coffee and tucking a strand of hair behind her ear, what she did know was that she wanted more of it. Whatever it was, she wanted more.

—

The following spring they watched, Michael's arm across Caroline's shoulders, as the removal company's lorry manoeuvred its way down the lane towards Coed y Bryn. As it lumbered towards them, rocking in the potholes, broken stalks of cow parsley shivered in its wing mirrors, as if it had been decorated expressly for this, its arrival at their marital home.

For the first week they went nowhere other than the local shops or takeaways. As they opened each packing crate and box, the objects of their previous lives began to fill the low-beamed rooms of Coed y Bryn. Lamps from New York, rugs from Kabul, a set of chairs from Berlin. Caroline, Michael discovered, owned two guitars, neither of which she could play. He, meanwhile, to appease her pleading, agreed to try on his student fencing kit she'd found, gutting it with glee from a musty kitbag. The creases in the jacket were stiff with age, but it still fit him, as did the breeches, streaked with long rust stains from the blades they'd been wrapped around. Pulling on the equally rust-patched mask, Caroline had picked up one of his épées, its coquille dented and scratched, and come at him with it, slashing at his arms, crying, "Defend yourself! Defend yourself!"

In the afternoons, despite her inexperience, Caroline attacked the garden with equal enthusiasm, working quickly and haphazardly. She didn't know what she was doing, but she didn't care. She wanted, she told Michael, to feel this turn in their lives between her fingers, in the soil of their new home, in its moisture seeping through her jeans as she knelt at the bramble-choked shrubs and bushes.

While the shadows of the May evenings lengthened over Caroline in the garden, a haze of midges blurring the air above her, Michael continued working inside, unpacking and arranging the furniture of their single lives. At night, whether it was cold or not, they lit the wood stove, opened a bottle of wine, and fitted themselves into a single armchair to talk about their future and watch the hills through the window turn inky against a darkening sky.

But already, even in those first months, Michael could sense the cottage alone might not be enough for Caroline. Their rhythms were complementary but different, and the move to Coed y Bryn had revealed this in a way their London lives had not. Both he and Caroline were storytellers, not of their own lives but of others'. It was this vocational territory, of exploring and shaping beyond themselves, that they'd first shared. It was what had first brought them together. But where Michael always retreated to his desk to tell his stories, Caroline had simply moved on to the next. For her their telling was a need, a hunger. Her belief in the truth being told was almost fanatical, whatever the outcome of a story's exposure. Where Michael would carefully weigh his content for repercussion or hurt, Caroline had always been fearless with consequence.

"Why wouldn't you be?" she'd once challenged him. "Anything that happens is only what should have happened anyway, if it was known in the first place. And what's the alternative?" she'd asked him, warming to her theme. "The untold story," she'd said, pointing at him like an accuser. "It's like landfill. We can bury it all we like, but in time it'll catch up with us."

Her passion was infectious and Caroline's commitment to her craft had been one of the traits Michael had most admired about her when they'd first met. But he also knew it wasn't without self-interest. For him the life of his subject was another country, one he discovered first in person, and then again on the page. Once back at his desk his stories travelled further than he had, went where he'd been unable to go, leaving Michael behind as a silent still point, a governing hand from afar. But for Caroline the stories of others were her fuel. She travelled for them and through them. Their birthing into the light was her nutrition, their telling what kept her moving.

"We can be still here." This is what she'd said to him when they'd first viewed Coed y Bryn and the estate agent had left them alone to talk. Michael had wanted to believe her, and as they'd bedded in over that spring, he'd continued to do so. But sometimes, when they walked to the top of the hill behind the cottage, or when he found her looking out of its windows on the landing, he'd catch a flicker in her expression, as if it wasn't freedom she saw in those hills, fields, and woods, but constriction.

On that first night they'd met at the Frontline, Caroline's manner had reminded Michael of a birdcage, her small body alive with wings brushing against her wire. On moving to Coed y Bryn he'd sensed those birds begin to settle, their wings fold, their alert heads become calm. But they were still there, inside her. Their lightness, their potential for flight. And this is what Michael saw in those moments on the hill, or on the landing, when something surfaced, briefly, beneath her features. The wingtip of one of those birds woken within her, its plumage flashing in her eye, its feathers brushing under her brow.

—

Within days of unpacking, Michael had begun work on his next book. Like *BrotherHoods*, *The Man Who Broke the Mirror* was to be a work of nonfiction, but novelistic in style and tone. Its subject was Oliver Blackwood, a brilliant but volatile neurosurgeon who in recent years had controversially, and often on the back of the work of others, "crossed the floor" to stray into matters of neuroscience. Although trained in the biological workings of the material brain, for the last decade Oliver had been making waves, and trouble, with his writings and lectures on abstract matters of the mind. Not that Oliver himself saw such a clear distinction between the two. "The material," he'd told Michael early on in his research. "It's all we've got, all we are. Anything else—memory, emotion," he'd tapped his finger roughly against Michael's head. "It's all created, for real or as illusion, by this, the spongy stuff inside our skulls."

At the time Michael met him, Oliver, with the determination of a Victorian explorer, had become fixated upon locating the neurological source of empathy. It was an emotion, he believed, born in "mirror" neurons, single cells in the human brain through which the actions and feelings of others are mirrored and therefore felt. "I'm telling you," he'd once told Michael before taking the stage for a panel discussion, "mirror neurons. They're the future. You watch, they'll do for neuroscience what DNA did for biology. Think about it, it's the source of everything. Everything!"

The book's title referred to Oliver's theory, but also to his capacity for self-destruction. Even without his ideas about neuroscience he would have made an arresting character study. An intellectual and a performer, imbued with the traditional arrogance of his craft, he was a man equally cast in temper and reason. But it was how the nature of his research sat within Oliver's own life that had convinced Michael that Oliver would be the subject of his next book. Oliver, as far as he could tell, was a man driven by an unacknowledged desire to fathom his own failings. To discover the neurological manifestation of the very emotion he himself most appeared to lack. It was this, beyond the colour of Oliver's life, Michael hoped his second book would be about. An intimate portrait of a search for why we feel for others, often beyond ourselves, conducted by a man whose default position was only ever to think of himself.

For the past two years Michael had accompanied Oliver to conferences, lectures, broadcasting studios, seminars, and operating theatres. Over the course of their time together, as other colleagues had fallen away, his presence in Oliver's life had grown to occupy the spaces they'd left. In time he became the kind of witness men like Oliver needed. At first Oliver had merely tolerated Michael's presence. But then he'd begun to court it. For the last year of Michael's research, he'd come to rely on it. Oliver was an actor for whom the public world of popular neuroscience had become a stage, his many critics and detractors an audience. But when they were no longer on hand, or had tired of his antics, it was Michael who'd remained; a dedicated audience of one, there to sit and watch Oliver's late-night rants in his London club, or to answer the phone in the morning and listen to his latest theories.

Michael and Caroline's leaving London coincided with Michael's leaving of Oliver. He'd reached that point in his process when he must turn away from the man himself, to the man he'd render on the page. The arc of the book, Michael felt, was complete. Oliver had written it almost perfectly, plotting over the last year a course in his private life in exact inverse trajectory to the ascendency of his public one. In this respect Michael's sense of a story had come good. During his time with Oliver he'd watched as the character traits he'd detected when they'd first met became inflated with attention to cause havoc with his marriage, his children, and the many colleagues who would no longer talk to him. At the same time, however, and with perfect symmetry as far as Michael was concerned, just as Oliver was being ostracised by his family and friends, so his ideas on mirror neurons and empathy were being accepted by the scientific community.

Michael set up his study in one of the cottage's upper rooms at Coed y Bryn, a simple table in front of a window through which, on a clear day, he could see the Severn glinting on the horizon. Although he still fielded calls from Oliver, and had agreed to meet him once when he'd come west to deliver a lecture in Bath, Michael knew he needed to withdraw into the necessary hibernation of his writing. After two years of fitting his life to Oliver's hectic schedule, he wanted to slow and still his days so he could both immerse himself in, and take himself out, of his story.

As Michael worked on his book upstairs, Caroline began a new job in Bristol. Before they'd left London she'd applied for a producer's position at Sightline Productions, a TV company specialising in news and investigative documentary. The directors of the company had been thrilled to welcome someone of Caroline's experience. Although she'd fallen short of becoming a household name with the satellite channel, she'd garnered a growing respect within the industry. There was personality to her reports and by the age of thirty she'd already broken two international stories herself.

Twice a week, when Caroline travelled into the Sightline offices to attend forward planning and development meetings, Michael was woken by the gruff engine of their faded red Volvo filtering into his sleep. Ten hours later her return was heralded by its headlights sweeping the hedges. For the rest of the week Caroline worked at home, editing scripts, making calls, and viewing cuts downstairs on the kitchen table.

The majority of Sightline's work dealt with issues in the South West. Half-hour investigations following the local news: slave labour among immigrant work gangs, care home abuses in Bath, the environmental battles over the Severn Estuary barrage. Occasionally a local story would provoke national interest: a study by Bristol University into pesticides and the declining bee population, the story of a Devon family's fight for their father's right to die. When it did, it was Caroline's job to work with the development team and chase the larger budgets of a network commission.

None of it satisfied her, and Michael knew it. The few times Sightline asked her to oversee a shoot, or whenever she set one up herself, Michael could sense the change in her as soon as she came through the door, her shoulders slung with cameras and bags of tape. It would stay with her through the night, as they ate, read by the fire, or watched TV. He would feel it emanating off her as she nestled into him. Even in bed, it felt at times as if their love-making was vitalised by her having tasted her old reporting life again.

When Michael asked her about it, she'd reassured him that this was what she'd wanted. It was she who'd suggested they move out of London. And she who'd said she had to put a stop to her travelling, to change her life from peripatetic to rooted. It would be fine, she told him. She just needed to get used to the different pressure points, the new rhythms of their lives. The foreign field-work, she'd explained to him one morning in bed, it had been like a drug. That was all. But she was coming off it now. For them, but mostly for herself.

—

Their first winter at Coed y Bryn was long, arriving with a sudden October frost furring the fields and icing the trees, before dragging on through to snow flurries in April. Despite the weather, or perhaps because of it, it was over these months that Caroline took to climbing the hill behind the cottage on her own. There was no mobile reception inside the house and Michael noticed she'd begun taking her phone with her on these walks. It hadn't worried him. He'd sensed no waning in her feelings for him. If anything, their relationship, still young, was only strengthening. Their life was finding its pattern, both mutual and independent. Ever since he was a teenager Michael had lived with a low-grade hum of concern that he would never be able to love. Not fully, beyond the initial attraction. Not with all of his past and all of his future as well as his present. But with every day together at Coed y Bryn, Caroline was proving him wrong.

———

She was preparing dinner when she told him.

"We got that commission," she said from the kitchen. "Pete told us today."

She was chopping vegetables, the tap of her knife on the wooden cutting board steady and quick.

Michael was editing a chapter at the table. "That's great," he said without looking up. "Network?"

It was late April and the evening beyond the French windows still held a hint of the day's light. The previous autumn, without telling Caroline, Michael had planted an arcing *C* of daffodil bulbs at the top of the lawn. The letter had shown itself in March, before pausing in the spring frosts, the tall stems still budded. Only the previous week had it finally thickened into the bright yellow of full bloom.

"Yes," Caroline said. "Transmission in October. If we can make it work."

"And can you?" Michael struck his pen through a paragraph and turned the page.

"I think so." Picking up the chopping board, she tipped the slices of courgette and red onion into a saucepan. "The uncle's agreed to contribute. He's our in, as long as we keep him on board."

There was something about the way she'd said "our" and "we" that made Michael look up from his editing. The words had been possessive more than inclusive.

She was facing away from him, her head bent as she crushed garlic cloves with the flat of the knife. Her hair fell either side of her neck, revealing a nub of vertebrae at the top of her spine. Somehow, all through the winter her skin had held its honey colour, as if it knew where she really belonged.

"The uncle?" he said. "Sorry, love, which one is this again?"

She turned to face him. Her expression was like that of a nurse imparting news to a relative.

"The one about the boy from Easton," she said, leaning back against the kitchen counter and crossing her arms. She still held the knife in her hands. The scent of the garlic pulp on its blade came to him. "The kid who went to Pakistan. His uncle's agreed to go back. To make the introductions."

He remembered now. Three young Muslim boys recruited at a mosque in Bristol. They were only seventeen, eighteen years old. Like backpackers on a gap year, they'd left for a training camp on the Afghan-Pakistan border. Two of them had returned, but a third had not. Sightline had approached his family about making a documentary. That was all she'd told him, months ago now.

He put down his pen.

"That's amazing," he said. "Well done. Sightline must be over the moon."

She smiled and looked down for a moment. And she was right. Suddenly it was funny. Suddenly they both knew what was coming, and the knowing of it made her wary attempt at disclosure seem ridiculous. Michael decided to go with the smile, even though a dull ache was already lodging between his ribs.

He leant back and put his feet on a chair. "But who's on their books who could handle something like that?" he said. "I wonder . . ."

She looked back at him. "It would be two weeks. Max."

"When?"

"As soon as we can get visas and travel sorted. And a fixer, but I've . . ." She trailed off.

"But you're already on to that," he said.

"Yes," she said quietly.

And then it wasn't funny anymore, as if the humour they'd discovered had been sucked out of the room with her confirmation.

Pushing herself from the work surface, she came to him, lifting his legs and placing them on her lap as she sat down.

"It wouldn't be Afghanistan," she said. "We'd do it all from Pakistan."

"Would it be safe?" he asked.

She shrugged. "As safe as it can be."

She leant forward and took his hands.

"It's a really important one, Mikey. His uncle, the sources he's mentioned. No one's had this kind of access before. No one. I mean anywhere. We'd be the first. And the group he's with, this kid, they actually want to talk. They want to tell their side of the story. And so does he."

He knew, as he stroked the back of her hand and she squeezed the fingers of his, that he could only go with this. He could only ride the contours of her desire, and that somewhere under that deepening ache in his ribs, that was also what he wanted. It was what they'd promised each other from the start. To help each other be happy, whatever that meant.

He lifted his feet off her lap and leant forward, taking her face in his hands. "Just," he said, kissing her lightly, "be careful."

Her lips were warm, and as she kissed him back, pulling him to her, her mouth tasted of the onion she'd been eating as she cooked.

"Thank you," she whispered, putting her arms about his neck. "I owe you one Mikey boy."

CHAPTER
FOUR

WHEN CAROLINE WAS killed, Michael brought so little back to London he made the move himself, loading his belongings into the back of their Volvo. He'd decided to sell Coed y Bryn fully furnished. Everything within it was resonant with her. Over the last week Caroline's family had flown over and passed through its rooms, taking certain personal items and anything else they wanted. Michael, too, had kept a few of the smaller mementos: photographs, a box of ticket stubs and cards, a Dictaphone recording of the answer-phone message she'd left him that night in Hammersmith. But everything else he'd let go. The buyers of the cottage took the furniture. He gave her clothes, which he kept seeing filled with her body, to a local charity shop. He wanted to remember Caroline, but under his own volition, not ambushed by the objects around him.

He'd arrived late in South Hill Drive, the car's engine sounding too loud, too clumsy between the curving banks of town houses, their windows lit with autumn domesticity. There was no space outside Peter's flat, so Michael double-parked to unload his belongings onto the pavement. He wondered for a moment whether he should leave them unguarded as he parked the car farther up the street. But a glance along its tree-lined camber reassured him.

The gentle incline was unpeopled and split into a loop that went nowhere but back on itself. In the aerial view Michael had seen online the shape of the street resembled an old-fashioned tennis racket strung with trees, an accidental growth ballooning from London's mosaic into the green spaces of the Heath.

Michael was returning to collect the last of his belongings when he first saw Josh. He was walking up the street, a trench coat slung over his shoulder, a briefcase in the other hand. He wore a dark suit and a loosened blue tie. Michael could tell he was drunk. There was a looseness to his body too, a detachment about his gaze.

Michael bent to pick up a couple of boxes. As he arranged them on top of each other he became aware of Josh nearing, then coming to a stop. He looked up. Josh was rooting for a set of keys in the pockets of his coat. As he pulled them out he returned Michael's look, then glanced up at the block of flats beside them.

"Seems we're neighbours," he said, raising his eyebrows. His accent was American, tempered by Europe.

Michael stood, hitching the boxes in his arms. "Almost," he said.

Josh looked at him blankly, as if seeing him for the first time. He wasn't as tall as Michael, but he was broader. His dark hair was stitched with grey, a fringe falling in a tight crest above a pair of wire-rimmed glasses.

"Well," Michael said. "Good night."

He went to move towards the flat.

"Lemme give you a hand." The thought seemed to come to Josh suddenly, stirring him with its arrival.

"No, really, it's—"

But Josh had already pocketed his keys and was swinging Michael's fencing bag over his shoulder. Hooking his briefcase over his wrist, he bent to the last box on the pavement.

"Guitar?" he asked, shifting the bag on his back as he stood.

"No," Michael replied, leading the way into the flat. "Fencing kit."

"Fencing?" Josh said from behind Michael as he pressed the timer switch for the hallway light with his elbow. "Never tried it myself."

Something in Josh's voice suggested he never wanted to, either.

"Gave mine away," he continued, as they took the first flight of stairs. "Guitar. Gave it away. Can't remember why now."

As they climbed the stairs up to Peter's flat Josh carried on talking, telling Michael how much he'd like the street, how the other neighbours were "okay, you know, no trouble," and how much his two girls loved the Heath.

"Like having London's biggest garden on your doorstep. I mean, the Queen, she's got nothing on this, right?"

At the turn of the third floor Josh's conversation gave way to a laboured breathing. Michael was grateful. As they'd ascended he'd felt himself growing tense in anticipation of the question he didn't want to answer. But it never came, and Josh fell silent with the exertion instead.

Inside the flat, Michael added his boxes to the pile already in the living area. "Just here's fine," he said, as Josh entered behind him.

Josh lowered the box and swung the kitbag off his shoulder. As he straightened he kneaded at his lower back with his knuckles. He wore a wedding ring, a gold Rolex, silver cuff links. He was breathing heavily.

"I'd offer you a drink, but—" Michael gestured at the empty room by way of finishing his sentence; the ghosts of hung pictures faded the walls in a series of squares and rectangles. The shelves were empty, the kitchen bare. It smelt of packing tape and old tea.

Josh waved a hand, dismissing his aborted offer. Taking off his glasses, he cleaned them on his shirt as he walked over to the windows, the same ones Michael had seen in the first email Peter had sent him, two long frames taking up most of the wall looking over the Heath.

"You know," Josh said, turning to Michael, "five years I've lived on this street, and this is the first time I've ever been in this building."

He tapped the glass, as if trying to touch the night. "You see this view?"

"Not yet. I mean, not here."

"Great view," Josh said, ignoring Michael's qualification. "Great view."

He turned back to the window and looked into the darkness. A single lamp on the Heath burned orange through a gauze of mist, illuminating the edges of the turning trees. "Seven years and still not tired of it," he said, speaking to the window.

But when he looked back at Michael he did look tired, as if the climb up the stairs had brought a painful memory to the surface of his skin. Josh nodded, as if in agreement with his own observation.

"Well, thanks again," Michael said.

Josh looked up at him, as if trying to decipher who his new neighbour might be. For a moment Michael returned his gaze, unsure as to what to do.

"Don't mention it," Josh said eventually, crossing the room and picking up his coat and briefcase. "Josh," he said, holding out his hand. "Joshua Nelson."

"Michael," Michael answered. They shook, a short, business-like chop. Josh, Michael felt, shook hands a great deal. Now that he was closer to him he could smell the drink and smoke on him, lacing his breath. "Good to meet you," he said. "And really, thanks for the help."

"You should come round," Josh said, as he went into the hall-way, putting on his coat. "My wife, she's always having drinks, par-ties, you know. She likes meeting people. New people. You should come."

"Thanks, I will."

Raising a hand in farewell, Josh walked out the door.

"See you around, Mike," he called from the stairwell. "Happy home."

—

Michael closed the door and went back into the living room, its drift of boxes and bags abandoned on the carpet. He turned towards the windows and saw himself, the lamp on the Heath burning in his chest. Slowly, he approached his reflection. As he did, the lamp's sodium glow slipped into his stomach, and then his groin. He stopped short of the window, as if facing down the man staring back at him. A tall man in a blue sweater and jeans, his long arms hanging at his sides, his blond hair receding.

This is where they would start again, he and this man in the window. In this flat with its view of the Heath, its stained carpet and its forgotten yet remembered pictures on the walls. This is where he would have to make peace with his past, and with the man in the window who'd let it happen.

His phone began ringing and both men reached into their pockets to check the screen. It was Peter. He'd already called Michael twice that day. Both times Michael had let the phone ring out in his hand, as he did again now. He took another step towards the window and put the phone on the sill. A single print, from where Josh had poked the glass, was smudged over the dark pond below. Michael rested his head against the pane and allowed the night to cool his brow.

Below him his phone vibrated with a message, lighting up and turning on the sill like a dying fly. Michael glanced at it but left it alone. There was nothing else to say. Caroline was dead and he'd been left holding the shell of that truth, bereft not only of her, but also of the man she'd been making him.

—

Caroline never told Michael she'd chosen Peter. A week before she'd left they'd picked her "proof of life" questions together, but that was all.

What was the name of her cat in Adelaide Road?
What was the colour of her neighbour's truck in Melbourne?
What gift did she take her host when she last visited Cape Town?

These were the questions someone from Sightline, probably Peter, would have asked her captors down the line. Their answers, should she have been kidnapped, would have proved she was still alive.

MISTY
ORANGE
MARMITE

They'd made a game of choosing the questions, sitting outside the French windows at Coed y Bryn in front of the opened *C* of daffodils, a bottle of a wine and an Indian takeaway at their feet. Together, they'd gone hunting for stories she still hadn't told him from her life. Anecdotes from her childhood or student days in Boston. Family fables that still left her creased with laughter from across the years.

It was standard procedure, that's what she'd told him. Nothing to worry about. Which was when Michael had wanted to ask her. Because he knew what else would be standard procedure. He'd had friends in New York who did jobs like hers. So which colleague or friend had she chosen? Who had she decided should be the person to come and tell him? But he hadn't asked her and she hadn't offered. As if in superstition of some jealous god, they'd left it unspoken as they'd picked up the glasses and cartons and, with a chill edging the evening air, headed inside to bed.

So the first Michael knew of Caroline's choice was when Peter arrived at the cottage a few weeks later. It was late in the afternoon, grey clouds piling above the hills, the River Severn flashing in the distance like a falling coin. Michael was out the back, heaping branches and brambles onto a bonfire. At first he'd mistaken the crackle of tires on the gravel as the sound of the flames. But then he'd heard an engine cut out and the slam of a car door. When he'd come round to the front of the house he was still wearing his gardening gloves, a fistful of blackthorn bunched in one hand. Peter was standing beside the front porch. On hearing Michael's footsteps he'd turned towards him. The look in his eyes, like that of a child, stopped Michael in his tracks.

Michael had met Peter only a few times before. At a Sightline Christmas party, at some drinks for Caroline's birthday. There had been a dinner once, too, with him and his wife at their house in Bristol. Michael liked him. He had the easy, dry manner of a man who'd decided to avoid arguments. Not because he couldn't win them, but because he didn't want to have to. According to Caroline, if he'd wanted, Peter could have risen high in broadcasting. But he'd chosen to stay at a level that kept him close to the making of programmes instead. "Close," as he once said to Michael, smiling in resignation, "to the stuff they're actually about."

For a long second, as they'd faced each other outside Coed y Bryn that afternoon, neither man had said anything, the gaps in their mutual knowledge growing between them. But then Peter had said his name—"Michael," and that's when he'd known. Caroline had chosen Peter. Peter was the man who'd bear her last message, the man who'd come to him across the gravel as he sank to his knees, whose voice would say his name again—"Michael"— and whose hands would come to rest lightly on his shoulders as he buried his face in his gloves, inhaling their scent of wood smoke, the blackthorns scratching at his skin.

CHAPTER FIVE

THE NELSONS' HALLWAY was flooded with light, the frosted pane above its front door bright with afternoon sun. As Michael walked its length he passed a series of black-and-white photographs hung on the wall to his right. A couple kissing on a bench in Washington Square; an elderly Chinese man looking into an out-of-frame glare; the skyline of Manhattan, miniature between two leaves in the foreground. To his left, halfway along this line of images, a broad staircase climbed the other floors of the house.

The photographs were taken by Samantha. Beneath them she'd hung framed drawings and paintings by her daughters, garish with primary colour. In the first a palm tree arced out from a yellow beach beside a blue sea. The artist's name was written in crayon above its jagged green leaves—*Lucy, age 4.* Next to this was a crooked picture-book house bordered by a scribbled hedge, another darker scribble describing smoke from its chimney—*Rachel, age 6.* As he walked on Michael passed horses, Mummy and Daddy, a red fire engine, and there, at the end of the wall before the door into the front room, a tall stick man wearing a red T-shirt and brown trousers, his hair a rough patch of yellow and his name written above in blue—*Michael.*

Pausing at his portrait, Michael turned towards the stairs and listened for movement from the floors above. There was nothing. He glanced at the front door to check it was fully closed, which it was. Perhaps it was simply a mistake. It was a beautiful day, so why would they have stayed inside? Josh had probably taken the girls to fly a kite on Parliament Hill, or to swim at the lido below it. Dealing with both of them on his own, he'd maybe just forgotten to close the back door.

Turning from the stairs, Michael went into the front room. He knew he was cutting it fine. If the screwdriver wasn't in there, then he'd have to leave without it. The room was lit by three tall windows, buttresses of sunlight falling through their draperies. The furnishings were pale, the carpet oatmeal, the shelves white. It was a cabinet of a room, a display case of a shaped and presented life. Artefacts from around the world, art books, travel guides. An oil painting of the Norfolk coast. Side tables deep with photographs of parents, the girls, Samantha and Josh on their wedding day. An old trunk served as a coffee table at its centre. Standing within this lit order Michael held his dirty hands in front of him, palms up, like a surgeon before an operation.

—

When Josh's promise of an invitation had arrived, it had brought Michael to a party in this room, which is where he'd first met Samantha and the girls. It was a clear Saturday afternoon in November. A week of strong winds had blown the last leaves from the trees on the Heath. The sky was a high blue, a last gift before winter, the air crisp under it. Michael had been to a fencing lesson that morning, one of his first. As he'd returned across the Heath his breath had steamed before him, his footprints leaving a trail through the frosted grass. The dog walkers were scarved, the joggers wearing gloves. As he'd approached the ponds behind the street he'd noticed most of the weekend swimmers were wearing caps.

It was Samantha who'd answered the door. The folded note

Michael had found a few days earlier on the doormat at the bottom of his stairwell had been written by her, too. A confident, flowing hand. His name on the front and a simple message inside—*We're having a party on Saturday. From around 2pm. Do come if you can. Samantha and Josh.*

"Oh, hi! Great you could come," she said. "Come in, come in."

She wore a long-sleeved red dress, a grey cotton belt tied above the slight swell of her stomach. Michael could tell she didn't know who he was.

"Michael," he said, as he stepped inside. "From next door?"

"Yes, of course!" She had an easy, natural smile. "Josh told me all about you."

Michael offered her the bottle of Sancerre he'd brought.

"Oh, you shouldn't have," she said as she took it. "Honestly, no need. Thank you."

There was a swell of voices in the room behind her, a cacophony of registers and conversations. Leading Michael towards them, Samantha called over the heads of her guests.

"Josh? Josh? Look who's here."

"Who?"

Michael recognised his voice from the night he'd moved in. Authority laced with surprise. She touched his arm.

"Oh, God, I'm sorry," she said, looking genuinely alarmed. "I'm useless with names."

He reminded her and she called to Josh again. "Michael," she said, leaning into the crowd, one hand on the door frame. "From next door."

She turned back to him, flashing another smile. "I'll just pop this in the fridge. Josh'll sort you out."

He watched her walk away. Her blonde hair was up, held by a clasp in the shape of a red flower. Her heels, also red, were sudden and sharp on the kitchen tiles.

"What can I get you?"

Josh's question arrived with his hand, firm on Michael's back, guiding him into the room. It was loud with people, more smiles, drinks. Children holding glasses of orange juice in both hands passed between the legs of the adults, or offered bowls of nuts and crisps to the friends of their parents. As Josh led Michael towards a table of bottles and glasses he seemed markedly different from the man who'd looked out at the nighttime Heath a few weeks before, a man on his first drink, not his last.

As Josh poured him a glass of wine, Michael tried to listen to what he was saying. But the room's activity had caught him unawares. His attention was already scattering in anticipation. He'd been back in London for five weeks now, but he'd yet to open himself to a social occasion like this. His recovery, he'd already learnt, would rely on routine, in avoiding anything that might accentuate the space of Caroline at his side. His memory had become a minefield. He'd never known his body to respond so quickly to thought, or imagined his mind could produce such physical pain, such tears. He was not used to crying, but even now, six months after her death, a thought of Caroline, the shadow of an image, the recall of how she tied up her hair before a shower or dabbed spots of moisturiser on her cheeks, could be enough to make his chest thicken, his breath shallow, and his eyes fill.

To avoid such uninvited memories, he'd kept himself away from older friends, or from anyone who'd known him and Caroline as a couple. He'd declined his editor's invitations to book launches, and had only agreed to meet with his agent at a restaurant away from his office. Cinemas, galleries, or theatres to which he and Caroline had once gone together were out of the question. In this way, London had been diminished by his grief, and so though familiar, made strange again, too.

As Josh poured himself another glass of red a child appeared at his leg, a girl tugging at his shirt. Her blonde hair had come loose of its bow. Smudges of chocolate were smeared across her T-shirt, its patterned hem hanging wide from her belly.

"Hey," Josh said to her. "You come to say hello?" He bent to pick her up.

"This is Lucy," he said, hitching her in the crook of his arm. "And this," he continued, prising Lucy's knuckle from her mouth, "is Michael, our new neighbour."

Lucy buried her face in her father's shoulder. Grasping at his collar, she rubbed its crease between her fingers.

"Oh, gone shy on us, have you?" Josh said to her, winking at Michael. "We'll see how long that lasts, eh?"

——

Josh knew his daughter well. Less than half an hour later Lucy came to find Michael in the crowd, a doll in each of her hands. He was sitting on the arm of a sofa, on the edges of a conversation about the local hospital.

"This is Molly," Lucy said by way of introduction, thrusting one of the dolls towards him. "And this"—she pushed out the other doll, its face marked with blue crayon—"is Dolly."

"Well, hello," Michael said. "Good to meet you. But what happened to Dolly's face?"

"Well," Lucy said, as if Michael had asked her opinion on the conversation behind him, "it started yesterday, you see. Molly was very cross with Dolly."

With an ease that seemed foreign to the child he'd met earlier, Lucy began explaining the root of the dolls' disagreement. As she talked she frowned down at them, both naked, one blonde, one brunette, absorbed in their story. Occasionally she raised her eyebrows, too, dramatically but with sincerity, as if trying out the expression for the first time.

Michael listened, grateful for the length of her explanation and happy to let her talk. He didn't want to disengage from the party, but the truth was Lucy's story, the solipsism of her age, had come as a relief to him. Earlier Josh, guiding him with his hand on his back again, had introduced him to a group of other guests. "This is Michael, our new neighbour," he'd said, before moving on to greet others arriving in the hallway. Michael had shaken hands with them, and appeared to talk easily enough. But beneath the conversation his mind was double-tracking all the time, trying to keep one step ahead so as to steer it away from any question that might force him to mention Caroline or her death.

In the end he needn't have worried. None of the other guests had seemed perturbed by his reticence, or anxious to question him in return. Ben, a colleague from Josh's bank, owned a holiday cottage in Cornwall not far from where Michael had been brought up. Within minutes he'd been able to navigate them towards swapping recommendations on restaurants and galleries, coastal walks between shingle coves, hidden pubs. The one woman in the group, a young lawyer who'd introduced herself as "Janera, but call me Jan," had been eager to tell him about a play she'd just seen. She'd gone on her own and it had made her cry. She couldn't remember the playwright's name, but she'd been at college with one of the actors. He'd had a full head of hair back then, but now he was completely bald and it was this, more than the play itself, about which she appeared most excited. The third guest was an older man in a blazer whose name Michael didn't catch. He asked whether Michael's flat had a view of the ponds on the Heath? When Michael said it did, the man, whose cheeks were rosy with capillaries, told him how he'd once swum in them on a Christmas Day in the sixties. He'd done it to impress a girl, whose name he'd forgotten now. There'd been a skin of ice at the water's edge. She'd waited for him on one of the benches, wrapped in both their scarves, laughing.

As Michael listened and talked, nodded and smiled, he felt as if he'd stepped through a looking glass and was observing a world he'd left behind, a more simple, childish world, untutored by death. He knew it wasn't true, of course. That every adult in the room would have lost. That each of them carried their own grief, however subdued, and that a fear of their own ends haunted them, too, whenever they allowed their thoughts to linger above that darkness. But none of that showed, and why should it? All of it was covered by the talk, the desire, the manners. And so Michael was left feeling adrift, the only seeing witness in a room of the chattering blind.

At their first interview for *The Man Who Broke the Mirror,* Oliver Blackwood had told Michael a man wasn't born until he'd had children. At the time Michael said he couldn't know, not having had any himself, but that he certainly agreed with the French when they said you became an adult only when you lost your parents. He'd spoken from experience. His own father had died while he was in New York. His mother, too, was seriously ill at the time. A year after that interview, she'd also died. Michael, an only child, missed them both terribly. In the months after his mother's funeral the comment he'd made to Oliver had surfaced in his mind every day.

Michael had only just begun seeing Caroline when he'd answered the phone one morning to hear a carer at the nursing home tell him his mother had "passed on" during the night. Caroline was in the shower, and when she'd come downstairs she'd found Michael, the phone in his hand, staring at the table. They were still just discovering each other. The night he'd find her waiting for him in his bathroom was months away in their future. Their knowledge of each other was shallow. And yet Caroline had accompanied him every step along the deepening shelf of his mother's death, nurturing him through the funeral and the quiet sadness afterwards. She was acquainted with it. That's what she'd told him. So he shouldn't see it as an imposition too soon, upon her or them. She knew death and what it did to the living, so he should let her help him, which he had.

But now, in the wake of hers, Michael couldn't help think that both Caroline and Oliver had been wrong. If he'd been able to speak to her, if her ghost should have visited him one night, he'd have told her you cannot be familiar with death; it can only be familiar with you. And if he'd known at that first meeting with Oliver what he knew now, then he'd have told him that there was a birth into maturity beyond having children or losing your parents. It was the birth of an amputated love. Of having found a person in whom life makes sense, someone who expands you, only to have their death suddenly close you again, like the teeth of a woodland trap. And in that closing to experience a slow tearing in the fabric of your days, your years. This, he would have told Oliver, is the truest birth into adult knowledge. A rare wisdom shared with life prisoners and locked-in sufferers, to have your future taken from you, and yet still remain alive.

—

"And so Dolly said sorry and now they are friends." Lucy punctuated the end of her story by jerking the two dolls in the air in front of her, shivering their synthetic hairstyles.

Michael smiled. "Well, I'm glad," he said. "It's more fun being friends than not being friends, isn't it?"

Lucy cocked her head in mock thought. "Maybeee," she said, drawing out the end of the word.

A woman in a petrol-blue shawl behind them began cracking pistachio shells into a cupped hand, the painted nail of her thumb prising them open. Somewhere by the door the greetings of old friends rose above the room's murmuring talk, like a piece of driftwood lifted on a wave.

"How old are you, Lucy?" Michael asked her.

"She's four," another voice said. Michael looked up to see an older girl looking down at them, her chestnut hair cut in a bob. She wore jeans, trainers, and a sweatshirt with the name of a boy band down one of its sleeves.

"Four and a quarter!" Lucy protested.

"I'm seven," her older sister said, as if she hadn't heard her. "My name's Rachel."

She spoke confidently, a child brought up among adults.

"Do you want to come and see my drawings?"

"What do you think, Lucy?" Michael said. "Shall we go and see Rachel's drawings?"

Lucy hit the sofa with Dolly's head. "They're stupid drawings!"

"Well," Michael said, trying to placate her, "isn't that for me to decide?" He stood up. "Do you want to come, too?"

But Lucy wasn't listening anymore. Michael's acceptance of her sister's invitation had instantly demoted him in her interest. Lowering herself beside the sofa, she was already talking to Molly and Dolly instead.

"Come on," Rachel said, taking his hand. "They're in the kitchen."

—

The question Michael had managed to avoid among the Nelsons' guests was eventually asked by Josh himself. They were standing together at the bottom of the garden, looking out over the ponds. Rachel, as promised, had taken Michael into the kitchen to look at her drawings laid across a coffee table in the conservatory. Samantha had been at the oven, sliding out trays of canapés.

"Now, don't take up all of Michael's time," she'd said, her face flushed in the heat. "Someone else might want to talk to him, too."

She needn't have worried. All Rachel had required was a brisk tour through her work before a request from her mother soon sent her back into the party, a bowl of olives in each hand. Michael asked Samantha if he might help, too. Giving him another of her smiles, she told him it was fine. She spoke to him as if they'd known each other for years. And yet her manner was also somehow distant, her air of familiarity defused, he suspected, by the generosity with which it was applied to all whom she met.

Removing a last tray of canapés from the oven, Samantha had followed her daughter down the hallway towards the voices at its end. Michael listened to her heels diminish down the wooden floor-boards. He thought about following her but didn't. After the crush of bodies next door, the quiet of the unpeopled kitchen was calming, as was the cleanness of the winter light falling through the conservatory. He needed time to collect himself before he entered the party again. Or perhaps he would leave. Perhaps it was still too soon. Perhaps, he admitted to himself, he shouldn't have come at all.

A copy of the *Herald Tribune* was lying on a chair beside him. Opening it, Michael began flicking through its pages, his eye naturally drawn to articles about the wars. The presidential candidates were filling their speeches with talk of surges and exit strategies. A group of road workers had been killed by ISAF bombing in eastern Afghanistan. An FBI investigation had concluded fourteen civilian deaths at the hands of Blackwater were "killings without cause." Michael was still reading the paper when Josh entered. He made straight for a drawer in the kitchen's island and took out a packet of cigarettes and a lighter.

"Smoke?" he said, holding them up.

"No, thanks," Michael said.

"Join me anyway?" Josh nodded at the back door, pushing his glasses up the bridge of his nose.

Outside, the afternoon light had pulled the Heath into focus, a palette of oranges, greens, and browns beneath the blue sky. As Michael and Josh walked down the garden towards the ponds, Josh lit a cigarette.

"Sam doesn't like it," he said, the smoke thickening his breath. "But, well, it's my weekend, too, right?"

As they reached the fence at the bottom, Josh took another deep draw. Leaning against the fence, Michael breathed in more deeply, too. The air above the water tasted of iron and fallen leaves. The trees beyond, which had just that morning been so busy with wind, were bare and motionless. A dog was swimming in the pond, only its golden head visible above the water. Its owner, a woman on the other side, was calling to it from the water's edge.

"Jasper! Jasper!"

"Christ," Josh said. "Jasper? No wonder it wants to stay in the fucking pond."

Michael watched the dog make a slow turn back towards his owner's voice, his nose high as he paddled into the shallows. Reaching the bank, he trotted up the slope towards her, the long hair of his flanks heavy with water, his paws dark with mud.

"You married, Mike?"

The question seemed to come from nowhere. Michael kept his eyes on Jasper as he stopped short of his owner and shook himself dry. After such attention among the other guests, he'd been distracted by this dog's brief escape. And now Josh had asked him, so he'd have to answer.

He turned to face him. Josh pointed with his cigarette at Michael's wedding ring. Michael glanced at it, too. It had never occurred to him to take it off. As far as he was concerned, he was still married.

"I was," Michael said, touching the underside of the ring with his thumb.

"Ah, shit," Josh said. "Divorced?"

"No," Michael replied, looking out at the pond again. "She died."

"Jesus."

Michael heard Josh take another drag, then blow out a thin plume. "God," he said, "I'm sorry."

Michael had never had to say those two words before. Since returning to London he'd avoided them. But now that he had, they felt untrue. As if someone else were speaking through his mouth.

"I like it best when it's frozen," Josh said, drawing his cigarette across the air in front of him, its tip glowing in the movement. "Last year all this, the whole thing, was ice. The girls wanted to skate on it, but, well, you know—"

Michael knew Josh was talking to fill the vacuum. He wanted to let him know he didn't have to.

"That's why I moved here," he said. "We had a place in Wales. But when it happened—"

Josh nodded in understanding, but also, it seemed to Michael, in calculation, too. Was he remembering the night he'd moved in? How they'd stood together in his flat, the meagre pile of boxes and bags abandoned in the living room?

"Was it an accident?" Josh asked.

"Sort of," Michael said, taking another deep breath and releasing it in a sigh. "But also not. She was in Pakistan. Well, in the border area—"

He broke off, unsure how to continue.

"Was she serving?"

"God, no!" Michael allowed himself a bemused smile at the thought of Caroline in the army. "No, she was a reporter. Wrong place, wrong time. You might have read about it. It was in the papers."

"What was her name?"

"Caroline," Michael said. "Caroline Marshall."

Josh took another drag on his cigarette. "That's terrible," he said, shaking his head. "I'm so sorry, Mike. Just terrible."

Michael nodded. He was right. It was terrible. That was the word, and it would always be the word for it, however much time passed, or however much his memory might fade. He ran his hand across the top of the fence, to feel the realness of its grain, the dampness of its wood against his skin.

"I'm sorry," he said. "I didn't mean to bring it up. I mean, at your party."

Josh reached out and held Michael by the shoulder, his grip firmer than necessary. "Are you serious?" he said. "Christ, don't be ridiculous. And anyway, you didn't bring it up, I did."

A drift of voices came down the garden. Some of the guests had moved into the kitchen.

"If there's anything we can do," Josh said, "just let us know. I'm serious. Please."

Michael nodded. "Thanks."

The back door opened and the chatter of the party became louder.

"We should get back," Josh said, stubbing out his cigarette and slipping the butt in his pocket. "Or at least I should."

"No," Michael said, letting go of the fence. "I'm fine. I'll come, too."

As they walked up the garden Josh touched Michael's arm again. "So what's it you do, Mike? To keep the wolf from the door?"

"I'm a writer," Michael said.

"Yeah?" Josh said. "Anything published?"

"One book. Too many articles."

"Hey, that's great!" Josh said with too much enthusiasm.

"And you're with Lehman's?" Michael asked.

"Yeah, in brokerage, mostly," Josh said, as if that's what everyone did. "Hey, listen, there's someone here I want you to meet. Old college buddy of mine, Tony. He and his wife have just moved over. He's a publisher."

As they neared the back door, Samantha appeared at the top of the steps. Her face was tense. "Joshua?" she said, showing her palms in exasperation.

"Is Tony in there, honey?" Josh asked. "I want him to meet Mike. Mike's a writer, did he tell you that?"

—

In the years to come, Michael would often think how it was Tony, more than anyone else, he had to thank for his friendship with the Nelsons. Or perhaps to blame, given what happened because of it. Had Tony and his wife, Maddy, not been at the party that day, then it was more than possible Michael would have remained no more than a neighbour to Josh and Samantha. Morning greetings, occasional conversations over the hedge dividing his communal garden from their private lawn, glimpses of them emerging from a taxi at night, a streetlight catching their clothes as they passed into the shadows.

Perhaps there would have been other parties, and maybe at one of them someone else would have performed a similar role to Tony's that Saturday in November. But Michael doubted it. There are narrow windows for certain beginnings. Multiple strands of personal histories, psychologies, emotions that intersect once only, and then never again. There is, in the end, a time for everything. This is what Michael told himself in the years afterwards. Sometimes in consolation, more often in regret. That however much he tried to unpick those threads, however much he attempted to locate the source moment of what had happened, he could not. There was always another beyond it, connected by the most fragile of strands, but connected still. Time had travelled through all of them—him, Caroline, Samantha, Josh, Lucy, Rachel—and there was nothing they could have done about it. None of their choices had been malign. And yet combined, they'd created darkness more than light.

For the other residents of South Hill Drive, the nature of Michael's friendship with Samantha and Josh was difficult to fathom. Viewed from a distance, it seemed both unlikely and imbalanced. Him, a young single widower, reticent with grief, a freelancer adrift on the hours of the day. Them, a young family busy with the tides of life, with the schedules and demands of their shared hours.

But it wasn't just the differing makeup of their lives that led others on the street to comment or question. It was also the momentum of their relationship, the speed at which they'd become so intimate following that party. Over the next seven months their involvement in one another's lives deepened to a degree that all of them had only ever experienced before after a period of years. Within a few weeks Michael and Josh were regularly to be seen leaving of a morning for their jogs on the Heath; when the girls came

home from school and nursery they soon got used to Michael joining them in their kitchen, having tea with Samantha or even helping with their homework as she prepared dinner. He and Samantha
often met during the days, too, at the cafés edging the Heath or
in the canteen of Kenwood House. Three or four times a week, as
Josh exited the Tube station in Belsize Park, Michael's phone would
light up with a text on his desk—"Come round for a drink?" By
the time it was Christmas it already seemed natural that Michael
should join them for lunch, arriving at their back door with an
armful of presents for the girls and a bottle of champagne for
their parents. All of which puzzled their other neighbours on the
street who followed, through windows and rumour, their accelerated friendship. What these neighbours couldn't appreciate, however, was that the source of their surprise was also its reason. It
was exactly because of its newness, its lack of depth, that Michael,
Samantha, and Josh had embraced their newfound companionship
with the familiarity of years.

When Michael had first met them that winter, there were
already undercurrents pulling at Samantha and Josh's marriage.
In their differing ways, despite apparently having achieved all
they'd hoped, both were honeycombed with disappointment. In
the last couple of years that internal fragility had begun to show.
Josh, Michael came to learn, beyond his public bonhomie, could
be spiteful and demeaning to his wife. Samantha, meanwhile, met
his outbursts with a deepening silence, an ingrained resentment
that increasingly manifested itself in an outward disregard for Josh
and his work. They both drank, Samantha for solace and reward,
Josh to rediscover the optimism of his youth; to feel the muscle
memory of when his life was just that, his. The first time Michael
had heard them arguing through the conjoining wall of his building and their house he thought maybe a burglar had broken into
their home. But then he'd recognised Josh's accent in the muffled
shouts, Samantha's pitch in her tearful retorts.

For both Samantha and Josh, Michael appeared at this stage in their lives as someone unattached to their pasts, or to any of the areas of their marriage in which its stresses were bred. He wasn't a work colleague of Josh's, a university friend of Samantha's, or a parent with a child at Lucy's nursery or Rachel's school. He was free of association with their histories, and as such their only shared acquaintance. All their other friends were either Samantha's or Josh's before becoming "theirs." It often felt as if in Michael's presence Samantha and Josh were able to forget their married past, and yet remember the best of themselves, too, and that this was why, beyond anything he ever brought himself, they'd become so attached to having him in their home.

In a similar way, Michael was surprised to find relief in Samantha and Josh's unfamiliarity with Caroline. Josh thought he may have once seen one of her reports when staying at a hotel in Berlin, but he couldn't be sure. What was certain was that neither of them had ever known her in person. Her death, for Samantha and Josh, was just another fact of Michael's life. Something with which he'd arrived at their door along with the rest of his past, rather than a loss with which he'd been burdened, as some of his older friends had seen it. To Samantha and Josh, Caroline existed only in Michael's telling of her. When he talked about her with them, he found himself speaking about her life, not her death. So for them, there was no "before" Caroline, but just this echo of a person, still sounding in the man sitting at their table, not as an absence, but as a part of him.

Over those first few weeks after meeting Josh and Samantha, Michael came to realise that rather than avoiding the questions of strangers, perhaps he should have been seeking them all along. In the Nelsons' lack of familiarity with Caroline he'd discovered a taste not just of what his life might be like in the years to come, but also what it had been like before her death, and even—and at this a sharp guilt would stab through him—of what it had been like before her.

—

"Michael Turner? The Michael Turner who wrote *Brother-Hoods?*" Tony pumped Michael's hand harder as he said yes, that was right, he'd written *BrotherHoods.*

When Michael and Josh had reentered the party Michael had said he thought he should be going after all. But Josh had been insistent. He must meet Tony. He was taking over the digital arm of a company here. He'd love him; he was a great guy. Josh had known him since sophomore year. Michael was a writer, Tony was a publisher. So of course he should meet him. With a hand on Michael's shoulder once more, Josh had guided him back into the talk and the drink of the front room.

Tony Epplin was a tall, balding man with the hollowed cheeks of a distance runner. On being introduced to Michael, described by Josh as "our writer neighbour," he'd extended a polite but wary hand. On hearing Michael's name, however, his expression discovered a new vitality.

"It's great to meet you," he said, finally letting go of Michael's hand. "That was a great book. I loved it, I really did."

"You two know each other?" Josh asked, looking up at Tony from between them.

"Yeah," Tony said. "Well, no. Not each other. But Michael's book? I know that for sure. It was a big deal. Everyone knew it."

Michael thought he saw a glimpse of their teenage dynamics in Josh's reaction. Smiling and nodding, he turned to look at Michael as if seeing him for the first time. "Yeah? That so? You should have said!" Tony, Michael felt, had long been in possession of a taste to which Josh aspired, perhaps since those early sophomore years.

"Hey, Maddy? Maddy?"

A woman, as tall as Tony, turned towards them. Michael had never seen her before, but he still felt he knew her, having often met women like her in Manhattan, at drinks parties on the Upper East Side, or sleek in evening dress at the Met. She was slender-necked, the crow's feet about her eyes somehow a mark of knowledge more than age.

"Maddy? Can you come here a moment?" Tony said to her. "Guess who Josh's neighbour is?"

Maddy came over, parting the bodies between them with fingertip touches on their backs. She wore many rings, mostly gold, with emeralds and amethysts inlaid in their galleries. Michael saw Samantha tracking her approach from over another man's shoulder. She seemed alert, ready to intervene at the first sign of trouble.

"This is my wife, Maddy," Tony said. "And this," he continued, laying a hand on Michael's shoulder, "is Michael Turner. The guy who wrote *BrotherHoods*?"

"Oh," she said, offering her hand. "Yes. What a wonderful book." Her voice was as self-possessed as her beauty, slow and natural. "Weren't they making a film of it?" she asked.

As Tony and Maddy told him how much they'd enjoyed certain passages of *BrotherHoods,* and how Tony had once missed his subway stop while reading it, Michael became aware of the room's interest contracting around their conversation. Tony's voice was strong and confident, rising above the other talk. His attention to Michael began to draw the attention of others, too. In the focus of his and Maddy's questions, and in the ripples it sent through the other guests, Michael felt a resonance once more of the success to which the lives of Nico and Raoul had led him.

Samantha came to join them. Out of the corner of his eye Michael saw Josh turn to say something in her ear. She slipped an arm about his waist, giving him a squeeze as if to congratulate him on his discovery.

"How did you first meet them?" Tony asked, giving a twitch of his chin in professional interest. "Was it a commission?"

Josh had left them to get a couple of drinks. As he returned he handed Michael another glass of wine. Michael thanked him, took a sip, then began telling Tony about his trip up to Inwood Hill Park that day, about the cop on Dyckman and the story he'd told him about two brothers who'd left Arden Street glittering with smashed glass and car alarms. "I think it was the name of the street," Michael said, when Tony pressed him on why he'd followed that particular story. "It seemed so incongruous. And yet suitable, I suppose."

"Why?" Maddy asked from her husband's shoulder.

"I don't know. I've always associated Arden with the forest in *As You Like It*. A transgressive environment, a place to break the rules." He laughed at himself. "A bit of a stretch, I know, but—"

"Stories breed stories!" Tony said, turning to Maddy. "Isn't that what I always say? Stories breed stories. Always have, always will."

Maddy closed her eyes and gave the slightest of nods to confirm her husband's assertion. When she opened them again she was looking directly at Michael. He felt adolescent in her gaze.

Soon Josh and Samantha were asking him questions too. They'd both lived in New York when they were younger. Josh had lived on the Upper West Side when he'd crossed the river from New Jersey, and Samantha had studied at Parsons downtown. Michael was surprised to learn she knew many of the streets he was talking about. How did he conduct his research? She wanted to know. Did the police ever accuse him of being implicated?

Someone else—Janera, the young lawyer—cut in, explaining that journalists, and therefore writers, she guessed, had a right not to disclose their sources. Michael wasn't convinced this would have applied to him and Nico and Raoul, but he stayed quiet as the conversation moved on. When Josh asked him what he was working on now, Michael told him about Oliver Blackwood. The older blazer-wearing guest said he'd known Oliver at university. "He was," he said, "an annoying little shit, even then."

Perhaps it was the drink, or just the relief of having been asked the question he'd feared for so long, but as the talk opened up—to Oliver, neuroscience, other books and writers—Michael, held in a cat's cradle of voices, and with an end-of-day light washing the room, felt something give within him. It was a subtle slippage, no more than a flake dislodging from a cliff. But it was movement nevertheless, a falling away. He was still far from at ease in these surroundings. In New York, at this type of gathering, it had always felt as if the occasion's energy was fuelled by questions. The people around him had been on quests, searching. The effervescence of their enquiries had always settled him, made him less anxious about his own unanswered horizons. At the Nelsons' that day, however, the party appeared to comprise those who'd found their answers. Whatever they'd set out to discover was now theirs. Their search was over, and as such, despite their praise for him, Michael, as he had in Maddy's gaze, felt juvenile in their presence.

He continued to field their questions, answering Tony, Josh, Janera as fully as he could. He hadn't talked this much for months. As he did, his imaginings of what Caroline would have said, too, had she been there, shadowed his words. And then what she'd have said later too, as they walked home together, or got into bed, what she'd have said about the people they'd met. How she'd have described them, judged them, done impressions of them: Maddy's imperial stance, Josh's eager hosting.

Whenever Michael thought of Caroline like this, projecting their past into an impossible present, although he had trouble seeing her he could always hear her voice clearly. Even now, beneath the crowded talk in the Nelsons' front room, he could hear her, like a subterranean stream running under a city. Her laugh. Her migrating swallow of an accent, her low whisper in his ear, telling him it was time to go.

—

The morning she'd left for Pakistan, Michael hadn't seen her leave, only heard her. The taxi had come at four in the morning. He'd wanted to be up with her, to kiss her good-bye at the door. But Caroline had got ready without waking him, so the first he'd known of her going was a kiss on his forehead, followed by her hushed voice, telling him simply, "See you in a couple of weeks, love." And then she was gone.

The front door of Coed y Bryn closing, the taxi turning on the gravel drive. Then, as Michael turned too, under the duvet, the cab's engine thick in the dawn, before thinning away between the hedges. That is how she'd left him. With words and sounds. So maybe that was why, as he half listened to Tony telling another anecdote, Michael could still hear her voice so clearly. Because it was the last he'd known of her, and so was the last he held of her.

But although her voice was with Michael in that room, Caroline herself was not. For the first time since her death, as he stood there in the middle of the party, he'd felt alone. Not because he was without her, but just simply alone. As a single man might be, or an only child. Alone and surviving. And this, Michael realised, as he got ready for bed later that night, is what he'd felt give. A loosening in his memory of her, in his dependency. Which was why, as he'd stood in their front room, talking with their friends, he'd felt such a flood of gratitude towards the Nelsons. Towards Lucy and her dolls, towards Rachel and her drawings, and towards their parents, Josh and Samantha, for inviting him into their home.

CHAPTER
SIX

MICHAEL APPROACHED A desk in the corner of the front room. A pile of art books was topped with a paperweight, a blue butterfly suspended in its glass. A green-shaded library lamp stood beside the books. As far as he knew, this desk was where Josh had put the screwdriver he'd lent him. Michael looked around the art books and behind the lamp. There was no sign of it.

The desk, like the rest of the room, was prepared rather than used. Michael glanced around at the other surfaces: the side tables either end of the sofa, the bookshelves, the trunk in the centre of the room. The screwdriver was nowhere to be seen. Just the sculptures, photographs, paintings, and books of the Nelsons' lives. The sunlight through the draperies lit shafts of slow-turning air. A car sighed down the street outside. Somewhere farther off, on another road, an ice-cream van began playing a tinny "London Bridge Is Falling Down."

Michael didn't want to start opening drawers, looking in the cupboards under the shelves. His hands were dirty and he would leave marks. He checked the time again. The broken blade was his only French grip. His fencing master, Istvan, had told him specifically to bring it this week. He went back to the desk and, hooking his little finger in the handle of its drawer, slid it open. Inside there was a pad of writing paper, a spool of Sellotape, two old cheque-books. He slid the drawer closed again.

—

The fencing lessons had been a suggestion of the bereavement counsellor he'd been assigned in Chepstow. At first Michael had resisted her idea. The thought that his grief might be sweated out like a fever felt crude, and somehow disloyal. At that stage he'd still been consumed with exposing those who'd killed Caroline, his energies channelled into sating his anger rather than assuaging it. But on leaving Coed y Bryn, he remembered what the counsellor had said and pulled out his fencing kitbag from under the stairs, trying not to recall the last time he'd opened it. "It can help," she'd told him, as she'd made them coffee in her office behind the library. "And not just the exercise," she'd said, bringing the two mugs to the table between them. "But also taking up a past activity." She slid one of these mugs towards him. "Something from before."

He'd found the club on the Internet, a small but dedicated group of fencers, mostly épée and foil, who met twice a week in a school sports hall in Highgate. The first time he'd attended a session was on a blustery night at the end of October. Banks of fallen leaves choked the kerbsides. Others swirled in eddies along the pavements. The hall, in contrast to the night outside, was bright, lit by strip lights buzzing overhead. His kit smelt musty, and his limbs were leaden, unfamiliar with the movements of his youth. But the counsellor was right. For a few seconds, maybe even minutes, he'd forgotten. For precious moments the parts of his mind and chest that had been constricted with Caroline's death had relaxed. For the first time since Peter had called on him that afternoon it had felt as if he was breathing to the full depth of his lungs. So Michael returned the following week, and had continued to return every week since, finding, behind the mesh of his mask, the anticipation and clatter of the fights, the ache in his thighs and forearms, a release. An action that was neither past nor future, but purely present.

—

Michael had lent Josh the screwdriver a couple of days earlier. The night before Josh had broken his glasses. They'd been sitting in the kitchen after dinner, the remnants of a lasagne in the middle of the table, their wineglasses showing the tide marks of a bottle of red. The girls, after a round of good-night kisses, had already gone to bed. Having settled them upstairs, Samantha had returned to Michael and Josh in the kitchen, where, once again, they'd fallen to talking about New York, a city they'd discovered they shared twice, as somewhere they'd all lived, and then again as a memory.

"But where did they all go?" Samantha said, angling a piece of Brie onto a biscuit. "That's what I want to know."

Josh was bent over his glasses, trying to tighten a screw in their wire frames. "What do you mean 'go'?" he said, not looking up. "Into shelters, hostels, given rooms."

"But how do we know that?" Samantha countered him. "How do we know they weren't just all shoved into New Jersey or the Bronx?"

"Because"—Josh lifted his head to look at his wife—"if they were, then I'm pretty sure New Jersey and the Bronx would have let us know soon enough."

"Not if he paid them enough."

Josh shook his head and went back to studying the wire frames. He'd changed into a loose-fitting shirt, one side of its collar frayed by the attentions of Lucy's fingers. He was tired, and looked it.

"You have to admit," Michael said, looking up from a *Vanity Fair* he'd been browsing, "it was pretty quick. When I first moved there people were still calling Bryant Park Needle Park, remember that? Then, in what felt like only months, they were screening films there, holding Christmas fairs."

"That's what I mean," Samantha said, tapping the table. "Too quick. Giuliani isn't stupid. He knew if they were off the streets of Manhattan, maybe Brooklyn, too, then that's all that mattered. Out of sight, out of mind."

"Shit." Josh ducked his head below the table. A concave lens lay beside his plate.

"The fucking screw fell out," he said from under them.

Samantha shook her head and drank the last of her wine.

"Got it!" Josh emerged again, his face flushed. A miniature screw was balanced on the tip of his index finger. For a few moments none of them spoke. Michael returned to the magazine, while Samantha stood and began clearing the table. Fitting the loose lens into the frame, Josh twice tried to drop the screw's thread into place. Both times it fell to the table instead.

"I've got a screwdriver for that," Michael said after Josh's second attempt. "In my blade kit. It's magnetic."

"Well, look at you, James Bond," Samantha said from the dishwasher.

"Thanks, Mike, that'd be great." Josh pushed back his chair. "I haven't got time to—" he continued as he walked out of the kitchen.

"I can take them—" Samantha started.

"I said it's fine Sam," Josh called from down the hall, cutting her off. "No drama. I'll fix 'em tomorrow."

The next day Michael called round early at the Nelsons' front door. He knew the girls would be having breakfast in the kitchen and his appearance at the back of the house would only give Samantha another distraction as she tried to feed and dress them before taking Rachel to school. It was Josh who answered his knock. He was recently showered, the hair above his temples still damp. He wore a laundry-pressed shirt, red tie, and polished shoes. Together with an unfamiliar pair of glasses and a fresh shave, he looked like the younger brother of the man with whom Michael had eaten the night before.

"For your glasses," Michael said, holding up the screwdriver. Its miniature size and transparent yellow handle made it look like a toy from a cracker.

"Ah, thanks, Mike," Josh said, taking it from him. He nodded at the towel over Michael's shoulder. "Going for a swim?"

"Thought I might," Michael said. "Seeing as I'm up. Beat the crowds."

"Well, all right for some, that's all I can say," Josh said as he went into the front room. From where Michael stood on the doorstep he could see the edge of the desk inside its door, Josh's glasses folded on its corner. Josh put the screwdriver next to his glasses and came back into the hallway. Samantha, in the kitchen at its far end, gave Michael a silent wave. She was standing at the island, pouring milk into a couple of bowls. Michael raised a hand in reply, but the sound of a spoon hitting a table had already made her look away.

"Lucy, please—" Michael heard her say as she slipped out of sight.

"Well, see you later," he said to Josh.

"Yeah, see you around, Mike," Josh replied, closing the door. "Don't swim too hard, now."

———

That had been two days ago. Michael hadn't seen Josh or Samantha since. Josh had worked late for the last couple nights. And Samantha, as far as Michael could remember, had left for a spa weekend with her sister, Martha, on Friday morning. From what he understood, it was a trip that had been decreed more than offered by Martha. Along with several of Samantha's friends, Martha thought her little sister needed a break. To get away for a few days. She and Josh had been having a difficult time. They'd

never spoken of it when Michael was in their house, and Josh rarely
shared details of their marriage on the jogs he and Michael took
on the Heath. But for several weeks now, he'd detected the surface
tremors of a deeper disturbance. The last time they'd had dinner,
the night Josh's glasses had broken, he'd sensed it in the air, and
in the girls, too, sensitive to the edge in their father's voice. In
Samantha herself, he'd seen no outward change. She and Josh had
bickered over the cooking, but no more than usual, and she'd held
the same determination she always applied to her arguments in
their conversation. But when she hadn't been talking, when she'd
been watching and listening, that was when Samantha had seemed
more fragile than Michael had seen her before. Her skin had lost
its lustre and the muscles of her jaw were tense. The lightest touch
in the wrong place, he remembered thinking, would have been
enough to send her fractures running.

—

In the end it had been Samantha with whom Michael had
talked the most at that first party in November. Aside from her
few initial questions she'd remained largely silent as he'd discussed
BrotherHoods with Tony, Maddy, and the others. Alert and listening, but quiet. As the party had begun to thin, however, she'd
remained in the front room to say her good-byes, as if she was
reluctant to leave Michael, or to speak to anyone else for too long
before she'd spoken more to him. Eventually Tony and Maddy had
also left, Tony helping his wife into a heavy fur coat before following another couple out the front door and into the winter dusk of
the street.

There was something of a royal departure in their exit. Saman-
tha kissed them on both cheeks, but with a formality at odds with
Josh's extravagance—his hugging of Tony and his grasping of
Maddy's shoulders as he told her, "It's been so good to see you guys.
Really, it's been far too long. Far too long." Maddy nodded her

assent with closed eyes, absorbing his enthusiasm with a benevolent smile.

When Josh showed them to the door, Samantha and Michael were left in the room alone. Putting down her glass, Samantha moved between the side lamps, turning them on. She seemed distracted, brittle. Tony's voice came to them through the windows. "If you say so, Josh," he called through a laugh. "But I'll believe it when I see it!" Samantha drew the curtains.

"Coffee?" she asked, as she turned on the lamp beside an armchair.

"Yes," Michael replied, surprised by his own reluctance to leave. "Thanks."

They drank their coffees on the sofa. "So Tony really liked you," Samantha said, prising off her heels and tucking her stockinged feet under her thighs. She pulled a cushion across her stomach and held it there, like a baby, close against her.

"He liked my book," Michael said. "Which isn't the same thing as liking its author."

Samantha smiled, a tired acceptance. "Well, whatever, you're lucky. Tony doesn't like many people." She took a sip of her coffee before adding, "He prides himself on his taste."

She said the last word as if its own flavour was bitter.

"Josh said they've known each other since college?"

"Yes. Tony was best man at our wedding."

She shifted her position, leaning in closer to Michael as she did. His head felt light with wine and he realised that she, too, must have been more than a little drunk.

"Josh has always looked up to Tony," she said. Then she laughed suddenly. "And not just literally, either!"

"And Maddy?" Michael asked. "Have you known her long, too?"

Samantha raised an eyebrow. "No. No, Maddy's more recent. She's his second wife. Mind you," she said, as if acknowledging the achievements of a rival, "he's her third husband."

"Impressive," Michael said, although it sounded more impossible to him than impressive. With Caroline gone, he couldn't imagine the existence of a second, let alone a third, wife. Marriage felt like a finite resource to him, a rare ore he'd already exhausted with Caroline's going.

"It must be wonderful," Samantha said.

He looked up and realised she'd been staring at him. She was smiling in a new way, as if she was proud of him. "To live by your writing. To live by what you want to *do*."

Her emphasis suggested the idea was as impossible to her as Maddy's third marriage had been to Michael.

"It can be," he said. "But often it isn't. Being your own boss. I don't know, that isn't always a freedom."

She looked at him as if he hadn't understood her. "Perhaps," she said, looking away to the bookshelves across the room. The lamp at her side lit the fine hairs on her cheek and her upper lip. She wore diamond earrings, small, neat. Her cheekbones were high, and Michael saw how once she must have been beautiful, in quite a remarkable way.

"What would that be for you?" he asked her. "Your 'do'?"

"My 'do'?" she said, laughing. "Christ, where to begin?"

—

Samantha's parents, she'd told Michael that evening, had divorced when she was eight years old. From then on much of her holidays from boarding school in Sussex were taken up with travelling between them. Her mother remarried a New York doctor, leading to Samantha spending a chain of summers and Christmases in Montauk and Vermont. These were the environments of her teenage experiences. On a windy beach at the bottom of a cliff with a surfer, the hairs on his stomach dusted with salt. In woodland huts softened by fir trees and snow. Drinking her first beer as she ate a lobster roll, watching the last train carriages clatter in from Manhattan towards the end of the Long Island line.

From eight to eighteen, despite her frequent visits to the East Coast, Samantha no more than brushed against Manhattan itself. The city was her point of arrival and departure, but never anything more. A handful of afternoons touring the Fifth Avenue window displays in winter, another handful in a bright and sticky Central Park Zoo in summer. A total of twenty days, half of them hot, half of them freezing.

"I suppose that's why I chose Parsons," she said, uncurling her legs but still holding the cushion across her stomach. "I mean, I could have gone anywhere closer to home. Central Saint Martins, Kensington and Chelsea. Not Oxbridge, I suppose. I don't think they do photography, do they? Anyway, that's not the point. I was determined. New York or bust." She shook her head. "God, my poor parents. I must have been a right pain in the arse."

Her teenage desire had been fuelled not just by her own glimpses of Manhattan but also those of others. The work of Nan Goldin, Robert Frank, Garry Winogrand. Through the lenses and frames of these photographers, New York became a kaleidoscope of event for her, a maelstrom of the human and the built. All through her first year at Parsons she'd worked diligently to follow their example, spending whole days immersed in the chemical scent of the darkroom. But then one day towards the end of the summer semester, stepping back from her pegged prints bathed in the red bulb, Samantha had seen that she had nothing new to say, or to see. She was twenty years old and beyond the bar or the bedroom it was her first discovery of her adult self.

"Lucky, in a way," she said, undoing her hair. Running a hand through it, her fingers worked to untangle a knot, as if arranging threads on a loom. "I mean, some people spend their entire lives not learning that. Imagine, all those years producing crap, without knowing it."

"Those photos in the hall," Michael said. "You took those, didn't you?"

She looked at him as if he was trying to catch her out. "Yes."

"They're not crap," he said. "They're good."

She nodded slowly, allowing him his point. "They're not bad. But that's what I mean. I wouldn't have taken them if I hadn't first realised everything else I was doing was so derivative. I mean, it really was, honestly. Terrible stuff. I suppose those are all right. But that's why they're on the wall. Because they're the only ones that were."

—

In her final year, Samantha had to submit two end-of-course projects. The first of these she titled *The Choice*. For three weeks she sat in a Midtown deli between Lexington and Third. Arriving early, she'd position herself at a table next to the chilled food cabinets of sandwiches stretching the length of one wall, their shelves white with light. Taking a novel from her bag to read, and putting another on the table on which she angled her camera, she'd wait, the Midtown traffic washing the avenues, the button of a cable release under her thumb, under the table.

Over a single lunch hour she sometimes took as many as fifty or sixty photographs, the noise of the deli obscuring the slide and click of her shutter. The framing of most of them was out, her contact sheets full of chins and the tops of heads. But sometimes she'd capture a face in its entirety, features and skin tones from across the world, from all walks of life, from the basement to the penthouse. And all of them looking into the brightness of those shelves. All of them wearing expressions of thought, confusion, sometimes even wonder, as if they were looking into an ark, not a fridge.

For her second project, *Mirage*, Samantha left the city to see the city. Once or twice a week, sometimes after a whole day in the deli, she'd catch the A train east into Queens and Jamaica Bay. With a tripod strapped to her rucksack, she'd tramp out into the salt marshes to spend the evening crouching there, framing Manhattan's keyway skyline between the leaves and bushes as planes landed at JFK above her and flocks of waterbirds broke across the sky.

—

"I fell for the city all over again out there," she said, adjusting herself to allow Lucy to join them. Lucy nestled into her, fitting herself into the curves of her mother's body before bowing her head to the pages of a picture book, sucking on the knuckle of a forefinger as she did. Samantha placed a hand on her daughter's belly and held her close, just as she'd held the cushion.

Josh's colleagues had left by now, and Michael was the last remaining guest. He'd been about to go himself, but then Josh brought them both another drink, a Baileys for Samantha and a whisky for him. So he'd stayed, and Samantha had continued talking. As she did, Michael could hear Josh in the kitchen, loading the dishwasher, turning on the radio. From somewhere upstairs came the sounds of a DVD, the bright talk of a Disney movie.

"It looked—" Samantha frowned and shook her head again. "God, I haven't thought about this for ages."

"It looked?" Michael asked.

"Manhattan. From out there in the marshes. It looked, oh, I don't know. Vulnerable. Small. I suppose that's what I was going for. I wanted it to look like an Inca ruin, something like that."

"You did."

"Maybe."

"So what happened?"

"Happened?"

"I mean, why did you stop? You did stop, didn't you?"

Samantha laughed. "I got engaged. That's what happened." She looked down at Lucy, stroking her head. Lucy didn't look up from her book. "Why don't you go and watch the film with Rachel, honey?" Samantha said. "It's *Finding Nemo*. You like that, don't you?"

Without a word, Lucy slid off the sofa and went to join her sis-ter. As she went, Michael gestured towards her. "Well, that didn't turn out so bad."

"Oh," Samantha said. "Not to Josh. That was years later. No, this was to Ryan." She gave a short sniff of a laugh. "Ryan McGinnis."

—

On some evenings in her final year at Parsons, Samantha would come home from Queens, or from a session in the darkroom, to find a note on the table of her shared apartment on MacDougal—*Trading night?* The note would have been left by one of her two housemates. Occasionally Samantha would leave the same note for them. The phrase had become a joke to them, established a few weeks after they'd moved in together. But since then it had increasingly become something of a way of life, too, an escape. The three of them, all art students, were young, attractive, and living in downtown Manhattan. But they were also broke, the interiors of the Zagat-rated restaurants and cocktail bars they passed each day far beyond their means and reach.

"It was terrible, really," Samantha said, shaking her head at the memory. "If Rachel or Lucy ever did something like that I'd be livid. But at the time it seemed only fair. I mean, they were on safari downtown, so why shouldn't we do a little hunting, too? That's how we saw it, anyway."

—

The men they chose were often barely more than boys them-selves. Graduates working the lower rungs of Wall Street. All three of them—Samantha and her housemates—walked miles through the city every week. One of them, a girl called Jade from Ohio, had swum for the state as a schoolgirl. They had firm bodies, good legs.

So it was never difficult to get attention. "A short dress from Century 21, arch the back, high heels. Pathetic, really, but that was all it took. We saw it all as another trade I guess." She paused, drank from her Baileys. "And I think they did, too."

The men paid for the drinks, the checks. Sometimes, in that final year, the drugs. In return, Samantha and her housemates gave them attention. A display of attraction. But that was all. Most trading nights ended with one of them raising an arm as if officiating at a race and the three of them climbing into a cab, scribbled numbers and business cards in their purses. Occasionally, though, four bodies rode that cab, not three, the night's trading having evolved for one of them into a more significant exchange.

At thirty-one, Ryan McGinnis aspired to the gravitas of middle age the way his older colleagues wished they could recapture their youth. After ten years as a currency trader for JP Morgan, he owned an apartment on the Upper East Side and a five-bedroom antebellum house in Greenwich, Connecticut. When he'd first met Samantha, Ryan had been drawn to her accent and the shape of her neck. But also to her knowledge of art and Europe. Three times a week he trained in a gym with a view over Central Park, mixing creatine with his protein drinks in the changing room. He shaved his chest and had a CD pack of *Teach Yourself Italian* on his bedroom shelf. He made Samantha laugh and looked at her in a way that made her feel prized.

Unlike the other men Samantha had brought home from their trading nights, Ryan wanted more. Within weeks of his buying her a French 75 on the rooftop of 60 Thompson, placing it in front of her like a checkmate, her life had changed. She knew it was impossible to live in New York and not feel the slipstream of the money flowing through its veins, to escape either its residual heat or the shadows cast by its light. But with Ryan, Samantha suddenly found herself at the financial heart of the city. As a consequence her life became strangely split, between the final weeks of her student days—completing course work, hanging prints, sending off CVs and portfolios—and a nightlife of privilege. Cipriani, the Rainbow Room, diamond earrings left on her pillow in the morning.

The Parsons end-of-year photography show was held at a gallery in Chelsea. A broad industrial space on the first floor of a decommissioned warehouse. Ryan accompanied Samantha, moving through the crowds like a fish in the wrong shoal. They were going out for dinner afterwards, and Samantha was painfully aware of how angular his suit looked among the hoodies and T-shirts, and how exposed she felt in her own strapless top. She watched him look. He paid close attention to the hung work, his eyebrows raised in quizzical amusement, as if everything he saw held a secret joke. When Samantha saw him nod at another student's father as they crossed in front of a print, she'd felt more like his daughter than his lover.

Before they'd left for dinner Ryan bought one of Samantha's *Mirage* prints: Manhattan's skyline miniature on a far horizon, escalating between two hackberry leaves, gigantic in the foreground, an ibis taking flight across the South Tower of the World Trade Center. "For Greenwich," he'd said, as they'd stepped onto the street. "It'll look good there." He swung his jacket about her shoulders. "Above the fireplace, or maybe in the kitchen."

When they'd woken the next morning, Ryan had asked Samantha to accompany her photograph. It was time, he said, for him to move out of the city, and he wanted her to move with him. His place in Greenwich had been empty for three years. They were lying in bed in his apartment, the hum of the air-conditioning already contending with the heat outside. From where she lay she could see the tops of the trees in Central Park. "It'll be great," Ryan said, running the knuckle of his forefinger along her jaw. "C'mon, trust me."

Samantha said yes, as much because she didn't know what else she'd do if she didn't as through any desire to stay with him. Her father, having neglected the child of his first marriage, was now absorbed in the lives of those from his second. Her mother, meanwhile, had broken it off with the doctor and returned to Britain. In the apartment on MacDougal they'd all talked about finding assistant positions, of sending portfolios to photo editors. But so far nothing had come of it. After three years of studying, the months ahead of Samantha were empty, unknown. Ryan was offering to fill them. They moved to Greenwich the next month. A few weeks later, on a bench beside Long Island Sound, Ryan proposed, and again Samantha said yes.

Whenever she travelled back into Manhattan to visit her Parsons friends or her old flatmates, Samantha felt fortunate. Many of them were working in retail stores now, or waiting tables. Some had found jobs in galleries, organising private views, sitting for long hours at front desks in cavernous spaces. One of them was stripping in a lap-dancing bar. Life after university had been pared of the certainties of their student days. The aspirations they'd once fostered seemed suddenly out of reach. In comparison, Samantha had few worries. No rent to pay. A steady relationship. And time. This is what Ryan had also promised her. Time to pursue her photography, free of the constraints of shifts in a diner or a cocktail bar, or any of the whole messy business of living.

But on her return journeys to Greenwich, twisting the engagement ring on her finger, Samantha often found herself staring for long minutes through the train's windows. How had she come to call the destination on her ticket home? It was not her home. And it wasn't Ryan's, either. The house was too large, too unlived in. Like all the houses in their neighbourhood, it felt outsized, as if it had been built for a larger species than humans. Their neighbours were older, polished, and settled. Some had children of Samantha's age, or even grandchildren who came to stay on vacations. When she and Ryan visited them for drinks, her heels sinking into their soft lawns, Samantha had to resist breaking the scene. She wanted to scream or tear off her clothes, just to see what would happen when their calm waters were disturbed.

From Monday to Friday every week Ryan woke at six-thirty a.m., showered, dressed, and drove his Porsche Boxster down Interstate 95 to work in the city. Sometimes he stayed there overnight too. Samantha would get up later, alone in the echoing house. She began making plans for photographic projects.

—

"I wanted to try and get under its skin," Samantha said, shifting a leg from under her. "Have you ever been there? Greenwich?"

Michael shook his head. "No."

"It's beautiful. But—" She broke off, frowning. "It's as if the place is vacuum-sealed. Like there's no way in."

—

For a few weeks she tried photographing the wives in their cars: tiny women lost in monstrous SUVs, their painted nails clutching the steering wheels like the feet of caged birds. Stopped at the lights, checking their lipstick in the parking lot. But Ryan soon put a stop to that. A member of his country club said something to him after a tennis match. It was a passing remark, but enough, about his wife preferring to look at paparazzi photos rather than be in them. "For chrissakes, Sam," Ryan had said when he'd come home. He was still in his shorts and T-shirt, a sweat patch between his shoulder blades like the map of a long country. He poured himself a neat bourbon. "Set up a darkroom, hire a studio, do whatever you need. But just leave their fucking wives alone, will you?"

—

"I should have known, really," Samantha said, laughing at her younger self. "But I was so naïve. For a bit, anyway."

"Known?" Michael asked.

The TV was playing in the kitchen. Josh was watching a sports quiz. The intermittent sound of buzzers and applause reached them where they sat in the front room.

Samantha sighed. "Let's just say Ryan wasn't very good at choices." She paused, correcting herself. "No, actually he was good at choices. Very good. He just never saw them as exclusive, that's all. I mean, when he bought that place in Greenwich he didn't sell the apartment in Manhattan. And when he couldn't decide between a Lexus and a Porsche? He just bought one of each."

She smiled weakly, looking down at her feet. "And when he proposed to me he carried on screwing his secretary."

—

There'd been something in the woman's voice that had made Samantha ask her directly. Something in the way she'd responded when she'd told her who she was. A knowledge. Ryan was in a meeting, the girl said, but could she take a message? Samantha paused for a moment, then asked her outright. "Are you," she said, trying her best to keep her voice calm, "fucking my fiancé?"

There was an intake of breath at the end of the line, a brushing of fingers across the mouthpiece. "It's all right," Samantha had reassured her. She was sitting in the kitchen in Greenwich. A sprinkler on the lawn was spraying the window with dashes of water. The droplets caught the light with the fire of diamonds. They were probably about the same age, Samantha remembered thinking, she and this girl sitting at her desk high above Manhattan. She wondered what she looked like. Had Ryan wanted something different? Dark hair, dark eyes? Or, if they'd ever met, would Samantha have seen echoes of her own features, her own colouring? Another

her, but there, not here. "Really, it's okay. But I do need to know," she said. "Now."

When the girl answered, her voice was quiet. "Yes," she said. Then, her composure breaking, "I'm so sorry."

But Samantha had already hung up. Three hours later a Lincoln Town Car was taking her to the airport, her bags in its trunk and her *Mirage* print with its distant, lost skyline, angled between her legs.

—

"I got that bit right, anyway," Samantha said.

"What do you mean?" Michael asked her. "Right?"

"The leaving. I did it like in a film. Cut up some of his suits, soil on the carpets." She said this without emotion, looking away. There was no suggestion of anger in her telling. She took another sip of her Baileys. It was another woman's story now. From another life.

"And then what did you do?" Michael asked her.

She turned back to him, as if he'd disturbed her. "Oh," she said. "Came back here. To London. Had to earn some cash, so started temping."

"And the photography?"

Josh appeared at the door. He looked irritated. "Honey?" He held a hand towards Michael. "Sorry, Mike," he said, before turning to Samantha again. "Lucy wants you."

Samantha raised her eyebrows, as if to say This—this is what happened.

She put her glass on a side table and rose from the sofa. "Okay," she said. "Tell her I'm coming."

"I should be going," Michael said, also getting up from the sofa.

Josh leant into the hallway. "Mummy's coming, honey!" he shouted up the stairs. "You know how it is," he said to Michael as

Samantha passed him, laying a hand on her husband's shoulder. "Have to get the kids down."

Out in the hallway, as he was going to the door, Samantha turned and came back down the stairs. She waited until she was close to Michael before she spoke. "Josh told me about your wife," she said, looking up at him. Without her heels, she wasn't much taller than Caroline. She took his hand. "I'm so sorry," she said, her eyes searching his, as if looking for the debris of Caroline's death.

"Thank you," Michael replied.

She gave him another smile, a tired acknowledgement, and Michael recognised again that she was far from sober. How much, he wondered, had she meant to tell him? Letting go of his hand, she returned to the stairway, Lucy's cry drifting down from above, "Mummy!"

"Coming, sweetheart," Samantha called up to her daughter. "Coming."

—

As Michael had climbed his own stairs next door he couldn't help seeing, in his mind's eye, the Nelsons' staircase tracing his ascent on the other side of the wall. Unlike theirs, his was communal, shared with the other occupants of his building. On each landing he passed two numbered red doors, each leading to the homes and lives of others. Through the bare wall beside him the Nelsons' stairway, with its dark wood banister and red carpet runner, rose through their lives only. The girls' bedrooms, Samantha and Josh's bedroom, a playroom, the bathrooms, a spare room. On the top floor, Josh had mentioned, a study.

They were the same generation, Michael and the Nelsons. Samantha was a year younger, Josh a few years older. And yet to Michael their lives might as well have been decades apart. Everything he'd lost in the shipwreck of Caroline's death had washed against the shore of Josh and Samantha's thirties with ease. The house, the children. Their grounded life, solid and settled in comparison to his own, newly cut loose as he was, living in a set of rented rooms four stories up in the air.

Reaching his door, Michael turned the key in the lock and opened it. His flat was dark, the scent of its air still not his own. He went into the kitchen without turning on the lights. A TV in the flat below played a Saturday-night talent show. His head was fuzzy with the long afternoon of drinking. He ran himself a glass of water from the tap, drank it down, then ran himself another. Taking the glass to the long windows at the end of the room, he looked out over the Heath. The lamps lining the path had come on, the branches of the trees lit along their undersides. This was the view he'd looked out on every day since first moving in. The dark waters of the ponds, the suggestion of a swan drifting along one of their banks. The concrete path, the foot-worn tracks, the wind-stripped trees. In the distance, more of London's streets, edging in on the Heath's green. The same view, and yet that night, as Michael looked over it again, drinking his water, somehow different, shared as he now knew it was, with the Nelsons next door.

CHAPTER
SEVEN

TURNING FROM THE desk, Michael took another glance over the side tables in the front room. The screwdriver was nowhere to be seen. He thought about where else Josh might have put it. In his study? In a drawer in his bedside table? But he couldn't very well go searching the house. It was one thing for him to be there, another again to start rifling through bedside tables. He would just have to do without his French grip. He could ask to borrow one of Istvan's, but he already knew what he'd say.

"It's a relationship." That's what Istvan had told him as they'd zipped up their jackets at the beginning of their second lesson, his Hungarian accent eliding into his English. "Do you use other men's wives?" he'd said, pulling on his glove. "No. Or if you do, you get into trouble, yes? So don't use another man's blade. It will only end up hurting you, not your opponent."

Coming back out into the hallway, Michael paused at the foot of the staircase. The stairs were wooden, painted white, with a red carpet running down their middle secured by silver rods in the crook of each step. In all the months he'd known the Nelsons, Michael had never been up these stairs. All the dinners, conversations, drinks they'd ever shared had been confined to the kitchen and the conservatory. Only when other people had also come round had they ever moved into the front room. The ground floor had been the extent of his jurisdiction within their home.

Another car passed down the street. In its wake, Michael heard a pushchair trundling down the pavement. Standing in the hallway, he listened as its wheels grew louder, kicking over the edge of a paving slab prised up by a sycamore's root. As the pushchair faded down the street he saw that root clearly in his mind's eye, its bark polished to worn leather by the thousands of shoes that had stepped on it. Farther off, the ice-cream van started up again, a tinkling rendition of "Yankee Doodle Dandy." Closer, somewhere in the front room behind him, a fly was needling at a window.

Michael looked back down the hallway towards the open back door. He knew the front door beside him was secure, the tongue of its deadbolt buried in the mortise. Despite the heat of the day, he'd seen no open windows in the house. Would Josh really have left without locking the back door, too? What if he had, and it wasn't just a mistake after all? Michael's mind began working on this conjecture, making any number of scenarios suddenly seem all too possible. The Heath had been full of people ever since the heat wave began. From across the other side of the ponds the houses on this part of the street presented an attractive and vulnerable prospect. Over the decades, successions of owners had set more and more windows in their back walls, as if the houses were thirsty and could never quite get enough of their view of the water, the Heath. Looked at from the other way, however, these windows made a gallery of the houses, especially in the long evenings of summer. It wouldn't be difficult, from far away even, to track the movements inside one of them.

A little farther up the street there was a tangle of hidden paths between the ponds and the gardens. Michael and Samantha had taken the girls looking for late conkers along them just a couple of weeks after they'd all met. Now, in summer, the foliage over those paths was overgrown. Someone could easily sit there out of sight for hours, watching a house for when its owners left.

Michael felt a chill at the back of his neck. He thought about calling out again, but if there was an intruder in the house he didn't want to alert them to his presence. They'd have already heard him shout for Samantha and Josh from the door, but how much sound had he made since? Would they think he'd left when he got no answer? Or were they still waiting for him to leave now? Waiting to hear the back door close, so they might make their own escape?

He looked up the stairway towards where it turned, curving behind the wall. His pulse was beating in his temples. It was only right he should check the other floors of the house. To make sure.

As quietly as he could, Michael walked towards the stairs. As he climbed the first few steps, the carpet runner softening his tread, he stared intently at the turn above him, half expecting someone to appear around its corner. Which is when it happened.

A stab of recognition, so immediate Michael couldn't say from where it had emanated. Whether it had been a taste, a scent, a touch, or a sound. All he knew, with a painful clarity, was that it was her, Caroline. As if, just for an instant, he'd woken beside her again and she was alive once more, as fully alive as he was.

Michael froze, stilling himself. He was breathing rapidly, his heart thumping in his ribs. All thoughts of an intruder flooded from him. He looked up towards the turn in the stairs again, his mind trying to gain a purchase on what had just happened. The strength of the sensation had been such that now the only person he expected to come down the stairs was no longer a burglar, but Caroline, miraculously brought back from the dead. First her feet, then her shins, her thighs, her waist, her hands, her arms, her breasts, her neck, and, at last, her face, all revealed in the tantalising fractions of her descent.

But Caroline did not appear. She did not come to him. There was just the stairway's red runner disappearing around the corner, the dark banister tracing the same curve, and the blank whiteness of the wall.

Michael listened. The ice-cream van in the other street had

stopped its tune. The fly in the front room buzzed, paused, then buzzed again. But from beyond the turn in the stairs there was no sound. He shook his head, as if to wake himself. He did not believe in ghosts. In all the months since her death, never once had he thought Caroline was still with him. Her absence had been the most certain thing he'd ever known.

But she had been. Just now. He'd felt her, with absolute experience. And he still could. It was fading, the resonance cooling, but it was there, as if he were slowly walking backwards from a fire, retreating into a cold night. But he did not want to walk away. He didn't want to grow cold. For all its painfulness, he wanted to feel that warmth again. Like touching a bruise or a half-healed wound, he wanted the pain of feeling her again.

He took another step up the stairs, but then stopped. He wasn't thinking clearly. He was in his neighbour's house. He was late. He should go. If there had been an intruder, then they must have heard him already. Had he made a sound? Just now, when he'd caught that sense of Caroline? He didn't know. It had been so sudden, like being hit from behind. Whatever, it no longer mattered. He should go. He should leave by the back door through which he'd entered and close it behind him.

But he could not. He could not walk backwards, not while the warmth of what he'd felt was still on him. Not when it might be felt again. He had to know where it had come from, that sensation. When it had happened it felt as if he'd walked into it, as if its source lay above him. So he must go forward, not back. That was the only way. He had to carry on.

Placing a foot on the next step, Michael began ascending the stairs once more. As he did he listened to the house. It was silent, still. As if he were moving through a photograph. As if he were alone.

CHAPTER EIGHT

ON THE DAY Caroline was killed, Major Daniel McCullen woke early in his second-floor bedroom in Centennial Hills, a suburb in northwest Las Vegas. As he had every morning for weeks, he woke with his body damp, his heart racing. It had been the same dream again. Of the motorcyclist. Of the children playing soccer; that celebration after the goal. Except, as always, it had been worse than a dream, because it was a memory too, more real for him each time it returned.

He turned over. His wife, Cathy, was still asleep beside him, one bare shoulder showing from under the duvet. She was facing away from him and for a moment he just watched her breathe, trying to match the shallow rise and fall of his ribs to the steadier tempo of hers.

Daniel was still in love with his wife. From what he could tell, compared to a number of his colleagues in the air force, this was something of an achievement. For many, their marriages had been the first casualties of their service. Men who'd kept their heads under fire collapsing in the face of a relationship gone sour. Women flight officers volunteering for another tour, rather than slugging it out back home with a husband who no longer recognised them. But Daniel had always been determined. Cathy and the girls would come first. That's what he'd promised Cathy when they'd married, and he'd tried to stay true to that promise ever since.

In the world in which they'd met it hadn't seemed like such a difficult vow to keep. But back then, twelve years ago, everything had seemed possible. On the afternoon he'd first approached her, strolling across the lawn at his younger brother's graduation, the years ahead of Daniel had looked like the skies into which he flew when he broke through a bank of cloud—open, rare. His. Just the year before, within months of his own graduation, Daniel had flown his first combat missions in Bosnia. Somewhere below him, in the wake of his jet's roar, he'd taken his first lives. But—as their commanding officers had told them, and the newspapers, too—they'd saved many more. They'd done good with their might, and Daniel had returned a hero. So as he'd introduced himself to Cathy on the lawn that afternoon, as he'd made her laugh, and later, as he'd led her to the dance floor, he'd never suspected that one day the certainty of his life would become so fragile. That one day his sense that these years—even their wars—had been created for him might be turned on its head, until he'd feel like a plaything of the world, and not the other way round.

Wiping his palm on the sheet, Daniel reached out and laid a hand on Cathy's shoulder. Her skin was smooth, warm under his touch. She didn't stir. Judging from the light filtering through the shore pine outside their window it wasn't even six o'clock yet. Daniel thought about waking her. Gently, with kisses, pressing himself against her from behind. Perhaps, after a night's rest and with the girls still asleep, they'd be able to make love as they once had. He knew they needed it, to feel each other instinctively, without thought.

But he did nothing. The anxiety of his flashback was still active within him, its residue too unreliable, threatening like a faulty screen to flicker into life at any moment. So he just watched Cathy sleep instead, moving his hand up to stroke her hair where it flowed across the pillow.

Even with their recent troubles, this waking together still felt like a gift to Daniel. The knowledge that they'd be sharing the same bed that night, that they no longer had to worry about orders coming down the line, about watching the news with one eye on what it would mean for them in a couple months' time. This was why they'd moved to Nevada. For this waking, this knowledge. To feel their future as firmly under their feet as their present. As soon as Daniel had learnt what they'd be doing at Creech, he'd put in for a transfer. He'd been on three tours since they'd got married. Two in Afghanistan and one in Iraq. All three had been hard on Cathy and the girls. And, in a different way, on him, too. It was on those tours, in two-minute sat-phone conversations and jumpy Skype sessions, that Daniel had come to understand the value of his family. When he'd last returned from Afghanistan, Kayce, just six years old back then, had hugged him round the legs and asked him to promise he'd never leave like that again. Daniel told her he'd do what he could. Which, when he saw the email about Creech and the future reactivation of the 432nd, he did.

What they had planned for the 432nd at Creech seemed like the perfect answer to Kayce's request: a chance for Daniel to have it all. To still be flying missions, to be doing his duty, but to be with his family too. To see his daughters grow, not across periods of months but over days, hours. To have this waking with Cathy, and know it wouldn't be taken from them.

"Be careful what you ask for." That's what his mother used to say to him as a boy. When he'd wanted to play with his older brother's football team. When he'd wanted a more powerful dirt bike. When he'd been picked for the college boxing squad. Maybe, if she'd been in Langley with him when he'd filed his transfer request to the 15th Reconnaissance Squadron, she'd have said the same again. And just as she had when he was a boy, she'd have been right to as well.

He and Cathy had tried talking about it a few nights before. They were sharing a drink on the deck while the girls did their homework, a bottle of Sonoma fumé blanc sweating crisply in the last of the sun.

"Not if you're flying missions at the same time, Dan," Cathy had said to him, looking down and shaking her head.

Daniel laughed, exasperated. He knew she was right, but he wasn't going to admit it. Not after all they'd done to be here. Moving across the country, taking Kayce out of school. This was the best it could be, that's what he wanted to say to her. She should be grateful, not resentful.

"C'mon," he said. "Has it really been so bad?" He tried to keep his voice light. She looked up, as if she didn't recognise him.

"Yes," she said. "And it's getting worse."

He felt his chest tighten. He took a sip of his wine.

"You're not sleeping," she said. "And when you do, you talk, shout. And with the girls—"

"That was once," Daniel snapped. He hadn't meant to sound so sharp. "Once," he said again, more softly.

—

There'd been a reason why he'd yelled at the girls like that. Why he'd done what he had to Kayce. There'd been a cause for his actions, but he hadn't been able to tell Cathy what it was. He would never be able to tell her.

He'd just finished a shift at Creech. There'd been an engagement, one they'd been planning for weeks. The target was achieved, the missile had connected, but other aspects of the operation hadn't gone well. At the last moment, with six seconds to impact, two boys riding a bicycle had come round the corner, one of them sitting on the handlebars, the other pedalling behind him.

Maria, his sensor operator, was sitting beside him. "Shit," she'd said, when they'd come into view.

"Are those kids?" He'd heard his own question echo in his headphones. Elsewhere, in other darkened rooms in America, and

8,000 miles away in Afghanistan, other uniformed and suited men heard him, too.

"It's too late," Maria said.

Up to six seconds to impact, and she could still steer the targeting laser on to their abort location. Daniel glanced at the counter in the corner of his screen as it descended through four, three, two. He and Maria watched as the visuals across the monitors wiped white.

When the smoke and dust had cleared, Daniel circled the Predator while Maria zoomed in. The target's car was a twisted and blackened wreck, flames licking at its frame. Twenty feet away the boys' bicycle was also screwed out of shape, its front wheel still spinning. A severed leg, wearing a sandal, was trapped under it.

Daniel had typed a chat message to the intelligence coordinator: *Possible child fatalities?*

The reply had come back at the speed of speech: *Two possible teenagers confirmed. Male.*

An hour after that reply, Daniel was back home, sitting on the decking, watching Kayce and Sarah play in the garden. The coordinator's *possible teenagers* had both been about Kayce's height. She was nine years old. As he watched the girls they'd begun arguing, each of them pulling at the handlebars of a red bicycle. Daniel hadn't meant to scare them. He hadn't meant to scare himself. But it had been too much, too soon. The spinning wheel. That sandal.

—

Cathy leant forward, her glass of wine catching the light. A peach-white star flexed on the decking between them. She took a deep breath and exhaled it as a sigh.

"Is this about Barbara?" Daniel asked her.

"No," she replied, shaking her head again and biting her lip. "You know it isn't about her. I told you. We agree to disagree. That's it."

Barbara was another teacher at Cathy's school, a high-end primary school in the west of the city. A couple of months ago, along with other members of the Nevada Desert Experience, she'd been arrested outside Creech. Daniel had seen the demonstration when he'd arrived for his morning shift. A small crowd strung out along the perimeter fence, their homemade banners breathing in the breeze: *Not in Our Name! Say No to Drones! U.S. Air Force—Killing by Remote!*

If Daniel had known Barbra was among them he'd have got out and tried to speak with her. Not to give her hell, but just to set her straight. He understood the origins of the group. Subterranean nuclear tests cracking the earth upwind of your homes, your kids' schools. He'd have probably joined those demonstrations himself. But this was different. This was a different kind of war, and what they were pioneering at Creech wasn't threatening anyone who lived nearby. It was, though, saving hundreds, maybe thousands, of lives elsewhere. Daniel was convinced of that. They had the figures, the projections, to prove it. And every month they received emails from grateful troops on the ground, thanking them for their work.

By the time Daniel drove home at the end of his shift, the demonstration had gone. Apparently it had only been there for a couple of hours before the police had arrived and made their arrests. But it had still got more attention than Daniel liked. He believed in what he was doing at Creech and he wanted Cathy to as well. So it made him uncomfortable to think of her going to work every day alongside Barbara and her talk.

—

Daniel leant back in his chair. The shadow of their garden fence was inching up the lawn towards them. "Good," he said to Cathy. "Because Barbara doesn't have the facts. She doesn't understand."

"Yeah, I know," Cathy said. She sounded tired.

He let out a long sigh of his own. "So what do you want to do?"

He looked out at the roofs of other houses beyond their garden, the sky towering above them, its blue darkening to indigo. "What do you think *we* should do?"

Cathy shrugged, watching the star of light thrown by her wine. "I don't know," she said. "I don't know."

Daniel looked at her, trying to read her expression. A frown was creasing the skin between her eyebrows. He didn't understand when their conversations had become like this. So stilted, guarded. There'd been a time when they'd told each other everything, however difficult the truth. He waited for her to look back at him, but she didn't. He wanted to say so much. About how much he loved her. About the terrors of the world. About how he wanted to protect her and the girls from them. About how, without her, he couldn't do any of it. And he wanted to say sorry, too. They'd come to Las Vegas to remove the wars from their lives. But now Cathy came home to it every day. Not because he was away on tour, but because he wasn't. Because in staying away from the war, he'd become it. But Daniel said none of this. It was as if his throat was blocked. As if to speak those words would shake their foundations and bring everything down. This was as good as it could be. That's what he'd told himself. If he questioned it, where would they go? What would they do?

"It's just . . ." Cathy began.

Daniel leant towards her. As he did she finally looked up at him. There were tears in her eyes, lensing the blue of her irises. She smiled at him despite them, like she did when trying to explain something to the girls. Something grown up, something difficult.

—

The sound of the bedroom door brushing across the carpet made Daniel turn in their bed.

"Hey, kiddo," he said, his voice still raw with sleep. "What's up?"

Sarah, their youngest, stood in the doorway, her favourite picture book, *The Very Hungry Caterpillar,* fanning from her hand.

"Is it morning yet?" she asked. She wore a pair of Disney pyjamas, a blonde princess crowned across her belly.

"I guess it is, honey," Daniel whispered. Rising on his elbows, he sat on the edge of the bed and slipped on a T-shirt.

"What say we let Mommy sleep, eh?" he said, going to Sarah and picking her up. As he carried her out of their bedroom and down the landing, her picture book tapping against his hip, Sarah put her thumb in her mouth and leant her head against her father's shoulder. Daniel inhaled the scent of her hair. It smelt of a child's sleep, of dreams, not memories. And, Daniel thought, as they entered her room and he sat her on the edge of her bed, reason enough for everything he was doing, and for everything he'd done.

—

In 2007 Centennial Hills was one of the newest suburbs of Las Vegas. Sometimes in the weeks after they'd first moved there, as he'd reversed their Toyota Camry out the driveway, Daniel was sure he could still smell the paint drying on its fences, the tarmac off-gassing from its streets. The local hospital was half under scaffolding, and all the houses, theirs included, had a model suburban hacienda look, as yet unworn by the lives of their inhabitants. Even the desert trees and shrubs lining the bald streets and cul-de-sacs were older than the houses they shaded, brought in by the developers to lend the neighbourhood a strangely youthful maturity. At his last posting, in Langley, Virginia, once the shell of Walmarts and gas stations had been broken, you could still find evidence of the men and women who'd first settled towns like Smithfield and Suffolk. Their names were on the street signs, their descendents on the council, and their fingerprints dried into the stoops and wooden sills of the older houses. In Centennial Hills the only fingerprints left in the paintwork were those of the Mexican labourers hired by the contractors to finish the job. The street signs, from what Daniel could tell—*Rockridge Peak Avenue, Danskin Drive*— had been chosen by a downtown city planner, and he didn't even know if a local council had been formed.

As a counter to their immaturity, the streets of Centennial Hills, positioned as they were on the edge of the city, framed an ancient view. It was this view that greeted Daniel as he began his drive to Creech that morning: the Charleston range, its ragged peaks rising through a milky light to the summit of Mount Charleston itself. A bare, pleated mountain looking over the sprawl of Las Vegas like an implacable god.

In recent weeks, as he'd driven down his street towards this view, Daniel had found himself giving the mountain a silent salute. As if there was some luck, or maybe wisdom, to be mined from its craggy slopes that would still be there long after the city had been extinguished by the sands on which it was built. Despite their proximity, Daniel had never been into the range. His mountain bike was unpacked but unused in the garage, and his hiking boots sat expectantly in the utility room. So as he reached the end of his street that day and turned left, slipping the mountains from his windscreen into the passenger window, the Charleston range still remained unknown to him. They were his daily view but not yet his landscape, a feature of his geography but not yet his territory. Unlike those other mountains, 8,000 miles away.

Those mountains Daniel knew intimately. He'd never climbed in them, either, but he was still familiar with the villages silted into their folds, the shadows their peaks threw at evening and the habits of the shepherds marshalling their flocks along their lower slopes. Recently he'd even been able to anticipate, given the right weather conditions, at what time the clouds would come misting down the higher peaks into the ravines of the valleys. Over the last few months he'd begun to feel an ownership over them. Were they not as much his workplace as that of those shepherds? For the troops operating in the area they were simply elevation, exhaustion, fear. They were hostile territory. But for Daniel they were his hunting ground, and as such it was his job not just to know them but to learn them, too. To love them, even, so that from the darkness of his control station in Creech, he might be able to move through their altitudes as naturally as the eagles who'd ridden their thermals for centuries.

As he swung into an intersection, Daniel's phone began to ring. Glancing at the screen, he slipped the hands-free over his ear.

"Hi, honey."

"It's Kayce's soccer tonight," Cathy said. "I forgot."

Her voice sounded tight. Daniel guessed Sarah was still playing up over her breakfast.

"Okay," he said. "It finishes at five, right?"

"Can you take Macy home, too? Emily just called to say she'll be working late."

He slowed at a stoplight. A truck drew up beside him, the sun flashing off its chrome fender. The sky above the road was a cyan blue. It was going to be a beautiful day. "Sure," Daniel said. "Just text me their address."

"Thanks," Cathy said.

Daniel heard a muffled wail in the background. The clatter of a spoon falling. "Is she still not eating that?" he asked. But Cathy had already hung up.

Daniel's operator, Maria, lived farther west, fifteen minutes closer to Creech. She shared a car with her husband, so on most shifts Daniel picked her up on the way in. At the end of their day he'd often drive her home, too. As she got into the Camry that morning, she was already talking, but not to Daniel.

"Waddya mean?" she said, her phone cradled under her neck as she pulled the door closed and reached for her seat belt. Daniel drove away from the kerb as she buckled up. "You tellin' me that?" she continued, her Hispanic pitch nailing whoever was on the other end of the line. "You really tellin' me that? Well, lemme tell you something, lady. That ain't good enough. You hear me? I work, you know that? I work. Eight a.m. to six p.m.? What kinda window do you call that? *D'mio!* That ain't no window, that is one mutha of a hole. Uh-uh. No way. So waddya goin' do about it, eh?"

Daniel turned on the radio to try and tune out Maria's conversation. Slim Whitman's "My Heart Is Broken in Three" filled the car as they rose on the slip road to join 95 West. As they picked up the highway's speed, Las Vegas fell away from them, reducing block by block from strip malls to suburbs, to half-built streets, to open desert, until all that was left were a few exploratory SUVs and a group of surveyors, their hard hats bright in the sun. When Maria eventually hung up she offered Daniel no more than an exasperated shake of her head in explanation. Turning to her window, she watched the desert scroll past, the cacti and shrubs, the tan hues of its sands. When they drove out here on earlier shifts, Daniel found this landscape beautiful, amber under a low sun, the smallest of stones bestowed with long shadows. But now, with the sun higher, the desert's light was already flat and strong, its warmth matured into a threatening heat.

Daniel didn't ask Maria about her phone call. He was grateful for her silence and he knew she'd feel the same—that she, too, needed this stretch of road uninterrupted by conversation. Driving westward on Highway 95, they had a chance to prepare; to begin their daily transition between the compartments of their lives. Later that day, when they'd drive the same road back east, it would be different. Then the car and the highway would become their decompression chamber. They'd talk, ask about each other's families, tell jokes. But now Highway 95 was their road to war, and as such it demanded silence more than speech.

Daniel knew that people like Barbara saw this daily commute as the epitome of American cowardliness, the leading edge of a new era of asymmetrical warfare. Fighter pilots going to battle without having to fight, without risking anything more than a speeding ticket or a traffic accident. But it wasn't that simple. War, as Daniel had learnt, was never simple.

It was true there were still days when he wished he was back in the cockpit 8,000 miles away, risking his life with the patrols on the ground rather than just watching them work. And it was also true he missed the flying itself. Not just the valour of it—the thread that unwound back to the code of medieval knights—but also the pure experience. The victory over gravity, the surge and press of an F-16's afterburners, the delicate touch of such power, whole countries rushing under his wing. The smell of the plane's metal, and the sound of it, straining at 60,000 feet. On his very first training flight Daniel had fallen in love with the sky up there, a treasure to be owned only by those anointed to fly at such height, such speed. The blue of glazed porcelain, their contrails like fine paint strokes across its finish.

It was a romance, he knew, but a powerful one. And it had, after all, been this romance that made him want to be a pilot in the first place. His grandfather had flown F-86s on the Yalu River in Korea. His stories of those days, illustrated by a handful of black-and-white photographs, had caught the imagination of the young Daniel. Tales of single combat against MiG pilots they never met or knew, but with whom they shared those skies like brothers. The silver flashes of a sortie returning, the roar of their accelerating engines each morning. The beautiful routine of hunting, together and alone, in foreign cloudless skies.

It was his grandfather's stories, as much as his family or the troops on the ground, that Daniel was increasingly trying to protect when he piloted a Reaper or a Predator from his screens in Creech. The inheritance of his grandfather and every other pilot who'd taken to the skies in combat. Because as well as being one of the country's first Unmanned Aerial Vehicle pilots, Daniel would also be, he was sure, one of the last to have ever flown missions in a manned craft. Already the military was training young marines, eighteen, nineteen years old, who'd go into missions with no prior experience of aerial combat. The joystick he now handled through each shift had recently been remodelled on that of the Sony Play-

Station. Daniel didn't like it, but he knew it made sense. Without knowing it, under the eyes of their parents and siblings, America would train her future pilots in bedrooms and living rooms across the country. They would fight as if the world was a free-fire zone, cocooned within the hum of servers and computers, but never the sounds of the sky, of an engine's torque, the wing's strain, the purity of its thinning air.

For Daniel, who'd felt the tipping of a wing, who'd known the adrenaline of fear, it had become part of his duty to translate the essence of those manned decades into the control stations of Creech. The knowledge of being both the harbinger of death and its prey, of hearing the sound of your speed, of feeling, at one and the same time, vulnerable and invincible. A respect for the threat of the earth. A memory of air.

—

Thirty minutes after he'd reversed out of his drive in Centennial Hills, Daniel and Maria were pulling up outside the gates of Creech Air Force Base. As they waited for the guard to wave them forward, Daniel looked along the perimeter fence. Creech, it had to be said, still didn't look like much of a base. Indian Springs, the town it edged, was small, only 1,500 people at most, but its outer streets drifted up to within touching distance of the highway at Creech's border. Trailers and caravans, even an old Slipstream, all listed within sight of the huts and hangars inside the fence. When Daniel had first started there, over a year before the 432nd was officially reactivated, they'd had problems with local cats getting in, giving birth to litters of kittens in the garages. The only building next to the base was the Indian Springs Casino, a faded two-storey structure with a café, a handful of slot machines, and the Flying Aces Bar. After that, as far as Daniel knew it was just more desert, dotted by a few nature reserves, all the way to California and Yosemite National Park.

The guard called them forward, took the briefest of glances at their passes, then waved them through with a curt salute. He was one of the older guys, maybe stationed there since before the renaming. A veteran of the Gulf, perhaps. As Daniel drove through he wondered what he must think of them, arriving like this. Creech might not look like much of a base, but then he and Maria, in their sneakers, T-shirts, and shorts, well, they didn't look much like a flying crew, either.

But they were. And this is what Barbara and their other detractors always forgot. They weren't risking their lives when they flew. They weren't exposed, physically, to the war. But that didn't mean they weren't exposed. There were still pressures, other risks, ones Daniel was only just coming to understand, the contours of his combat experience altering as fast as the technology he flew.

For Daniel, and although they never discussed it, he suspected for many of his colleagues too, the greatest pressure of flying UAVs was one of witness. They were paid to watch. This was their job. To record hundreds of thousands of hours of footage that was then watched again, processed by soldiers and analysts in Afghanistan and back at the CIA in Langley. When necessary, they were expected to strike, too. And then watch again. Which is something Daniel had never done before. In Bosnia, Iraq, Afghanistan, by the time his bombs detonated, his missiles hit, he was already miles away, flying faster than the speed of sound, outrunning even the faint thuds of his own ordnance. At Creech he still didn't hear his munitions detonate, but despite being even farther from the battlefield, he saw everything. He saw them explode and he saw what they did, sometimes to people he'd followed for weeks. To people he knew. Like the motorcyclist.

—

Daniel had always known the motorcyclist would have to die. His photograph, along with the head shots of others, had been up

on the wall in Creech for months. His misdemeanours listed below
it dated back to the very start of the invasion in 2003. Daniel had
wanted him to die. Even more, he'd wanted to be the pilot on the
mission that killed him. The motorcyclist's name was Ahmed al
Saeed, and he had the blood of American soldiers on his hands.
Should he get the chance, Daniel, with Maria beside him focusing
the cameras, guiding the lasers, wanted to be the pilot to avenge
them.

For a period of months they'd tracked al Saeed through the
streets of southern Baghdad. They'd watched him drink coffee
on plastic garden chairs in the street, visit his grandmother, liaise
with a team of insurgents laying IEDs. He'd led them, over those
months, to others who were, in turn, followed by other drones,
other pilots, and other operators who'd also watched their homes,
their cars, their children on screens across America. But Daniel and
Maria had stayed with al Saeed, as he'd weaved through the back
streets of the city on his motorbike, as he'd collected his son from
school. As he'd lived.

He became a familiar, like the regular colleague you see across
the office, but to whom you never speak. Daniel started anticipat-
ing his weekly routine. His Wednesday game of chess, his coffee
after Friday prayers. He was thirty-six years old, just a couple years
younger than Daniel, and like him also had two children, a girl
and a boy. Then, one day, the order came through. It was time
to kill him. It was time for Ahmed to die. According to a source
on the ground he would be setting up an ambush for a U.S. convoy. But before Ahmed could hit that convoy, Daniel and Maria,
watching from above, would hit him.

On the day of the mission they'd followed him from early in
the morning. He must have been in good spirits. Three times on
his journeys through the city he'd stopped to kick down the stand
of his bike and join in with a kids' soccer game. It was something
they'd seen him do before, sometimes even pulling a U-turn to
double back for a kick-around he'd glimpsed down one of the

alleys. It was around the time Kayce had got into soccer. Daniel had recently bought her her first pair of cleats. Just that week Cathy had allowed her to put up a set of David Beckham posters in her bedroom. At the first game Ahmed played that day Maria had zoomed in close as he'd dived the wrong way to let a kid score. At the third game, less than an hour before they'd killed him, Daniel had watched as another boy rode his shoulders in celebration of a goal.

The intelligence was good. After that final game, Ahmed had ridden on to an outer suburb, where he'd met with two other insurgents. One of the men was already known to them. The other was not. Listening to the weapon confirmations from the screeners in Okaloosa, Florida, Daniel and Maria continued their observations as the men unloaded two RPGs and three AK-47s from their van. The group was still getting into position when Maria achieved a lock and, confirming a clear blast area, Daniel fired a Hellfire from his Predator.

Perhaps Ahmed was more experienced than the others. Or maybe he just had better hearing, quicker reactions. Whatever the reason, with five seconds to impact, he'd recognised the missile's sonic boom and begun running away from the van, as if he'd known what was about to happen.

When the smoke cleared the other two men were dead. Ahmed, however, lying farther off, was still alive, rolling from side to side, clutching at the stump of his left leg. His head was tipped back, his neck strained as he screamed. This, Daniel had told himself, as Maria tightened focus, is what he'd wanted. They'd saved American lives. The mission was a success.

Turning away from the real-time visuals, Daniel had looked across at the thermal imaging screen. The same scene, rainbowed by temperature, was in focus, a hallucinogenic abstract with a pool of bright orange spreading from its centre. As Daniel watched that puddle of human heat grow, like the slow bubble of a lava lamp, he'd also watched its source, in the shape of Ahmed, change colour like a chameleon. From orange, to yellow, to green, until, leaking from his limbs towards his core, his body cooled to blue, eventually melting into the colour of the ground, the dust.

—

"Tracking white twin cab and blue pickup."
"Check, sensor."
"Holding altitude."
"Check, sensor."

Maria's voice came to Daniel twice, once muffled and distant from where she sat on the flight deck next to him, and again, intimate in his headphones. The ground control station was dark, lit only by the fourteen monitors and control panels in front of them. The servers' hum was harmonised by the whir of the air-conditioning, making the desert's heat no more than a memory on their skin. They both wore their flight suits, sleeves rolled to their insignia patches: a black owl clutching three thunderbolts with the wing's motto beneath, *Victoria Per Scientiam*—Victory Through Knowledge. Their flasks of coffee, two hours cold, stood on a shelf behind them, above which a banner bore the wing's unofficial, more commonly quoted, motto—*If you can't lower heaven,* the banner told anyone entering the room, *raise hell.*

Daniel and Maria had had their Predator in the air for more than an hour when the mission order came down the line. The Karachi station had received intelligence on the movements of Hafiz Mehsud, number three in the Tehrik-i-Taliban Pakistan. Daniel was familiar with the name, and with the face of the man who owned it. His photograph was also on the walls in Creech, just three portraits along from the crossed-out face of Ahmed al Saeed. According to a human source, and supporting chatter surveillance, a rendezvous had been arranged at a location in the mountains northwest of Miranshah. A ground team had already identified his convoy leaving a compound on the edge of town, a white twin cab followed by a blue pickup.

Within minutes the other members of the kill chain introduced themselves, either by voice in Daniel's headphones or by chat messages on his screen. The safety observer at Creech, an intelligence coordinator in Langley, a pair of screeners at Eglin Air Force Base in Florida. Others would be watching the mission, too. Maybe even some White House staff. Daniel never knew how many, or where they were, but these others were always there, even on a last-minute mission like this. Watching his flight, listening in, recording the results.

"No ground unit?" Daniel asked.

"Negative," the coordinator replied. "This is cross-border."

—

It was in the hours following the al Saeed mission, after he'd watched Ahmed's body cool into blue in that dust, that Daniel first established his post-strike routine, one he'd kept to ever since. After the debrief he and Maria had driven out of the base and into the parking lot of the casino next door. While Maria went to the bathroom, Daniel ordered a couple beers from Kim, the barmaid at Flying Aces. Kim, a motherly blonde in her forties, gave Daniel a nod in acknowledgement but didn't break her stream of conversation with another customer.

"I love those Italian ones," she'd said as she'd drawn Daniel's beers. "With the tomato and the mozzarella?"

"Caprese," an older guy said from across the bar. He wore a *Vietnam Vet* baseball cap and spoke without looking up from his drink. "They're called caprese."

"That's the one," Kim said. "Yeah, caprese. I love those."

Above her, four large TV screens, each hung at an angle, faced every side of the bar. They all played the same video-clip show:

animals slipping on ice, bike tricks going wrong. There were screens in the bar itself, too, for gaming, with slits beside them for feeding in bills from one to a hundred dollars. A woman next to the Vietnam vet was knitting a blue baby's sweater, while across from Daniel four young guys he recognised from Creech tapped at their phones.

As he'd waited for Maria, Daniel looked around the rest of Flying Aces. Its walls were decorated with black-and-white photographs of 1940s bombers, their noses painted with their logos and names—*Puss in Boots, Wishful Thinking, The Uninvited*. Below these, snapshot montages of nights in the bar were propped on each of the side tables.

When Maria returned they'd taken their beers to one of these tables. With the sound of the clip show behind them and a photo of a stag party in fancy dress at their elbows, she'd raised her glass in a toast. "To Ahmed." She'd meant it as a joke, but as they'd touched the rims of their glasses, neither of them had smiled. It was the first time they'd watched someone bleed out, and something about that spreading pool of orange had altered the air of their success. For a while they'd spoken about other things. The colonel at the base, Maria's son's upcoming basketball trials, improvements to their respective houses. Eventually, draining their beers, they'd left, walking through the lobby's dusk chorus of fruit machines and dime games out to Daniel's car in the parking lot. Pulling onto the highway, they'd driven it east together in silence, back towards their families, their homes.

Except Daniel hadn't gone home, not right away. Instead, after dropping Maria, he'd turned the car around and driven the highway back into the desert, turning off at a side road a few miles beyond the city. The road soon became a track, the Camry trembling and shaking over its stones, then nothing at all. Daniel texted Cathy, telling her he'd been ordered to an unscheduled briefing, then turned off his phone and got out of the car. For the next hour he'd remained there, sitting on the hood of the Camry until

the sun dipped below the Charleston range. As he'd watched the
view darken he'd tried to fill his eyes with the disappearing desert
before him: its low shrubs, its sand and rocks burnishing towards
evening. Its unblemished sky. He'd wanted to unsee the al Saeed
mission. Delete it from his memory. He'd wanted to extinguish
the image of Ahmed lifting a boy onto his shoulders in celebration, diving the wrong way in goal, rolling from side to side, side
to side, screaming. But he could not. And he still couldn't. There
had been many other missions since then, and many other strikes.
But through all of them Ahmed the motorcyclist had remained,
a stubborn residue bleeding out under Daniel's eyelids. Victory
through knowledge.

—

"Creech?" The screener's voice sounded unsure, a degree off the
usual protocol. "We have two times vehicles approaching south-
southwest. Approximately eight pax total."

"Can we get a feed?" Maria asked.

Within seconds a visual appeared from a Global Hawk, a surveillance drone watching the watchers.

"Guess that's the rendezvous?" The coordinator's chat message
popped up on another monitor.

"Intel on their source?" Daniel typed back, keeping one hand
on the Predator's controls.

"Negative," the coordinator replied. "Langley picked up the
trail in deep country."

"Double-tap," Maria said quietly from her seat. "Double-tap,
baby."

Within another thirty minutes Mehsud's convoy had reached a
small compound high up one of the eastern valleys, half in shadow,
half in light. In another ten minutes the second convoy, tracked
by the Global Hawk, also came within their visual range. A minivan trailed by another pickup. Daniel watched as the two vehicles

revved and stalled up the steep track towards the eastern valley. At one point they both stopped and a door of the minivan opened. A man got out, walked to the side of the track, and took a leak.

Higher in the valley, in the mud-walled compound, a single figure, a man, from what Daniel could tell, came out into one of the three interconnected courtyards. There was a tree in the corner, and for a moment he disappeared under its shadow. When he emerged back into the light he was throwing his arm before him, again and again. A scattering of dark dots gathered at his feet, moving erratically. They were chickens, Daniel realised. He was feeding chickens. As Mehsud's convoy approached he paused in his feeding and looked up. The lead vehicle, the twin cab, came to a halt at the compound's walls and two men got out. Both carried rifles.

"That's a weapon confirmation, Major," one of the screeners said in Daniel's ear. "Two times rifles."

"Do we have ID?" Daniel asked.

"Negative," the coordinator replied. He had a West Coast accent, like a surfer. "If Mehsud's there," he continued. "He's still in one of those vehicles."

Daniel eased the joystick to the right and circled the Predator. Maria adjusted the sensors in response, keeping them focused on the compound. Their screens were always silent, but there were times when Daniel thought he could tell if there was real silence on the ground too. Like now. He could have been wrong, but the scene looked strangely peaceful. The tree—a fig tree, he'd have guessed—the two guards resting their weapons and waiting in the shade of the compound wall. The pickup and twin cab, also waiting. Everyone was waiting. He, Maria, the screeners, the coordinator, the observer. Somewhere, the pilot of the Global Hawk. And, they all hoped, in the back of one of those vehicles, Hafiz Mehsud was waiting too.

"Okay, people, eyes front." It was the coordinator again, marking the arrival of the second convoy. The minivan pulled up first, and then the pickup. The van's door slid open again, a growing dark on Daniel's monochrome screen; from slit, to square, to rectangle.

"We have two, three, four, five. Five, repeat, five, pax confirmed. All male."

The last man to exit was carrying something, hoisted on his shoulder. The third to get out now also reached back into the van to lift out an object. It looked heavy, and slightly shorter than whatever his colleague was carrying.

"Is that a weapon?" Daniel asked.

"RPG?" the coordinator guessed down the line.

"Too short," one of the screeners said.

"Mortar, then," the coordinator countered.

"Do we have confirmation?" Maria asked them both.

"Possible weapon confirmation," the coordinator replied.

"Okay, here we go," Maria said, as another man got out of what they hoped was Mehsud's pickup. He, too, had a rifle slung over his shoulder.

"That's three times weapon confirmation," one of the screeners logged.

"Possible four times," the coordinator reminded them.

Another man followed. He was slower, older, leaning on a stick.

Maria zoomed in on this last figure. He wore a combat jacket over his tribal clothes and carried what looked like a briefcase, holding it close to his side.

"That's him," the coordinator said. "That's our guy."

Daniel felt his pulse quicken. There were now nine men out of their vehicles on the ground. They were moving towards one another, bunching.

"Sweet target," Maria said in confirmation.

Daniel breathed deeply, trying to control his adrenaline. He remembered the list of alleged offences below Hafiz Mehsud's photograph on the wall. Not the detail, just the length. And now here he was, the same man, joining these two meeting groups. In a few minutes they'd move inside, or some of them might begin to leave. He scanned the territory of his screen for any others. Which is when he saw a movement in the minivan, a light patch in the dark of its opened door.

"Minivan door," he said.

"Check, sensor," Maria replied, tightening focus on the van.

"What's the problem, Major?" the coordinator asked. For the first time he sounded urgent, pressed.

"Was that a woman in there?" Daniel asked.

"A woman?" the coordinator replied. "No way. Not at a meet like this."

"Screeners?" Daniel asked. The van's open door was filling half his screen now, but all of it was dark.

"No way to tell," one of the Florida voices said.

"I saw something . . . ," said the other.

"I saw a man," the coordinator said, cutting in. "Possible tenth pax."

"Eyes front," Maria said. The two groups had come even closer together. They were talking, the armed guards hanging back a few feet. The man from the courtyard had also come round to the front of the compound now, to watch.

"What you got, Creech?" the coordinator asked.

"Two times Hellfires confirmed," Daniel replied.

"Okay, Major, you have Intel clearance."

"Permission to engage?" Daniel asked, slipping into his kill protocol.

The observer's voice was in his ear before he'd finished the question. "Good to go, Major. Permission to engage."

There was no word from Florida, so, pulling the joystick hard left, Daniel brought the Predator tight around into an attack trajectory. Soon, somewhere in those hills, the faint hum of its blades would be heard.

"Missiles armed."

"Check, sensor."

"Paint target."

"Check, sensor."

"Target lock."

"Check, sensor."

"In three, two, one. Missiles deployed."

The two Hellfires disappeared from their rails in a diagram of the Predator on Daniel's monitor. As he watched the scene of their destination—the shadow of the tree, the stilled pickups—the low buzz of his headphones filled his ears, and beneath that, six sets of breaths held on the lines. The counter to his left descended. Through ten, through five. The man feeding the chickens had moved closer. A lighter patch appeared in the van's door again. Four, three, two. It was a headscarf. One.

The visuals flashed white, blanking in the glare.

"Impact," Maria said beside him.

Daniel watched as definition slowly returned to the screens. Maria zoomed in close. The vehicles were burning. The few bodies left were prone. The hum of the servers, the conditioned air of the control station, a surfer's voice, close in his ear. "Good job, Major. Well done."

CHAPTER NINE

AS MICHAEL REACHED the turn in the stairway a floorboard flexed under him, its creaking making him pause. Without going any farther, his heart a tight fist in his chest, he leant forward and looked around the corner.

There was nothing. Just more stairs, then a landing carpeted in the same deep red as the runner descending behind him. No ghost. No intruder. No Caroline. Just a part of the Nelsons' house he'd never seen before.

He thought about turning and going back down the stairs. But now that he was there, higher in the house, shouldn't he at least check the rooms on this floor? For whoever might have come in through the back door, if not for whatever had conjured that sudden essence of Caroline. This is how Michael convinced himself to take the last few steps up to the landing. But in reality he knew the only intruder he was searching for now was her. The resonance of the sensation he'd felt was still fading in him, as if she'd only just vacated the air on the landing before him, leading him on an impossible game of hide-and-seek.

This, at least, was what Michael's body was telling him. His mind, still trying to keep a rational purchase on what had happened, was already dismissing what he'd sensed as no more than grief, still having its way with him after all these months. Caroline was dead. All that remained of her was in his memories, and so this, his mind cautioned him, was all he was feeling. Memory, triggered by some unseen, unheard association. Michael wanted to believe the certainty of this rational voice. But he could not. It was a voice winnowed of mystery, and devoid of that most seductive of drugs, hope.

Stepping onto the landing, Michael found himself standing between three wooden doors, one on either side of him at the ends of a short corridor, and a third ahead of him, just off to his right. This last door was closed, as was the one to his left. The door on his right, though, was open. As he walked towards it Michael saw the foot of a bed in the room beyond, the corner of a rug, and, as he got closer, an armchair collapsed with clothes—a pair of trousers, some tights, a tangle of shirts and blouses, as if their wearers had evaporated mid-embrace. Entering the room, he stood before the bed, studying its heaped duvet for the shape of a body. But there was none. Just as there never had been. Just remains, that was all that had been left of her. And that's all they'd buried too. Not Caroline as Michael had known and loved her, but just her remains.

—

Michael had never been a violent man. The tinder he'd witnessed fire up in others was an unfamiliar fuel to him. Over the years he'd spent with Nico and Raoul in Inwood he'd learnt the contours of violence, but as an observer only. The way it entered a room, or took possession of a man's face, drawing the tendons in his neck, flushing his cheeks with blood. He'd seen the suddenness of its flaring, too—the staccato jerk of a punch, the sardine flash of a blade. And more than once he'd been in the presence of the weight of its threat, the heaviness of a pistol on a table, the tightly bedded bronze of an ammunition clip. But never, even when he'd been threatened himself, had he felt its compulsion to harm. Until they'd killed Caroline.

The desire had risen in him a few hours after he'd discovered Peter waiting for him by the porch of Coed y Bryn. It was evening, the woods across the valley already a swathe of darkness. The sky above them was showing its first stars. Peter was still in the house, cooking them both dinner. He'd said he thought it best if Michael wasn't left alone. But for a few minutes, when Michael had gone upstairs to change, he had been.

On entering their bedroom he'd seen the chair on Caroline's side of the bed, piled just like this chair in Samantha and Josh's room with her discarded clothes. Dropping to the floor beside it, Michael had slowly pushed his hands under their weight, as if reaching for eggs under a sleeping hen. Drawing them to him with both arms, he'd pressed his face into Caroline's dresses, T-shirts, and the jumper she'd worn on the first night they'd met, its neckline falling from her one bare shoulder.

He wanted to kill them. These faceless men who'd murdered his wife from the air. The planners and officers and spies who'd played with her fate like gods. He wanted to find them, expose them, turn their hidden warrens and nests inside out. He wanted to make them pay.

For the following weeks these thoughts spread through Michael like a virus, an anger masking his pain. As the story broke across the world, as the comment pieces mounted, as Caroline's name was spoken again and again on radio and TV shows, he learnt all he could about the U.S. drone programme. Long into the night and the early morning, ignoring advice to sleep, to rest, Michael trawled blogs, forums, and chat rooms for information. About the bases from which the Predator might have been operated. About the innocents killed or unmentioned in mission reports. About the missiles that blew apart his wife.

The more Michael learnt, the more the injustices continued to deepen. Caroline and her team had been in Pakistan, a country with whom America was not at war. This was why their vehicle had been unmarked, why Sightline or their fixer hadn't contacted the U.S. military. Why warzone protocol had not been followed. Although the strike had been a covert operation, under pressure the Pentagon had issued a statement acknowledging the incident. It was, the statement read, a tragic accident. There would be an internal investigation. As well as Caroline, her British director, a Swedish cameraman, and their Pakistani interpreter and driver had also been killed. Among the dead was a fourteen-year-old boy. The British, Australian, and Swedish governments demanded answers. There would be a review of operating procedures, they were told, of lines of command. There would be answers. But the Pentagon statement also made mention of the journalists "working undercover," of "entering a high-risk area." They had known, it was implied, the dangers of their actions. And, the same statement reminded the world, an influential terrorist had been successfully targeted. The weight of blame, Michael knew, from the moment it happened, was being dissipated, thinned.

At night, when he couldn't sleep, he thought of the interviews he'd give when he was able to face a camera or a microphone. How he would broadcast his anger. How he would make sure the story was never allowed to slip from the public conversation. How he'd demand those responsible should face justice, a glaring light, not an obscuring darkness, and how in its illumination Caroline's death might yet prevent the future deaths of others. He would find a way, somehow, to visit pain upon those who had killed her.

Then, just as quickly as it had first washed through him, so the swell of Michael's vengeance ebbed. It left him overnight. On waking in the small hours one morning, he'd simply known he wanted none of it. That rather than broadcast anything, he wanted to curl up from the world, to hibernate with his loss. This was, he realised later, perhaps the true moment of Caroline's death for him. A quieter, more complete acknowledgement of what Peter had told him as he'd knelt on the gravel beside him and laid his hands on his shoulders. A lonely and terrible reckoning with the facts.

In the following months Michael refused all interview requests. He made no statements, he pursued no more enquiries. Caroline's remains were repatriated in a Royal Air Force transport plane. A week later he and her family buried them in the chapel he'd first seen with Caroline through Coed y Bryn's kitchen window. The coffin, Michael had known, was mostly empty. He watched it lowered into the ground, threw a handful of soil across its wood, then turned his back on it. He would let the world clamour over her death. He would let others discover the details, the reasons. Because for Michael there was only the one truth to learn, and he'd already discovered it that night when he'd sat on the floor of their bedroom pressing Caroline's clothes to his face: in her scent, fading by the hour, and in the sheets of their bed, still creased by her body, which was no longer whole, and no longer here.

—

A tall window rose above the armchair in Samantha and Josh's bedroom, its frame filled with the leaves of the sycamore outside their house. Opposite was a king-size bed, above which hung an abstract landscape: the suggestion of hills, sky, perhaps a river. On either side the bedside tables marked out the room's territory. On the right a pile of novels, women's magazines, a ceramic bowl filled with earrings. On the left a book on the American Civil War, a glasses case, the lead of a phone charger. On the wooden floor, copies of the *Financial Times* and *Herald Tribune.* The bed itself was unmade, the duvet a cumulus at its centre. At the other end two pillows were stacked against its head, their shape still holding the depression of a back.

Michael looked over the bed, the clothes on the armchair. So often, over the last seven months, being in the Nelsons' house had been like reliving echoes of a past life. As he'd helped Lucy build a LEGO car, when he'd watched Samantha and Josh fill the dishwasher or, once, each carry a sleeping daughter up the stairs to bed.

But such moments were visions, not echoes, glimpses of a future life that had been taken from him along with Caroline. A life of children, family. Even this bed before him was such a vision. The bed he and Caroline had shared had always been new. A bed of promise, not years. And it was the years Michael wanted, the accumulation of sharing. A lifetime, not just a marriage.

He turned from the bed. Whatever trace of Caroline had led him up the stairs wasn't to be found in here. And this wasn't for him to see, anyway. He felt as if he'd strayed from the corridors of a cruise liner to find himself, unexpectedly, in its engine room, the mechanisms unprepared for public eyes, the working parts worn with keeping an even keel, whatever the seas. He glanced out the window at the quiet street, the sycamore leaves filtering the afternoon sunlight. As he did, he seemed to surface back into the day, into the facts of its ordinariness, the city subdued under the heat. What if Josh were to come home now to find him in their bedroom? How would he explain? What had he been thinking, in coming up the stairs at all? He hadn't heard a sound since he'd entered the house. Would an intruder really have remained so quiet for so long? The open door was just a mistake, that was all. He should leave now, while he still could. Write a note for Samantha and Josh, close the back door and leave.

CHAPTER
TEN

ALTHOUGH IN THE months after her death Michael had lost his desire for full knowledge of what had happened to Caroline, there was one question that continued to linger in his mind. Who? That was all he'd still wanted to know. Not why, but who? Who had pressed the button? Who was the person behind the pilot, the operator, the contractor?

Who was the man or woman who'd killed his wife?

What did they look like?

How did they dream?

Who did they love?

What was their name?

—

On a March morning, four months after he'd moved into South Hill Drive, Michael learnt the answer to that final question, when Major Daniel McCullen wrote to him.

The letter had been addressed to his publishers in New York. An intern or mailroom worker had inserted it into a new envelope and written Michael's address on it in a rounded, flowing hand: *Flat 6, 34 South Hill Drive, London, NW3 6JP, United Kingdom.* The letter was handwritten, too. A controlled script with little variance, even around the fifth line, where Michael felt surely it should have betrayed something—a break in a descender, a deeper impression on the page—as the mind guiding the pen had written the words *I regret to say I was the pilot that day.*

Michael first read that line while sitting on the bottom steps of his communal stairwell. He'd been lacing his trainers when the letter, along with the rest of the day's mail, had slipped through the front door and fallen to the mat beneath. Charity brochures, bank statements, a travel magazine for a long-moved-out tenant, and, bearing a New York postmark, a letter addressed to *Mr. Michael Turner.*

For the past two months Michael and Josh had been meeting twice a week to walk and jog on the Heath. The days on which they met were dictated by the shifting pattern of Josh's work schedule, which was, in turn, defined by the state of various foreign markets. But whatever the day, they'd always managed to keep their agreement. For Josh it was part of a New Year's resolution to lose weight and counter the hours he spent each week under office lights and on the Tube. For Michael the exercise was to get fit for his fencing, to break the day in his flat between waking and working, but also to ease his sciatica, the consequence of a schoolboy injury that had recently returned from across the years to cramp his right leg each morning. He didn't know what had brought it on again— whether it was the fencing or having returned in earnest to *The Man Who Broke the Mirror,* the long hours at his desk. Or, even, he sometimes found himself wondering, was it another process of his grieving? A slippage of whatever leaden weight had sat in his chest since Caroline's death down his body to cannonball itself in his calf instead. Whatever the cause, its electric grip on his lower back, the muscles in his right buttock, had Michael limping from his bed to the bathroom each morning. It was only after thirty minutes of extended walking that his leg would begin to loosen and he could once more flex his right foot freely again.

As Michael, sitting on the stairs, read that fifth line, he'd felt the heat leave his body. The stairwell seemed to pulse about him, his vision to blur. He returned to the letter's opening. *Dear Mr. Turner,* it read. *I understand this is a letter you most probably do not want to receive, but I hope on reading it you might come to appreciate why I felt both compelled and morally bound to write to you.*

Michael flipped the page over, scanning to the letter's end. An unreadable signature, its letters printed below. *Daniel McCullen.* So that was his name. That was the name of the man who'd killed his wife, written in ink by the same hand that had held the controls of that Predator, that had released, via touch, fibreoptic, satellite, hydraulics and hinge, two Hellfire missiles, their thrusters burning, into the clear mountain skies above her head.

For a while Michael did no more than stare at the name. *Daniel McCullen.* Eventually, as his focus returned, he turned the page again and read the letter from the start once more. *Dear Mr. Turner.* When he reached the signature for a second time he folded the letter into its envelope, then folded the envelope into the pocket of his shorts before standing, his head light, to take himself and this new knowledge, burning at the front of his mind, out into the city's winter morning.

All through his walk and jog with Josh that day—around the men's pond and up the eastern side of the Heath to skirt the grounds of Kenwood House and back through the woods to Parliament Hill—Michael had felt the letter's edges rubbing against his thigh, its words distilling, like the slow release of a drug, through his body and his mind. The day was overcast, the Heath's sandy soil waterlogged under their feet. Lone walkers followed their dogs through the bare woods. A single woman was swimming in the mixed pond, her blue cap making slow, bright progress between a swan and a resting gull bobbing in her wake.

At first, as they'd walked, it was Josh who had talked. About Samantha wanting to go back to work, or to college. "It's doesn't seem to matter to her which," he'd said, as they'd strode along the lower paths. "Which is my problem with it. I mean, I don't mind her working, course I don't. Sure, it'll make things harder with the girls, and Christ knows she doesn't need to, but well." He'd paused, for breath, not thought. "If she's gonna make it more difficult, she may as well have some focus about what she does. You know what I mean?"

Michael could tell they'd argued. Josh only ever talked about Samantha at this length when they had. Usually he kept his conversation to work politics, current affairs. Sometimes football, although he knew Michael didn't support a team. But occasionally he'd use their sessions on the Heath to talk about Sam, the girls. Never anything too revealing, but still more, from what Michael could tell, than he perhaps shared with his work colleagues or other male friends.

As the cramp in Michael's calf eased, they'd broken into a jog along the façade of Kenwood House. Almost immediately Josh's talk gave way to his now-familiar heavy breathing, his face flushed with the effort, the boyish lick of his fringe bouncing above his brow. They ran like that, in silence other than the sound of their clouding breaths, until the end of their route. Reaching the crest of Parliament Hill, as had become their habit, the two men sat on one of the benches and looked out over London, craned and grey, spread like a sieging army before them.

Michael leant forward, his elbows on his knees. Josh rested against the bench beside him, his legs stretched and his arms spread across its back, as if to invite as much air as possible into his lungs. Their calves and shins were spattered with mud, their shoulders steaming. Michael could feel the sweat pricking at his temples. Removing his gloves, he took the letter from his pocket, unfolded it from its envelope, and handed it to Josh.

"What do you make of this?"

"What is it?" Josh said, as he took it. Michael just nodded at the letter, as if to say Read it and see for yourself.

While Josh read, Michael looked out over the city, keeping

his eyes on its skyline as Josh let out a whispered "Fuck." A plane coming in to land at Heathrow laboured across the sky, its under-carriage a dirty white against the darkening clouds. Somewhere, Michael found himself thinking as he'd watched its descent above the towers and terraces, at this same instant, Daniel McCullen was lying asleep in his bed. Perhaps beside his wife. He'd mentioned in the letter he was married. It was, it seemed, part of his reasoning. *As a husband,* he had written, *I can only imagine I would want to know how my wife came to die.* He disagreed, he also said, with the secrecy of the Pentagon's internal inquiry. With the limitations imposed upon him. He'd apologised, too, more than once. But not, Michael felt, so much for himself as for the situation. For the movements of the world that had led them all to this. He wrote like a victim. As if Caroline's death was something that had happened to him, rather than something he'd caused.

"Jesus, Mike," Josh said, returning the letter. "Have you shown this to anyone else?"

"No," Michael said, slipping it back in the envelope. "It came this morning. Just before I met you." He looked down at the original postmark. "From San Francisco."

Josh looked at him, as if in admiration. "That is insane," he said, shaking his head. "Insane." He laid a hand on Michael's shoulder. "I am so sorry. What a shitty letter to get. What a shit!" Taking his hand away, he turned to the view. "The fucking gall!"

"Maybe," Michael said.

"Maybe?" Josh looked back at him, his palms up in question. "What do you mean maybe? The guy—" He broke off, unable to finish the sentence. "You should inform the inquiry," he said, with more authority.

"Why?"

"Why? Because he can't do this." He seemed genuinely upset. "It's fucking manipulative. He doesn't have the right. Because it'll jeopardise the process. That's why."

Michael nodded. "Yeah. I guess I should."

Josh looked back out at the city, at Saint Paul's, the London Eye, the pyramid of Canary Wharf steaming in the east. "How can he do that?" he said, sighing heavily. "It's all so fucking ridiculous. I mean, I know what Caroline was doing was important. But the war? Afghanistan? Iraq? It's all a fucking distraction. Meanwhile, China is rubbing its hands, loving it. Doing what they fucking want. I'm tellin' you, China, that's where we should be focusing. Not a bunch of countries with a GDP the size of Birmingham."

—

In any other circumstance Josh and Michael would not have been friends. Their patterns of conversation were divergent, their rhythms at counterpoint. Josh often talked in this way, laying down the law with certainty, as if he had a privileged insight into the matters of the world. When he spoke he rarely left room for a second voice or alternative view. Michael, through character and training, preferred to listen, to probe, parry, and deflect as a way to spiral to the nub of a discussion.

But the manner of their first meeting, together with Michael keeping a territory close to his flat—a square mile comprising the Heath, the streets of South End Green and Belsize Park—meant they had, almost by accident, become close. From early on Josh had adopted something of an older-brother attitude towards Michael. In the week following their party in November he and Samantha had invited him over again, to have dinner with Maddy and Tony. And he'd joined them again soon after that too, when they'd all dined at Tony and Maddy's new house a few streets away.

At both these dinners Michael had felt like the younger sibling of the other two men, not so much through years, which he was, as through the lesser volume he appeared to displace in the world. His grief had made him light, and Josh had picked up on this. Whenever he laid a hand on Michael, as he often did—on his shoulder, his back, his arm—it was as if he were attempting to evoke solidity back into his being, to draw the focus of him to a physical level.

With Tony it was more subtle. As a publisher and reader he held Michael in high regard. But still, Michael's lack of institution, his lone existence in the world, meant Tony too had detected a lightness in Michael he'd also felt a need to bolster. Not with fraternal ease, like Josh, but with attention to his topics of conversation when in his presence, with asking, too often, for his opinion, as a teacher might of a shy but promising pupil.

Tony's interest in Michael never outlasted their shared company. As far as Michael knew Tony liked him, was pleased he'd met him, but invested little more in his recovery than the usual good wishes of one human to another. With Josh, however, as his neighbour, Michael had become more of a long-term project. In the last month alone Josh had twice invited a female work colleague to dinner on the same night they'd asked Michael round. Although he'd been under strict instructions from Samantha not to press the point, his intentions were clear enough. After the second time this happened, Michael had called him on it at the end of the night. They'd been clearing the table in the kitchen, Michael bringing the bowls and dishes to Josh at the dishwasher.

"Are you trying to set me up?" he asked him, as he put a stack of plates on the counter. Emily, another broker at Lehman's, had ordered a cab and just left. Samantha was upstairs, sorting through a basket of washing. Josh looked at Michael with mock surprise, followed quickly by a juvenile grin. "A man's gotta eat, Mike" he'd said, shrugging. "That's all I'll say. A man's gotta eat."

"Got to eat?" Michael said.

"Hey, c'mon," Josh countered. "Emily is great, isn't she? She's funny, clever. Great tits," he said, with a connoisseur's nod. As usual by this time of the evening, Josh was drunk.

"She's very attractive," Michael said. "And she seems lovely. But—"

"I know," Josh cut across him, the smile slipping from his face. "I know," he repeated, bending to drop knives and forks into the plastic grid. He straightened up and turned to lean against the counter. "But you've got to start living at some point," he said, as if suggesting the inevitable. "At some time you gotta get back on the horse."

"I *am* living!" Michael said. He spread his arms in illustration of the room, the dining table, them. And it was true. He wasn't ready for an Emily yet. It was still less than a year since Caroline had died. But after the last two months in London, he was, slowly, beginning to feel as if he was living again. Caroline's death had numbed him, like an arm deadened in sleep. But now the blood was returning to his emotional capillaries, as if he was waking. He'd recently rediscovered an enthusiasm for *The Man Who Broke the Mirror*, for carving a shape to his years with Oliver and threading his theories into the weft of the story. The fencing lessons, meanwhile, although reawakening his sciatica, had also reinvigorated him physically. When he showered each morning now he could taste, just, the hint of a future that didn't have to be an echo of his past.

Josh took Michael at his word and hadn't attempted any more introductions since. But their conversation at the end of that night had marked the genesis of another shade to their friendship. A conspiratorial tinge in relation to women, which, on two separate occasions since, had been strengthened further. The first of these had been planned by Josh. The second was not.

Josh's boss had tasked him with entertaining a delegation of Mexican hedge-fund owners and investors over in London from Guadalajara for the week. They were, he told Michael, cultured men who'd relish the opportunity of having dinner with a successful author. Would he do him a favour and join them for the evening? It would be at the bank's expense.

A few evenings later, over dinner at a restaurant in Mayfair,

Michael found Josh's estimation of his clients to be accurate. Many of them, as well as being businessmen and investors, were also professors at the university, some of the leading Mexican thinkers in their fields, fluent not just in English and Spanish, but also French, German, and, in the case of one engineer, Chinese.

It was the first time Michael had been out in the centre of London since he'd returned to the city. As they'd walked from the restaurant to a private club, along Curzon Street and up into Queen Street, the capital seemed impossibly grand to him, its classical architecture underlit, a hinterland of solid centuries fortifying the narrow streets north of Green Park. The Mexicans seemed at home in their surroundings, and even more so at the club. They were well acquainted with power, familiar with its global language. As Michael drank with them, watching them flirt with the waitresses, slipping business cards from their breast pockets, they reminded him more of gangsters than professors. As if a faculty had been passed through the prism of Grand Theft Auto, emerging with a hint of danger to their tailoring, a threatening air to their polish.

After the club Michael wanted to go home. He'd drunk more than he had for years. But Josh, who seemed to have become more himself as the night edged towards morning, insisted. The director of the delegation, a venture capitalist and professor of sociology called Ramón, had loved talking to Michael about *BrotherHoods*.

"You're a hit!" Josh told him, laying an arm around his neck and clasping his shoulder. "He wants you to give a lecture over there and everything. C'mon, you're my guest tonight. A couple of hours more, then we'll grab a cab together. I promise."

The next venue, to which they were driven in one of the Mexicans' chauffeured cars, was a lap-dancing club entered through a plain door beneath an awning in a square south of Piccadilly. The same square, Michael realised, as they filed between the bouncers, that backed onto the London Library. This discovery, in a location he knew so well, deepened his sense of being a stranger in a city he thought he knew. As they'd passed down a narrow corridor and on into a low-lit lounge, the host had greeted Josh with a hug. Josh seemed to grow again in the man's embrace. Handing him his Lehman's account card, he ushered his guests through, pointing them towards a set of booths at the far end of the club.

The rest of the night was hazy for Michael, with just certain details pushing through to clarity the following day. The club, although apparently plush, had the air of a cross-channel ferry. Its low ceilings betrayed grey stains of damp about the air vents. The arms of the chairs were faded and frayed. From their booth the group had a clear view of the main stage, onto which a succession of women appeared, each heralded by the bars of a new song, to strip and perform on a polished steel pole. Michael couldn't help staring at them. It had been almost a year since he'd last gone to bed with Caroline, since he'd last been close to a naked body. Not that the women onstage were naked as Caroline had been that night. Their bodies, corded with muscle and spray-tanned, were sheened under the stage lights. Caroline's skin, despite her year-round tan, had always been matt. Her breasts, too, had been natural, small, but with the shape of a younger woman's. The breasts of the women onstage were often hardened by implants, strangely immobile across their straining chests as they held themselves in slow, descending positions on the pole. Whenever they bent over, or spread their legs, the pink of their labias blinked suddenly honest amid the show, biology briefly disturbing the fantasy of their dance.

In comparison to Michael, the others in the booth appeared disinterested in the women onstage, familiarity defusing the potency of their display. The dynamics of the group, it seemed, were more powerful than any performance beyond it. But then the women had begun to join them, and everything had changed. Some had just been on the stage, from where they'd sensed the weight of the group's wealth in the room. The Mexicans ordered bottles of champagne as the women introduced themselves with false names and foreign accents—Croatian, Romanian, Nigerian. As they did, the group's focus quickly fragmented. Each man, within the radius of a woman's attention, became individual again. Within minutes the group was breaking up, the Mexicans being led away, sometimes by one woman, sometimes by two, through a velvet curtain and into the private rooms beyond.

When they'd returned, Josh and his colleagues began pairing off with the women too. As Josh took the extended hand of Bianca, a tall Serbian brunette wearing a parody of a green evening dress, he'd called across the table to Michael.

"Hey, Mike! You wanna dance?"

Michael raised a hand and shook his head to show he was fine. Crystal, a petite blonde sitting beside him, leant in to whisper to him, a Russian childhood shadowing her voice. "No, come on," she'd said. "You must have fun, too. Please." As she spoke she'd tapped the stem of her glass with her flat-cut nails, chequer-painted.

"Ah, c'mon, Mike!" Josh said, as Bianca drew him away from the booth. "It's on me."

When Michael, smiling, shook his head again, Josh had raised his own hands in surrender and shrugged towards Crystal, as if to say, *I tried, but he won't learn.* Allowing Bianca to lead him on towards the curtains he'd pointed a finger at Michael, like a coach reminding his young charge his training was far from over.

After going for another two dances, one with Crystal and then another with Bianca, Josh had kept his word. Putting on his jacket he'd leant down from behind Michael and given him a tap on the shoulder. "C'mon, soldier," he'd said. "Let's get you out of here." He seemed suddenly more sober and Michael wondered, not for the first time, how much of the night had been an act on Josh's behalf, a display, like the girls onstage, for the benefit of the Mexicans.

As they'd made their way out of the club, the host enthusiastically shook Josh's hand with both of his. While they'd talked, Michael looked back at the booths, where the Mexicans continued to drink and talk with a new set of girls. Their earlier polish had left them and they seemed newly exposed, like children almost, under the glitter balls and the lights. The power with which they'd entered the club had been transferred to the women for whom they'd bought drinks, whom they'd paid for minutes of their time. The Chinese-speaking engineer, Michael noticed, sat on his own to one side, his tie undone, absentmindedly turning his wedding ring with his other hand. Michael watched as, with a sigh, he drank from the champagne flute before him, its rim smudged with pink lipstick.

"Don't worry about them," Josh said, as they'd collected their coats from the cloakroom. "They're big boys. They can look after themselves."

The next time Michael saw Josh after that night had been in his kitchen, a few days later. Samantha was giving the girls their dinner. Lucy, as she ate, was overseeing another battle of wills between Molly and Dolly, both of whom had received recent and drastic haircuts. Michael had come round to give Sam a couple of books—a treatise on photography and the proof of a friend's new novel. They were sharing a pot of tea when Josh entered, dropping his briefcase in the hall and giving each of the girls a peck on their heads. Drawing a bottle of red from the wine rack, he began to open it.

"So what did you think of those Mexicans?" he asked Michael as he'd poured the wine. "Pretty interesting guys eh?"

"Certainly more lively than my old professors," Michael said.

"You bet they are," Josh said. "Very interesting guys. Very interesting. And smart businessmen, too."

"Did it work out?" Michael asked, as Josh pulled up a chair between his two daughters. "The bank side of things?"

"Too early to say," he'd replied, reaching out and stroking Lucy's hair. "But that's where it'll be coming from soon enough. Mexico, Brazil. They're bucking the global trend. Christ knows, they're doing it better than us."

Whether Samantha had picked up on the subtext of Josh's

comments, or whether she'd just chosen to ignore it, Michael couldn't tell. But whichever, Josh had seemed to enjoy the private knowledge he and Michael were sharing in his home. As if, in however small a way, he'd initiated him into his life beyond this kitchen, this house, and in doing so had carved out a bit of Michael for himself alone.

Josh's reaction a week later, when Michael came across him and Maddy at a wine bar in Belsize Park, couldn't have been more different. There had been, in itself, nothing suspicious about what Michael had seen. He'd been returning from the supermarket with a couple of bags of shopping when he'd seen them through the bar's window. Had Josh not been looking directly at him, he wouldn't have disturbed them. But as it was, their eyes met and Josh had waved him inside. They were just finishing up, so Michael sat with them only long enough to ask Maddy how she and Tony were settling in, and for her to enquire after the progress of his new book.

Throughout the conversation Josh seemed on edge, looking at his watch twice in the same minute. Maddy, however, maintained the same distanced interest she'd always held on every occasion Michael had met her. As if the person with whom she was speaking was just one of many in an invisible receiving line on either side of her.

When Michael picked up his bags to leave, Josh waved him off casually enough. "Sure, I'll be there," he'd said, confirming their jog on the Heath the next day. "See you by the ponds at eight." But when they'd gone for that jog the following morning, it was as if their meeting in the bar had never happened. Michael wouldn't have expected Josh to bring it up, but he'd interviewed enough people to know when the omission of a subject was enough to conjure it.

At the end of that jog, as they'd sat on their regular bench on Parliament Hill, Michael had thought Josh was about to mention his drink with Maddy. He'd taken an intake of breath like the beginning of an explanation, or perhaps a request for Michael to keep what he'd seen to himself. But no such request had come. Instead, he'd just leant back against the bench and stared out over the city, as if, after all these years of working at its heart, he was still trying to figure it out.

—

Sitting on that same bench, months later, Michael folded Daniel's letter back into the pocket of his shorts. As he did, a couple of girls jogged past on the path behind them. They wore hats, fluorescent bibs, and Lycra leggings. Josh followed them with his eyes for a moment, then, as if taking his cue from their dropping below the hill, put his hands on his knees, took a deep breath, and stood up. "I'd better get home," he said. "I gotta be in the office at ten."

Together they'd walked down the path in the direction of the jogging girls. Neither of them spoke. From thousands of miles away, Daniel and his letter had silenced them both. Turning off the path, they'd passed through a copse of young ash and a huddle of blackberry bushes and onto a track that met the nearest street, its tarmac starting abruptly at the Heath's edge.

As they'd walked on between the terraced houses, morning lives stirring within them, Josh had begun to talk again. Michael heard little of what he said. The letter in his pocket was rubbing at his mind as it had against his leg during their run. A white noise behind his temples. He felt isolated by its words. Underwater in a vast and darkening ocean. And yet at the same time he felt strangely connected by them, in the most intimate of ways, to the man who'd written them. As if they'd eaten from the same plate, or shared the same woman.

Turning into a narrow alleyway, they came out into South Hill Drive and walked down its incline, past the gardens and gates of the houses higher up the street. Michael tried to catch the drift of what Josh was saying. For some reason he couldn't fathom, Josh was angry with the Lehman's Manhattan office. Something about real estate, sub-prime and toxic derivatives, college boys making bonds bets that had left him "fucking exposed with my balls on the wire."

At times, when Josh talked about his bank like this, Michael wanted to stop him, there and then in the street, and tell him about the missile that had killed Caroline. Its name, he wanted to tell him, was the AGM-114 Hellfire, a "fire and forget" weapon manufactured by Lockheed Martin. Since 1999, he'd explain, the Hellfire has been the Predator's missile of choice. In 1997, two years before the first pair were fitted to a Predator's wings, a limited partnership led by his employers, Lehman Brothers Holdings, bought a 50 percent stake in a new company called L-3 Communications. L-3, in turn, had been formed from ten high-tech Lockheed Martin units. L-3 became the manufacturers of the Predator's sensor and optic equipment, the same equipment that had, in all likelihood, filmed Caroline from 20,000 feet as she'd sat in the back of that white minivan. And it was L-3 equipment, too, that would have fired a targeting laser at that minivan's hood.

This is what Michael wanted to tell Josh. How with every drone flown, L-3's profits had soared. How his wages and bonuses, along with the wages and bonuses of banks and companies across the world, were fuelled by deaths in faraway places, out of any conventional camera's focus. How Caroline, in doing her job, had also been "fucking exposed," sitting as she had been at the brilliant centre of that Hellfire's 5,000-degree thermobaric blast. How, at that heat, flesh melts instantly, bone is vaporised, and the person you love goes, in less than a second, from being to not. How, despite its "fire and forget" name tag, once a Hellfire had been released there would always be someone who never would.

But Michael didn't stop Josh, and he didn't say anything. Daniel's letter had pulled his world tight, drawn in its threads so that once again, like a man gifted with X-ray vision, he could see the full array of the causal web spiralling towards Caroline's death. But he no longer wanted to see. He no longer wanted to be sensitive to how lives rubbed against lives, and greed rubbed against death, across the distances of oceans and continents. So instead of exposing Josh to his thoughts, he'd just carried on listening to him as they'd walked on down South Hill Drive, its sycamores budding above them. When they reached their homes, side by side in the street, Michael had turned towards his front door, pulling out his keys from a string round his neck.

"So what you going to do?" Josh said, as he'd approached his house next door.

Michael slid his key into the lock. "About the letter?"

"Yeah," Josh said. "You should inform the inquiry."

Michael looked down at his feet.

"You can't let him get away with this."

Michael looked back up at him, realising how in some ways his neighbour was a child in this world. "He's already got away with it, Josh. They all have."

Josh nodded in appeasement. "Sure, I know," he said, giving Michael one of his older-brother looks. "But this is specific. You can do something about this."

Michael said nothing. He shouldn't have shown Josh the letter.

"So you're going to, right?" Josh said.

"Maybe," Michael replied. "I don't know."

"Well, just let me know if I can help." Josh looked down at his watch. "Shit," he said, opening his front door. "I've gotta run. See you later."

"Yeah," Michael replied, stepping into his own communal hallway. "See you later."

—

But Michael did know what he was going to do. He'd already decided on the Heath, as they were running through the bare woods beyond Kenwood. He would write back. He would write to Daniel and ask him for more. He would ask him to live that day again, to tell him what it had been like. What had he dreamt? How had he woken? What was the weather? What did he eat and drink? And what, afterwards, did he do in those few hours when he still didn't know that he'd killed her, and Michael didn't yet know she was dead? How, in that caesura of distance and time zones, as Michael had worked in the garden, his grief coming for him from the other side of the world, had Daniel occupied himself? What had he done and what had he thought? As 8,000 miles away a mud-walled compound had slipped into shadow and a thinning plume of smoke had blown through the leaves of a fig tree, a scattering of chickens stabbing at the earth at its roots.

CHAPTER
ELEVEN

MICHAEL WAS COMING back out onto the landing when he sensed her again—a change in the air's texture, a fleeting intuition. He stopped and turned towards the door opposite the stairs. A seam of light ran the length of its frame, and he realised it wasn't fully closed. A scooter's engine, high and insistent, rose and fell on the street outside. Michael listened to the house in its wake, but again there was nothing. Just the sound of his own breathing and this penumbra of Caroline, refusing to let him go.

He pushed the door open with his foot. It swung easily, revealing a bathroom. A broad window, its blind half drawn, looked out over the pear tree in the garden and the crowns of the trees around the ponds. A cushioned seat inlaid in its sill was piled with women's magazines, their pages warped by moist air. In front of him was a toilet and a wooden cabinet above its cistern. To his right, a sink with a collection of toothbrushes in a mug and a rolled tube of toothpaste beside it. Above the sink a mirror reflected the window's light, while beyond it, along the far wall, was a deep enamel bath, a showerhead resting in its cradle, its steel hose curling into the tub. In a corner of the bath were Lucy's water toys. A purple floating octopus, a My Little Pony sponge, and, beached on its side, a plastic goldfish with which, just a few days earlier, she'd squirted Michael from her paddling pool.

—

Ever since that first party, Lucy and Rachel had often been the conduit to Michael's spending time with their parents. When Sam took them for walks on the Heath, or shopping in Hampstead, she frequently called Michael to ask if he'd like to join them. Similarly, when Josh had the girls for the day he'd begun to ask Michael along too, to fly a kite on Parliament Hill or visit a museum in the centre of town. Like Sam, he'd noticed how the girls tended to be better behaved with Michael present, their attentions to each other diffused to accommodate his as well.

The girls accepted Michael into their domestic orbit quickly. Rachel, at seven years old, was beginning to aspire to a maturity beyond her reach. For her, having Michael around meant an opportunity to experiment with projections of her older self, to practice expressions of speech and face, postures and poses, with an adult who was neither her family nor her teacher. A serious girl, Rachel had a tendency to want to take Michael aside to talk with him. Approaching him with a frown, she'd lead him silently into the conservatory or pull a stool up close beside him so he had to turn and talk to her and her alone. When she did this, Rachel often conducted herself as if her affairs—her drawings, her books, her tales of school—were of an importance far beyond the trivialities of family life or her peers. There was no pretence, and Michael never doubted her sincerity. She would, he thought, most likely maintain a similar course as a teenager, until hormones or a boy proved to her otherwise. But until that happened Michael could imagine her as an earnest academic or a campaigner, a powerfully strident woman, quietly confident that the world would, eventually, bend to her way.

In contrast to her sister's desire to escape the limits of her age,

Lucy revelled in the licence of hers. At four years old, her toddler's solipsism had recently been grafted with a nascent awareness of the privileges of being a child. To her, Michael was someone for whom she could perform, and with whom she pushed the limits of what she could get away with, without fear of parental retribution. When they walked on the Heath she often insisted on being carried on his shoulders, his height thrilling her with an adult's perspective and a safe breed of danger. Samantha would tell her to leave Michael alone, and Rachel looked on with an expression of wise disapproval. But Lucy remained impervious to either her mother's requests or Rachel's judgement. She inevitably got her way, and when she did she rode Michael's shoulders with unbridled glee, one hand clasped around his forehead, the other reaching for the lower branches of the trees.

For Michael, it was impossible to spend time with the girls without a low, settling sadness gathering below his throat. In time he barely noticed it, associating its resonance with the climate of their company. But there were other occasions, when Caroline was present in his thoughts, or an object or song brought a memory to the surface, when it became more discernible. At these times Michael was reminded of the conversations they'd had about having a child of their own. Michael had felt more ready than Caroline. For her part, she'd said, although she'd wanted a child intellectually, instinctively the thought scared her. Not the child itself, but her possible failure as a mother. Her life had been independent, self-centred. Which is why she'd asked him for more time. To allow her to grow that part of herself that might accommodate an infant, to learn, again, to see her hours and minutes as no longer hers, but theirs as well. Had Caroline returned from Pakistan, they would have begun trying that summer. This is what they'd hoped. A spring baby to come into the world with the early blossom, when the trees across the valley were coming into leaf.

—

In the other corner of the bath, opposite Lucy's toys, a collection of bottles, three deep, vied for space. Many of them were hotel samples—shampoos, conditioners, bath gels—collected, Michael guessed, from Josh's business travels, family holidays, or Samantha's spa weekends with Martha. As he stood in the doorway, it was these bottles that drew Michael's attention. His unconscious must have detected the scent long before his sensory mind, for it was only now, as he walked towards the bath and this crowd of sample-sized containers, that Michael could smell it for sure. A fragrance of amber, a smell and a memory in one. A subtle genie held in one of the bottles of bath oil, the same as Caroline had used that night she'd waited for him in Hammersmith. The night he'd found her up there, her knees to her chest, the undulations of her spine melting into the nape of her neck. She must have brought it with her to his flat that night. A hotel bottle, packed into her bag in any number of the countries in which she'd worked.

As Michael neared the bath, he closed in on that memory again, until, without any disturbance of translation, he was no longer alone and Caroline was there too, naked in the bath, looking up at him. And he was looking down at her, into her brown-and-gold eyes and her fine-featured face breaking, as he watched, into a smile full of promises.

He tried to breathe, but the air had been pressed out of him. The room was dimming, fading to a set of tea lights guttering in the steam. He reached out, for her, but also to find the bottle. The one among those many that had summoned her like this. He had to know which one it was.

He leant forward, his hand outstretched. But as he did Caroline began to haze. She was fading, leaving him already. It was like a second death, watching her go. He heard himself say "no," like a condemned man against the certainty of his sentence. But it was no use. There was no change in her expression, her smile holding as she left him, as if he, not she, had been the ghost.

Michael dropped to his knees, reaching to touch her disappearing shoulder. But it was more than the vision could carry, and as his hand fell through empty air, so the room returned to him: the sunlight through the window, the enamel tub, the miniature bottles, and beyond the door at his back, a noise.

At first Michael thought the sound was part of the apparition. But when all trace of Caroline had gone, he heard it again. A movement, something brushing against carpet. He froze, still on his knees beside the bath, straining to listen. A knock against wood. A floorboard giving under weight.

The air came rushing back to his lungs, and with it a sudden clarity. He was on his knees in his neighbours' bathroom, sweat prickling his neck, between his shoulder blades, on his brow. It had all been so quick. Time, with that scent and with her, had evaporated. It had ceased to mean anything. But now, he knew, it meant everything. He was not alone. He must leave.

Leaning his arms against the edge of the bath, he pushed himself up and rose to his feet. He listened again. There was nothing. Perhaps he'd been wrong. Perhaps it was the wind, blowing through an open window. But there was no wind. The day was becalmed. Had someone broken in before him after all? Or what if it wasn't an intruder, and Josh was still in the house? Whichever, he should take his chance while he could. He could be out of the bathroom, down the stairs, and through the kitchen in seconds. Within half a minute he could be in his garden. Within a few more in his flat. But he would have to go now, quickly and quietly. Otherwise it would be too late.

In two strides Michael was out of the bathroom door and onto the landing. Which is when he saw Lucy, standing at the head of the stairs, looking back at him.

She was wearing her pyjamas: pink bottoms with a pink-and-white striped top, a boat in full sail across her stomach. Her hair was flattened on one side, like hay under wind, her one cheek still scored by the creases of her pillow. For a split second her eyes were heavy with sleep. But now, starting at the sight of him, they were instantly alert, alive with panic at the cross-wiring of seeing Michael, his face wet with tears and his hands muddied, bursting from the bathroom where only her parents should be.

Her whole body flinched with the shock. At the same moment she stepped back, one bare foot reaching for purchase behind her where none was to be found. Michael lunged towards her, but it was too late. She was already falling, so suddenly her hands remained by her sides as she tipped backwards, her eyes still on Michael as once again he grabbed at nothing but air.

The force of his lunge sent him sprawling across the landing as Lucy's torso, legs, and feet slipped out of sight below the top of the stairs. He saw nothing else, but he heard everything. The terrible thudding and knocking of her body and head, sudden and loud in the stilled house. And then, just as suddenly, nothing again.

Clutching at the carpet and calling her name, Michael dragged himself forward. But it was pointless. He looked over the top of the stairway and saw Lucy lying below him, head down in the crook of its turn. Her right arm was behind her back and her left leg was twisted awkwardly under her. Her eyes were closed. The striped pyjama top had ridden up in the fall, furling the boat's sail and exposing her pale belly. From his prone position at the top of the stairs Michael stared down at that strip of plump flesh, the dimpled belly button, willing it to rise and fall with a breath. But it remained motionless, and so did Lucy.

CHAPTER
TWELVE

FOR THE FIRST three days after he left Las Vegas, Daniel drove
the Sonoma coastline, sleeping in his car and eating at roadside
diners or crab shacks on the cliffs. Cathy hadn't asked him to leave.
But she hadn't tried to stop him, either. Even if she had, Daniel
would still have gone. He knew he had to.

As he'd driven 95 north and then west, past Creech and on
towards Reno and Sacramento, Daniel had told himself this was no
more than what he'd done when he used to go on tour: to Bosnia,
Iraq, Afghanistan. Back then he'd left his family to keep them
safe, and it was the same now. He hadn't been sleeping, or when he
did he dreamt in infrared, or night-vision black and green. He was
becoming more erratic. He'd been drinking during the day. Twice
in the last month the girls had found him crying on the decking
out back. The dreams were getting worse. More frequent, but more
varied, too. The motorcyclist had been joined by the two boys
on the bicycle, by an old man walking along the other side of a
wall, by a young marine straying from his patrol onto a mine. And
now by her, too. No more than a blur of white in the back of the
van, a brushstroke of silk. But enough.

They'd told him and Maria the following day. When they'd
arrived at Creech for their evening shift, instead of going straight

to the briefing room as usual, they'd been requested to go to another part of the base. The hut they were directed towards was on the far side of Creech from the ground control stations. Daniel had never been there before, and as a guard escorted them across the airfield, its yellow guidelines curving towards the runways, he knew something wasn't right. Maria, too, looked uncomfortable. Neither of them spoke.

As they neared a long hut with no windows, Daniel looked through one of the hangars to their right. It was open at either end, silhouetting the domed heads and rotor blades of three Predators parked up at their stands. It was in one of those hangars Daniel had seen his first UAV, a Reaper Mark II. It had been on his first day at Creech, when he was still training. Their civilian instructor, an ex–fighter pilot called Riley, had stood before them, patting the Reaper's flank. Daniel had been surprised at how large it was, twenty-seven feet from nose to tail. And how blind. No windows, no cockpit. Just a grey ball slung beneath its head, housing a Multi-Spectral Targeting System of cameras, sensors, lenses, and lasers. "Think of it as a giant bee, gentlemen," Riley told them, pointing to the missile mounts under each wing. "A giant bee with one hell of a sting."

The wing commander, Colonel Ellis, was waiting for them inside the hut. A civilian in a suit sat beside him. "This is Agent Munroe, CIA," the colonel said. Agent Munroe nodded to them as Ellis, dismissing the guard, gestured for Daniel and Maria to sit down. Both men had open manila files before them. The colonel looked down at his sheaf of pages, lifting their corners to read.

The reports, Agent Munroe told them, were still coming in. But from what they knew so far, when the Intel patrol went in last night they'd found evidence of foreign nationals killed in the strike. "We also know," he said with a small sigh, "that a British film crew, with a Swedish cameraman, have been missing from their accommodation in Islamabad for over twenty-four hours." He spoke slowly, clearly, like a tired teacher.

He leant forward on the table between them. "Now, fuck knows how they got there, how the Pakistanis missed them, or what they were doing there. And fuck knows how we didn't know about 'em either, but as you can see, Major McCullen, Senior Airman Rodriguez, from where we're sitting, it doesn't look too good. Not good at all."

Agent Munroe questioned them for twenty minutes about the mission, flight conditions, the kill chain procedure, the weapons confirmations. Daniel knew he'd have already heard the mission tapes, and, no doubt, seen the chat-room conversations, too. As they'd answered his questions the colonel had looked on with a half-hidden expression of disgust. Not for them or for Agent Munroe, Daniel felt, but for the process as a whole.

At the end of his questions, Agent Munroe closed his file and reminded them both of mission confidentiality. He leant back in his chair. "I should tell you now," he said, in a less formal tone. "That if this is what it seems, it's going to get out there, at some point. We can exercise damage limitation to a degree, but only so far." He looked at them both, one at a time. "So my advice," he said, slipping the file into his briefcase, "is get ready for some turbulence."

The colonel, taking his cue, gave them a curt nod. "That'll be all for now," he said. "Thank you, Major, Senior Airman."

Maria and Daniel stood, saluted, and turned for the door. Before they reached it, Ellis spoke again. "Congratulations," he said from behind them. "You did a good job yesterday."

They turned to face him. He was standing, his shoulders square. "This is unfortunate," he said, gesturing to Munroe. The colonel had close-cropped grey hair, the traces of a strong jaw beneath his jowls. "But you took out an important terrorist," he continued, looking at them hard. "You upheld the American Airman's Creed, and you should be damn proud of that. Don't forget it."

"Yessir," they said in unison. "Thank you, sir."

There was no guard outside the hut, so they walked back to the ground control stations alone. Daniel's head was light. Maria was silent beside him. Eventually she spoke.

"There was no way to tell," she said.

"I saw her," Daniel replied. "In the van."

"You saw something," Maria corrected him. "You don't know what it was."

Daniel didn't reply. The sun was setting, casting a pink light across the bare ranges of the surrounding hills.

"The screeners confirmed everything," Maria said, as they approached the control station trailers. Her voice was hardening, as if in response to a silent accuser. "And the OB-4, too," she added. "One of Munroe's, I bet."

—

Daniel told Cathy that night. He hadn't wanted to, but he knew this time he had no choice. Agent Munroe was right. The story would break, and Daniel wanted Cathy to hear it from him before she saw it on CNN.

"A woman?" She'd looked away from him immediately, shaking her head, her mouth open. "A woman?" she'd asked again, as if willing his answer to change.

Daniel waited for her to say something else, or to look back at him, but she did neither. "Yes," he said.

He wanted to say more. A woman, a child, a man. What difference did it make? They were innocent and they died, that was the horror of it. But it was a war. She knew it happened.

Cathy's eyes were already welling.

"It's not the first time," he heard himself saying. "I mean, journalists. They get caught in the crossfire. They get killed."

Cathy dropped her head. Why wouldn't she look at him?

"But not by you, Daniel," she whispered. "Not by you."

———

When the story broke, it was worse than he'd thought. Somehow, they got to publish their names. Her name. Caroline Marshall. She was thirty-four years old, just recently married. They ran footage of her news reports. Cathy told him not to watch them, but he did, and he knew she did too. She'd been everywhere he had. Bosnia, Iraq, Afghanistan. She was pretty. Dark blonde hair pulled back in a ponytail or cut into a bob. Her features were delicate, birdlike. She was energetic on camera, as if she cared.

Munro and his team managed to keep Daniel's name out of it, and Maria's. "A U.S. drone strike." That was all the press release said. No mention of Creech, screeners, Intel coordinator, an operator, a pilot. It was as if the Predator had been genuinely unmanned. As if there had been no hand behind its flight, no eye behind its cameras.

The internal inquiry began the following week. Just a month later Daniel was medically discharged, diagnosed with posttraumatic stress syndrome by an air force psychologist, his case rushed through the usual procedures. On Daniel's final day at Creech, Colonel Ellis presented him with a file. It was several pages thick, detailing every mission to which he'd contributed while serving at Creech. Surveillance, house raids, buddy lasing, patrols, intelligence support, command control, search-and-destroy, targeted killings. "You can be proud, Major," Ellis told him, as he shook his hand. "You've done your duty. And we thank you for it."

Sitting in the car park at the wheel of his Camry, Highway 95 humming with traffic on the other side of the fence, Daniel opened the file and looked through its pages. On the first, at the bottom of a spreadsheet, a single number was printed in bold—1,263, the total number of enemy combatants killed as a result of the missions listed in the file. There was no other figure on the page. No other total, as if this, as far as the air force was concerned, was the entirety of his scorecard and any other reckoning would remain his, and his alone.

The next morning Daniel woke with a desire for the ocean. He'd been brought up in the Midwest. Among fields of wheat and dirt tracks leading to hills. The coast had never been his environment. And yet he woke feeling certain it was the ocean that could settle him. Only the ocean seemed vast enough to smother the harrowing of his anxieties. Simple enough to cleanse his eyes.

And so he'd left. Cathy had told him she understood, but he doubted she did. Despite sharing the house in Centennial Hills, over the last year they'd drifted further from each other every day, drawn apart by their different realities. She'd tell the girls he was working away for a few weeks. No, she didn't think he should see them to say good-bye. Reluctantly, Daniel had agreed, and a few hours later he'd left, throwing his rucksack onto the back seat of the Camry and reversing out their driveway to leave his home.

He drove for twelve hours straight, stopping only twice for gas and to go to the bathroom. Skirting San Francisco to his south, he'd seen the city's lights come on in the dark of his rearview mirror. Eventually, running out of land, he'd pulled up at a parking bay overlooking the mouth of the Russian River, his headlights swinging through a thickening of sea mist and spray. When he cut the engine the silence fell like a final breath.

He got out of the car. His legs and back ached. His throat was dry. There were stars above him and the sliver of a new moon. It was dark, and yet he could still make out the breakers on the rocks below, long ruffs of white pulsing along the shore. An oncoming breeze brought salt to his face, over his skin. He closed his eyes and let the wind blow his fringe from his forehead. He could feel, in its passing, the hairs moving on his arms.

And it was then, as he stood before the Pacific Ocean that night, with the river at his back, that Daniel decided what he should do. He would find her husband. He would find the man Caroline Marshall had married and write to him. He would tell him what had happened. Not because he should, but because he had to. Because he knew it was the only way he would ever be able to go on. He was tired of being unseen. Of being dislocated from his actions. Of witnessing but never being witnessed. He wanted to own his life, and he knew that meant owning all of it. If he'd thought he could find the others—the motorcyclist's wife, the boys' parents, the old man's son—then he would have. And perhaps one day he would try. But for now, he'd start with her husband. This is what he promised himself as the breakers hushed below him. He already knew his name, and what he did. The newspapers had told him that. He would not be hard to find. But not yet. First, before he found him, he must find the words. It would take time. But they would come. All of it would come. This is what Daniel told himself as looked over the ocean that night. Because in the end, everything does.

CHAPTER THIRTEEN

"DISTANCE! DISTANCE MICHAEL! It's your best defence!" Istvan hooked a thumb under the padded lining of his mask and slipped it up over his forehead. "You know this," he said. "If you are so close, how can you riposte? Come on." He rapped Michael's coquille with his blade. "Again."

With a tap on the top of his mask, Istvan knocked it back down over his face and took up en garde. He wore loose tracksuit bottoms, trainers, a T-shirt. A padded brown suede coaching sleeve protected his sword arm. His glove was coming apart at the seams. Two faded Hungarian flags were still stuck on either side of the mask's wire mesh.

With a quick clatter of blades, Istvan came at Michael again, his body upright and slow in contrast to the speed of his fencing arm as he disengaged to parry in sixte before sliding his blade down Michael's in a glisé attack. He hit Michael on the outside of the shoulder, almost exactly where he'd hit him before. Istvan stepped back into en garde. "Again," he said, from behind his mask. "And this time think!"

But all Michael could do was think. Within the closeness of his own mask, beneath its dark wire, he felt as if he were thinking with three brains at once, and none of them his own. A tangle of humming thoughts, of competing images and sounds, flashing then passing, too quick to hold.

He was trying to focus. On his blade before him, on Istvan's oncoming attacks, on the brightness of the sky through the high windows of the sports hall. On anything that might stop him, just for a second, from seeing the one image that remained constant: of Lucy, motionless on the turn in the stairs, her pale belly exposed, her one leg caught under her.

Everything else was indistinct. He didn't know for how long he'd lain there at the top of the staircase, looking down at her. Or, when, exactly, he'd got to his feet and, stepping over her body, descended it to leave the house. He knew he'd closed the back door when he'd left, and that as he'd picked up his shoes he'd brushed the step clean of their soil. But he couldn't remember entering his own garden, or his building itself. He knew he had only because the first thing he recalled was sitting on his sofa, his head in his hands, the lights and sounds of the day coming back to him. It was like surfacing from a deep dive, breaking through choppy waves into a terrible clarity of air.

As the minutes returned to him, so had the same instinctive voice that had persuaded him up those stairs just minutes earlier. But now the note of its desperation was different. Now it was telling him, while he could, that he must change the story. He must change the day's truth. Michael shook his head against it. He wanted, with a violent desire, never to have been in the Nelsons' house. Never to have climbed their stairs, never to have gone searching for Caroline. He wanted never to have gone into their bedroom, their bathroom. He wanted never to have been there.

The alternative was impossible for him to face. He'd only just, in these past months, begun rediscovering his life. He'd lost so much already: Caroline, their future, the man he'd have become with her. And with her fading from him in the Nelsons' bathroom it had felt as if these losses were just minutes old. He could not, he would not, lose again. This is what the survivor's voice had told him as he'd sat on his sofa, staring at the carpet. That if he was quick, he could still make it so. He could still shape the story. Lucy was dead. He knew that could never be changed. He'd never meant to frighten her, to cause her to start like that. If he could still save her, he would. But it was too late. So he would save himself instead. Something, he remembered telling himself, must be saved. Eventually, standing from the sofa, he'd washed his hands, collected his fencing kit from the hall, then left his flat, slipping the bag over his shoulder as he'd descended the staircase.

—

"Better! Good!" Istvan took two quick steps backwards. His body was heavy, but his feet were still light, a dancer's feet. Somehow Michael was following his lesson, muscle memory guiding his arm, his body.

"Now," Istvan said, raising his épée as if in salute, "when I lower my blade, attack in patinando, tempo or speed, up to you. Then counter in octave."

Michael bent his knees to en garde, his eyes on the switch at the end of Istvan's blade. As it fell, he took a short step forwards, then lunged, extending his arm towards Istvan's stomach. Disengaging from the parry, he pushed forward until he felt his own switch depress, and his blade flex in the curve of a hit.

"Good!" Istvan exclaimed, skipping backwards. "And again!"

—

When Michael had left his building there'd been no one else on the street. At the end of the path to his front gate, he'd turned up the hill passing the Nelsons' house, its windows as impassive as any other, then continued up the incline to turn left down a narrow path. Emerging from the shade of this cut-through, he'd crossed a tarmac walkway bisecting two of the ponds before leading on into the Heath itself.

Nothing was altered. A male moorhen ducked for food in the pond to his left, then paddled to a piled nest to feed his chicks. To Michael's right, farther off, the mixed swimming pond, in full sunlight, was pointillist with swimming costumes and bare bodies. He could make out a line of girls queuing for the showers. The red-and-yellow uniforms of the lifeguards, looking on. The white buoys, bobbing in the swimmers' wakes.

As he'd reached the Heath itself, here, too, the scene appeared unchanged from earlier in the day. Picnics, prone sunbathers. A boy on a scooter, about Lucy's age, was backheeling himself along the path, outstripping his mother, who was pushing a pram behind him. "Joseph!" she shouted as he crested a rise. "Joseph! Slow down!"

Michael had walked on. He'd wanted to keep his eyes on the ground, to avert his gaze from anyone who might see him. But at the same time he couldn't help glancing up at the Heath around him, at its life, so abundant and insouciant. A woman in a bikini was talking on her phone; a shirtless man in jeans spread himself across a bench, ridges of fat pinking around his midriff. Another man, propped on his elbows on the grass, tilted his head back, eyes closed to receive the sun.

How could nothing have been disturbed by what he'd done? Just minutes and metres away a life had ended. Two lives, perhaps. A four-year-old cache of memories, ideas, pains, favourite colours and toys had been extinguished. A genetic pattern, unique in the universe, had been snuffed out. Features and qualities of her parents, her grandparents, great-grandparents, had all died in the instant of Lucy's fall. And as they had, within seconds, his own life had been burdened with the weight of hers. In an attempt to see Caroline again, he'd taken Lucy away. There would be aching ripples of grief, coursing through Samantha, Josh, Rachel—and through hundreds of others he didn't know. Lives would change.

The hue of the years to come, although they were unaware, was already tainted for these people, the shade of their existence already darker. And yet out here, on the Heath, under an afternoon sun, nothing had altered. What Michael, and Michael alone, knew seemed to make a mockery of time and space, of the very meaning of those words. As if in causing Lucy's death he'd proved everything to be illusion.

But it was not illusion. This is what he'd also known as he'd traversed the Heath, his fencing bag slung over his shoulder. It might have felt unreal, there in the open air, beyond the walls of the Nelsons' house. But it wasn't. It was very real. It was true, and Michael had known he had only minutes to write himself out of that truth.

As he'd cut across a southern spur of the Heath towards East Heath Road and the streets leading to Rosslyn Hill, Michael had run through the timings of the alternative truth he was trying to create. His lesson with Istvan was at four p.m. It usually took him about thirty minutes of fast walking to arrive at the school in Highgate. From his first lesson he'd always walked, whatever the weather. Partly to avoid being stuck in traffic, but also to open up his sciatic cramp and warm up his body for the rigours of the session. The walk back to his flat was, similarly, his warm down. To arrive on time today, having walked his usual route, he would already have been halfway across the Heath when Lucy fell. It was as simple as that. No one knew he'd been in the Nelsons' house. No one had seen him enter or leave. If he could arrive for his fencing lesson on time, then he could delete the minutes he'd spent there, edit them from the day, just like when he redrafted a manuscript. A single key held for a few seconds, and a story could be altered forever.

He looked as his watch. It was ten to four. He must have remained at the top of the stairs, or on his sofa, for longer than he'd thought. His best hope now was to catch a bus to Highgate. Looking up, he saw a bus stop on the road ahead. He knew one of the Highgate buses stopped there. But on a Saturday there would be no more than three or four an hour at most. Quickening his pace, his right calf cramped like pig-iron above his ankle, Michael walked on, his leg short in the stride, as if manacled by a ball and chain.

He was still fifty or sixty metres from the road when he'd seen the Highgate bus approaching from South End Green. It was a single-decker, almost empty, carrying just one woman reading a paper towards the rear. Picking up his pace again, Michael had watched as with a painful ease the bus's left indicator flashed as it slowed to a pause beside the stop. The woman rose from her seat, walked down the aisle, and dismounted from its middle doors. Michael raised his arm, hoping the driver would see him in his wing mirror. He could hear the engine, turning over heavily beneath the shade of the trees. As he'd got nearer he'd kept his eyes on the right indicator, willing it not to take up the rhythm of the left. He'd thought about shouting, but he was wary of drawing attention to himself.

With a deliberate beat the right indicator began flashing, twice, three times, as the bus smoothly pulled away from the kerb and the driver worked through its lower gears to tackle the hill towards Spaniards Road. Michael, slowing in his walking, had watched it go, sensing as it went each of those printed minutes in the Nelsons' house becoming more indelible with every second.

—

"Step! And step! And—" Istvan, feinting for Michael's wrist, suddenly dropped, as if he'd tripped. But then Michael felt his blade jab into the arch of his foot. Istvan never tripped. "Come on, Michael!" he said as he rose back into en garde, his tone that of a disappointed parent. "You are slow today. Too slow. Again!"

Michael felt drained of all energy. As if a stopper had been pulled from his chest and his vitality was pouring from the hole.

The excitement of reaching the school in time had, he realised, fuelled him through the opening exercises of the lesson. But now, even as he parried and attacked, all he wanted to do was sleep, to lay his head on a pillow and wake up weeks from here and find none of this to be true or all of it to be forgotten.

—

The taxi had appeared from down the hill like a gift. Michael had continued walking towards the road in the vain hope of another bus coming to the stop. But as he'd reached the kerb, he'd seen the taxi instead: a black cab, its orange bar lit. He'd raised his arm, trying to look calm, his heartbeat hammering in his chest.

"You all right, mate?" the taxi driver had asked him as they'd pulled up at some traffic lights. Michael knew he'd been studying him in his rearview mirror since he'd got in. He'd replied to his disembodied eyes, "Yeah, fine. Just this heat, you know."

"You sure?" the driver pressed. "Cos you look a bit ropey, to be honest." He reached to his side and waved a bottle through the partition. "Want some water?"

"Thanks," Michael said as he took the bottle. "Probably a bit nervous, too," he added, after he'd drunk, pointing a thumb towards his fencing bag. "Got my instructor test today."

As soon as he'd spoken, he wished he hadn't. The story needed no more than for him to be there on time. But already he was lying, creating.

"Yeah?" the driver said. "Well, good luck, mate, sure it'll be a breeze."

Michael had given a nod and a brief smile to the mirror. He was trying to still his pulse, slow his breathing. "Thanks," he said again as he handed back the water. "I hope you're right."

He'd asked the driver to drop him a hundred metres or so before the school. As he'd driven off, Michael bent as if to tie a lace, waited for the taxi to round a corner, then picked up his bag and doubled back onto the Heath. Cutting through a bank of trees, he'd joined the path he usually walked to his lessons, a feet-worn track emerging from the foliage of the Heath across the street from the side entrance of the school.

Crossing the road, he'd glanced at his watch. It was five past four. As he'd walked on towards the sports hall, he'd felt his minutes inside the Nelsons' fading with every stride. As if, on passing through the sliding doors into the lobby, he'd be passing into another version of time. One where he hadn't gone next door, where he hadn't gone up the stairs, and where he hadn't come out of the bathroom, his face streaked with tears, to find Lucy in her pyjamas, her eyes wide and one bare foot stepping back into the air behind her.

—

"Distance!" Istvan shouted. A second later, as if to make his point, he landed a hit hard against Michael's coquille. The impact shuddered through his tired grip. Michael felt a swell of nausea rise in his stomach, chilling his skin. He dropped back two paces, away from Istvan, who was still talking. "This is why I told you to bring the French grip," he was telling Michael. "To stop you doing this. Again!"

But Michael could no longer hear him. Inside his mask, in slow motion, Lucy was falling again. Everything that had been too quick for him to see at the time, he was seeing now. Her foot travelling back and back, down and down, her toes missing the red carpet by centimetres. The tipping of her body, her left hand opening, as if to catch something. But her arms remaining motionless, as her wide eyes went back and back too, and her other foot lifted from the landing, and carried on lifting until it was higher than her head. Her flung blonde hair, which had already gone now, along with her eyes, and her arms and her feet, dropping below the top of the stairs.

Istvan was coming at him once more, but Michael raised a hand to stop him. Taking another step backwards, he dropped his blade and bent double. He was going to be sick. "Michael?" he heard Istvan say, as if from another room.

His goal of reaching the school on time had consumed him. It had been all that mattered. But now he was here the full tide of the facts had come flooding through. Lucy, who'd come to him with her dolls, who'd stroked her father's collars until they were frayed. Who'd squirted him with a goldfish from her paddling pool and who'd ridden his shoulders with one hand clasped at his forehead, the other reaching for trees. She was gone, and it was he who had killed her.

As he ran, Michael pulled his mask from his face, dropping it to the floor as he pushed through the doors into the changing rooms. He reached the sink with the first bile rising in his throat. Clutching at its enamel edge, his whole body retching, he vomited long and violently, his knees giving from under him as his body tried to evacuate the memory of what he'd done.

When it was over, he heard Istvan from outside.

"Michael? Michael? Are you okay?"

"I'm fine," he heard himself say. He wiped at his mouth with the back of his glove. "Something I ate."

He spoke with his head still bowed, his eyes closed. Slowly, raising himself on his elbows, he ran the tap and looked into the mirror above the sink. A man he no longer recognised was looking back at him. He was pale, the last week of sun washed from his complexion. Sweat had stuck his hair to his temples and forehead. His eyes were bloodshot, his cheeks hollow, the white of his fencing jacket flecked with yellow spittle. He looked exhausted. But what surprised Michael the most was that he also looked innocent. Just as there had been no mark upon the day, so there was no mark upon him. He'd been convinced Lucy's life, her death, would show; like a bruise of the soul, it would leak into his skin. That all who saw him would see her, too. But there was nothing. Just a tall, pale man bent over a sink, looking back at him, asking him what to do next.

—

It was evening when Michael returned across the Heath. The heat of the day was already leeching towards night. The lowering sun cast the trees with a corona, and midges hung in the air like dust in a workshop. Most of the families had gone, leaving the Heath for the drinkers and lovers, for those who'd come or stayed to see the stars and the city reveal themselves against the sky's deepening purple.

He walked slowly. The emptiness of his body felt religious, as if he'd been anointed. His mind, too, felt newly clear, as if this is what the consequence of a killing would be: a recurrent surfacing into more and more brilliant orbits of clarity, until the sharpness of it, the depth of its cutting, would become unbearable. It had happened in a second, and yet now it was his for life. This was the equation Michael couldn't make balance, the sum circling in his mind as he drifted from his usual homeward route into parts of the Heath he'd never seen before.

There had been no one else in the house. Just him and, unknown to him, Lucy, sleeping upstairs. It was a moment in time owned by them alone. And yet it was not just theirs. Already Michael could feel the bleeding of those seconds, breaking the banks of their intimacy. He'd gone up those stairs first as a concerned neighbour, and then in search of Caroline, of the chance of seeing her again. If she hadn't died, then nor would Lucy. So those seconds at the top of the stairs were Daniel McCullen's, too. Wherever he was now, at this moment as Michael wandered the Heath, he, too, owned Lucy's fall, as the furthest ripple of his Hellfire's blast, the most recent echo of his killing.

And even now, as Michael paused in a clearing, the aftershocks were expanding. Had Josh or Samantha discovered her yet? Or maybe Rachel, coming up the stairs, calling her sister's name, then trying to understand why she was lying in the turn, her leg caught under her? Michael walked on, following a path back into the woods. Once under the cover of their canopy, he stopped again and leant against the trunk of an oak. He ran his hands around its girth, to feel the solidity of its growth, its undoubtable bark. Why was he returning home? Shouldn't he be fleeing in the other direction? Leaving London, Britain? Someone must have seen him. He'd been in such a hurry he'd gone straight from his gardening to the Nelsons.' His hands were still soiled when he'd entered the house. He would have left traces. Footprints. Fingerprints. It would be known.

Stepping off the path, Michael put down his fencing bag and slid down the trunk. He pressed the heels of his palms against the sockets of his eyes and tried to think clearly. Because of the dirt on his hands he'd touched nothing. Or had he? He couldn't be sure. What about when he'd tried to catch her, or when he'd closed the door? But even if he had, what crime had he committed? He hadn't broken an entry. He was a regular visitor, so had he trespassed at all? His fingerprints were always on that door handle. And Lucy. He hadn't touched her, either. He'd just seen her, witnessed her fall. But would she have fallen had he not been there? Would she have even woken? Perhaps. There had been that scooter, after all, its sudden whining. And the ice-cream van, too. But where had Josh been? Had he, in fact, been in the house after all? And if not, then why had he left Lucy alone?

Michael opened his eyes. He couldn't leave. He had to return. He had to tell them, explain. He had to explain, to try, impossible though it seemed, to answer their questions. He had, now that his head was clear again, to undo his first panicked leaving, his first running away. Pushing himself up, he shouldered his bag, his blades shuffling against each other, and continued his slow drift south.

Emerging from the woods, Michael found himself walking into the full glow of the evening. The tall grasses, swayed by a breeze, were lit like the summer hairs on a woman's arm. Parliament Hill, where he'd sat so many times with Josh, was ahead of him to his left. The day's scattered crowds had gathered there to witness the last minutes of light. A jogger rose on the path towards the crest of the hill. A dog bounded through the dry grass in pursuit of a ball. Life, in the final moments of the day, had been coaxed to the surface in all its complex, simple beauty. As if to say, through the coming hours of darkness, do not forget this. This is what you wait for, what you work for, what you love for. This is what we are given and what we shape. This, one day, is what we will lose or have taken from us, whichever may come first.

Michael turned away from the hill and walked on, the grasses brushing his bare legs and his hands. Parliament Hill's view was not for him this evening. And nor was the company of its crowds. His destination was a house a couple of streets away. It had to be, he saw that now. The house in which he had seen his dead wife and where, with no intention or malice, he'd caused the death of his neighbours' daughter.

He took the longest route possible, remaining on the Heath for a couple more hours until he could no longer avoid the surrounding pavements and streets. Instinctively, he felt as if while he was on its sandy soil, among its plants and trees, he would be safe, suspended. A colonnade of London plane trees led him down towards the shops of South End Green. As he approached their lit windows, a waiter laying tables outside the Italian restaurant, Michael steeled himself for what would meet him on South Hill Drive. Any minute now, he thought, the blue pulse of a police car or ambulance would beat across the street before him, like the swing of a lighthouse, warning of what he'd done.

But when Michael neared the corner of the street there was no pulsing light. Just summer drinkers and smokers spilling into the garden of The Magdalena. A TV inside was showing a football game. Waitresses carried swaying towers of pint glasses. A tethered dog at the entrance lapped at a steel bowl of water.

Michael walked past the pub, listening for snatches of conversation and watching for expressions that might betray the news of what had happened on the street today. But there were none. Just as, when he reached the Nelsons' house, there was no squad car or ambulance. No police tape cordoning off the area. No stern-faced officer at the door. The house was dark and as silent as when he'd entered it that afternoon, just one of many in the street's grand curve, each as implacable and settled as the other.

For a moment, as Michael walked past its front door, he thought perhaps it had all been a vision. Caroline in the bath, Lucy appearing and then falling. Perhaps his wish it hadn't happened wasn't a wish at all, but reality. Reaching his front door, he felt a rush of excitement at the possibility. Had his mind conjured not just Caroline, but everything else he'd seen in the house, too?

He climbed his staircase, listening to his own footsteps, and for any other sound he might pick up from the staircase next door. As he reached the second floor another thought reached him. What if it had happened, exactly as he remembered, but no one had found her yet? What if Lucy was still lying there, alone, on that darkening staircase, waiting for her discoverer? Michael could still be that person. He could still be the one to find her, to call the ambulance, the police.

He let himself into his flat, dropped his bag in the hallway, and went on into the living room. As had become his habit ever since the first night he'd moved in, without turning on the lights Michael went towards the windows at the end of the room. He wanted to pause, think. Make sure he was making the right choice. He was no longer certain of what was fact or the creation of his imagination. And he had to be certain before he acted. Closing upon his reflection, on reaching the windows Michael placed his hands against their coolness and leant his forehead against their glass. Which is when he saw Josh.

From the windows of his flat Michael had only ever been able to see the far end of the Nelsons' garden. Their pear tree, mature and tall, obscured his view of the rest of it. But above the reach of its crown, even in spring and summer, he'd always been able to make out the last few tapering metres of lawn, the fence at its end and the willow tree beyond, draping its branches into the pond. It was a long garden, so at night the light from the kitchen or the conservatory only travelled so far down its slope. But far enough, with a clear sky and a moon, for him to sometimes see Josh down there, smoking a cigarette before bed, its tip glowing with his inhalations in the dark. Which is where Josh was again this evening, standing by the fence where Michael had first told him about Caroline. Only this evening Josh wasn't smoking, but was holding the fence with both hands instead, gripping its wood, his head bowed between his arms as he wept.

From his vantage point in his flat Michael watched from above as Josh's broad back shook and heaved. Balling one hand into a fist he began to beat it against the wood, not with force, but softly, steadily. Eventually, as if this effort had drained the last of his will, Josh slipped to his knees, which is where he remained, his face sunk in his hands and his back still shaking, coursing with the voltage of his daughter's death.

CHAPTER
FOURTEEN

WITHIN MINUTES OF Michael's leaving that afternoon, Josh had
returned home. He'd walked back to South Hill Drive quickly,
so although Tony and Maddy's house was just a few streets away,
when he'd come into the hall his T-shirt was already patched with
sweat. Closing the front door behind him, he'd held on to the handle, keeping the tongue of the latch from clicking so as not to wake
Lucy, then gone straight into the kitchen for a drink. Taking a
glass from the cupboard, he'd filled it with ice from the fridge, and
then water. As he'd drunk, one hand resting on the tap, Josh had
listened for his daughter upstairs. She'd been irritable since she'd
woken that morning, fractious and running a temperature. At first
he'd thought it was just the heat, but when she'd asked him if she
could go back to sleep he knew she must have been sick. Ever since
she was a baby, sleep was how Lucy's body had tackled illness. So
Josh had said yes, and put her to bed.

Samantha was away for the weekend with her sister, and he'd
dropped Rachel off at her friend's house for a daylong pool party
first thing. So, having put Lucy to bed, Josh found himself unexpectedly alone. It was a hot Saturday in June, and for once he had
no daughter to occupy. His time was his own. He thought about
taking the paper into the garden, or heading up to his study and

getting through some of the emails he'd been avoiding for weeks. But the day had seemed too good for either of those and he felt his free hours too much of a gift. Especially falling, as they had, on a weekend when not just Samantha, but also Tony was away.

Perhaps he'd sent Maddy a text then deleted it. Or maybe he hadn't even risked that, and had just gone around and surprised her. Their house was, after all, so close. However he'd done it, with text, phone call, or on the spur of the moment, Josh had gone. For only a short amount of time, perhaps. For less than an hour, certainly, but still, he'd gone. Leaving Lucy asleep in her room upstairs, and unaware of the hallway's shifting air drawing the back door open, he'd pulled the front door closed, and gone.

And now he was back, his body evacuated by the urgency of their sex, a boyish thrill of truancy ebbing to a pragmatic efficiency. It had been a risk, but now taken he must restore the day's rhythm and elide the minutes of his absence. Finishing his water, Josh stripped off his T-shirt, put it in the washing machine, and headed upstairs to take a shower.

He saw Lucy's hair first, blonde against the red. For a few seconds he didn't understand. But as each stair revealed more of her— her closed eyes, her ridden-up pyjama top, her pale belly—Josh realised he was looking at his daughter, motionless before him.

For a long time he just held her, rocking her against his chest on the stairs, feeling the warmth leave her skin. The coroner's report would say this was regrettable. That the body should not have been moved. The police, too, questioned Josh as to why he'd laid Lucy out on the sofa downstairs and hadn't left her as he'd found her. Although the report stated she'd most likely died instantly— from either the contusion to the back of her head or the break in her neck—there was a chance, however slim, that Lucy, had she not been moved, might have been saved. But Josh knew they were wrong. He'd known, as soon as he'd touched her, that his daughter was dead. Which is why he'd held her like that, tight against his bare chest, so he might harvest the last of her heat, so he might feel the blood and skin he and Samantha had made, that they'd known since she was a baby, cool against his own.

The police were the first to arrive, a squad car with two officers. Soon afterwards the ambulance Josh had called pulled up alongside. A group of shirtless boys on bikes gathered down the street, sucking on brightly coloured ices. Across the road, a woman three floors up, resting her folded arms on a windowsill, called back to her husband to come and look. A few doors down, an elderly man, an ex–classics professor, had been reading his newspaper in the sun at the front of his house. Standing up, paper in hand, he'd watched along with the shirtless boys and the woman at the window as the paramedics had carried out a stretcher, a blanket bunched at its centre. Later that day, the sun having moved on from his garden, he'd looked up again while folding his deckchair and seen police photographers ferrying their equipment into the house.

At the police station a detective sergeant, a young woman still in her twenties, took a statement from Josh. At the same time, down the corridor in a room with two desk fans turning at full speed, an officer from the family protection unit ran background checks on Lucy's name and the Nelsons' address. Halfway through his statement, Josh, still numb, had become angry. Why were they questioning him? She'd fallen. It was an accident. Did they really think he'd kill his own daughter? The detective sergeant had let him rant, watching him with tired eyes. Going to the corner of the room, she'd poured him a cup of tea and asked him if he wanted any sugar, and if he wanted to call Lucy's mother. Or they could send a female constable. It was up to him. As she brought him his tea Josh had nodded silently and then begun crying again.

Samantha was getting ready for dinner when she took the call. She'd just showered and still had her hair in a towel. Martha was already downstairs, waiting for her in the hotel bar. At first Josh wouldn't tell her why she had to come home. But she'd insisted. His voice was cracked, submerged, and thick. She'd never heard him sound like that before. When he couldn't finish his sentences for sobbing, she'd simply asked him, "Rachel or Lucy, Josh? Rachel or Lucy?" Which is when he'd told her. Although she didn't move, Samantha had felt herself fall from a great height. Holding the phone close to her ear, she, too, had begun to cry, as Josh repeated down the line, "I'm sorry, I'm sorry."

Martha drove her, straight to the police station to be with Josh. A policewoman had already visited the parents of Rachel's friend and explained. Yes, the friend's mother had said, holding her hand to her mouth and nodding, pale. Yes, of course Rachel could stay for the night.

Samantha and Josh returned home in a taxi, holding each other as they walked the short path to their front door. By the time Michael had seen Josh in the garden they'd already been back for more than an hour. Samantha had gone straight to bed, where she'd cried herself to sleep. But Josh hadn't been able to sleep so had paced the house instead, trying to understand. He'd opened a bottle of wine and drunk two glasses in quick succession, then he'd gone out into the garden, where, unaware of Michael watching him from above, he'd wept before the dark waters of the pond, hitting his hand again and again against the fence as he slid to his knees, succumbing to his tears.

—

Michael couldn't sleep that night, either. He'd come back from the Heath intending to tell Samantha and Josh everything. But the sight of Josh crying had flushed all resolve from his body. He'd remained by the window for as long as Josh had stayed by the fence, and had only moved away once he'd seen him get up and walk back towards the house.

Going to his bathroom, Michael had undressed and showered, standing with his head under the beating water until the tank ran cold. As he'd watched the dirt wash from his knees and swill down the plughole he'd thought, briefly, about killing himself. It was too overwhelming. The vision of Caroline, Lucy's falling, Josh's weeping. He wanted to leave it, escape. But then somewhere deeper, below thought, he'd recognised this impulse as chemical, a passing reaction he must let work through its process. Which it did, the urge subsiding as Michael dried himself then went into his bedroom to try and work out what it was he should do next.

Of one thing he was now certain. He could not confess. He could not tell Samantha and Josh he'd been inside their house. As he'd lain on his bed through the rest of the night, his eyes open in the dark, this is what Michael repeatedly told himself. That now, having set his course in those seconds on the landing, and then in his leaving, there was nothing to be gained from further accumulation of anger or grief. Lucy was gone. He had seen her die. But he had not killed her. He had witnessed, but he had not committed. Telling her parents would not bring her back to life. It would only, most likely, take him away from theirs, exactly when he might be of most help to them, as a friend and a neighbour.

Michael knew this logic seemed perverted and was also dependent upon him not being caught, on a trace of his presence not being found in the house. And even if he did escape suspicion, he was so disoriented he didn't know if he'd be able to justify his thinking in another hour's time, let alone the next morning. But he did know, in a bald sense, that it was true. He had to be practical, to think, now that it had happened, now that Lucy was dead, how the most good might be done.

As he lay on his bed, the dawn light rising up the wall beside him, Michael endlessly turned over combinations of reasoning until he'd convinced himself that this was the only way forward. That from now on all his effort, all his actions, should be directed towards healing, not blame. It was an argument, he decided, as the sun edged higher and the first swimmers arrived in the ponds beyond his window, to which he could hold only if it overwhelmingly became his defining purpose. And yes, his atonement, too, his penance. To carry the knowledge of Lucy's death alone, while doing all he could to help her parents recover from their grief, just as they'd helped him recover from his.

As Michael made these promises to himself he became painfully aware of the presence of the Nelsons' home, just the other side of his wall. Its weight seemed improbable and yet painfully tangible. All through the rest of that day, as he forced himself to get out of bed, to dress, eat, he could feel it pressing against his own small rooms. And the thought of Lucy, dead, pressed upon him too. It seemed unthinkable that her vitality could be stilled in such an instant. That all she was, all she had been—all her memories, the imagined lives of her dolls, her favourite toys and colours—had become, the moment she'd hit those stairs, no more than Oliver's description of a spongy organ, heavy with death inside her skull.

But most terrible of all was the fact that he'd been responsible for that reduction, that grotesque transition from body to corpse. This, beyond his grief, was the cutting edge of her death for Michael, the sickening knowledge he'd carry for the rest of his life. That it was he who'd caused Lucy to fall. He who had killed her.

Although for the rest of the day he kept to his flat, Michael was unable to stop himself constantly checking the windows. But however many times he looked he saw no more of Josh in the garden, and nothing of Samantha either. He kept his phone in his pocket. He listened for sounds from their house, but heard nothing. And yet he knew they were there, just next door, the two of them, scoured by the loss he'd caused, woken like childless newlyweds into their altered lives.

Around mid-morning, as he was filling the kettle at his sink, Michael saw a car pull up in the street. A woman got out, went round to the passenger seat, and opened the door. Rachel, a blue rucksack over her shoulders, stepped onto the pavement. Taking her by the hand the woman, who was short and tanned with a neat grey bob, walked her down the path to her front door. Minutes later the woman reappeared, got back in her car, and left.

Michael wanted to speak to them. He thought about calling, or sending a text. But he could not until he, himself, had somehow been told. These were the rules he'd set himself. Having deleted his minutes in their home, he must now act and react as if his truth was the only truth. As if he'd walked across the Heath to his lesson, and then he'd come back. He had slept and now it was Sunday. A quiet day, a high bank of clouds pressing a humid heat upon the city. A day when families stayed close, until later in the evening, which is when, often, Sam or Josh would call him and ask him to join them for dinner.

He couldn't work, and he didn't want to leave the flat, but he had to do something. So he sat at his desk in the study making the movements of work instead: arranging notes, printing out the last chapter he'd written. In it, Michael had described his first meeting with Oliver Blackwood, but had done so while removing himself from the scene. Having filleted their conversation, recalled his observations—Oliver's silver Mercedes SLK, the brightness of his tie—he'd recounted the action in third person as if he, himself, had not been there.

The occasion had been a friend's funeral, a novelist who'd died of a sudden brain haemorrhage. Oliver was the surgeon who'd operated on him. He'd failed to save him, but, as he'd told Michael in their first conversation at the wake, when he'd learnt of his patient's profession a few days later, he hadn't regretted his failure. "He'd have had no language," Oliver had said with a doctor's frankness. "No linguistic facility to speak of at all. A man of words, of letters, of meaning, robbed of all that." Reaching across Michael he'd picked a canapé from a passing tray, a roll of salmon bedded on a slice of bread. "No," he'd said, taking a bite from it. "Better like this in many ways. Sometimes it just is."

Although in the chapter before him Michael had removed his response to Oliver that day, now, sitting at his desk with the weight of the Nelsons' home beside him, he found himself repeating it from across the years. "Yes," he heard himself say, as if somehow the vocalised word might strengthen his resolve. "Sometimes it is."

—

Michael was staring at a pen on his desk when the entry buzzer sounded. His mind, still loosened by recurring images of Lucy, had wandered. A pulsing nausea swilled through him. All morning he'd paced his flat as if about to make an entrance into an auditorium, an uncomfortable nervousness in the pit of his stomach. So at first, on hearing the buzzer, distracted and confused, he'd done nothing. But then it sounded again, for longer, more insistent. Going into the hall Michael picked up the receiver and pressed the intercom.

"Hello?" His voice was hoarse, dry.

"Mr. Turner?" a woman asked.

"Yes," Michael said.

"Detective Sergeant Slater, CID. I was wondering if I could come up for a quick chat?"

Michael stared at the plastic grid of the speaker, his finger still on the intercom button. "Is everything all right?" he said.

"Just routine," she replied. "But I'd rather explain in person, if that's okay."

"Yes, of course," Michael said. "Fourth floor, all the way to the top." He pressed the entry button and heard the front door click open, then the sound of Slater's footsteps as she entered. There were no others following.

He heard her steps again a few seconds before she reached his flat. Delicate taps echoing in the concrete stairwell. He didn't wait for her knock but opened the door to meet her, greeting her with a nod.

"Thank you, Mr. Turner," she said, as he held the door for her and she entered.

She was small, petite, of a similar frame to Caroline. She wore plain clothes: a pair of jeans, a blouse, a navy jacket over her arm. She wiped at her forehead with her hand, hot from the walk up the stairs.

"Would you like some tea?" Michael said, closing the door.

She smiled at him, disarmingly natural. "No, I'm fine, thanks. Some water would be great, though."

She followed him into the kitchen and living area. As he ran the tap, testing the temperature with the tips of his fingers, she walked the length of the room, ending where Michael had stood watching Josh the night before. "Beautiful view," she said, looking out at the Heath, and then down at the Nelsons' garden.

Michael couldn't take the waiting any longer. He'd already surprised himself with his ability to slip into the stream of his altered yesterday. But he doubted he'd be capable of sustaining it under direct questioning. He had to know if she knew.

"Do you mind," he said, as he brought her the glass of water, "if I ask what this is about?"

She smiled again as she took the glass. She had close-cut brown hair, tomboyish in style. She looked no older than twenty-eight, twenty-nine. There was, Michael noticed, the scarring of a burn on her neck. "Just some routine enquiries," she said. She took a sip of the water. "Shall we sit down?" she asked, indicating the sofa.

As Michael sat she took out a notebook and a pen from her jacket, then joined him. "If I could just confirm your name?" she said, holding her pen above the page.

Michael laughed, a short expulsion of breath. "I'm sorry," he said. "But not until I know what this is about."

She looked up from her pad, her pen still poised. For a moment she said nothing, as if weighing his guilt. But then she smiled again. It was, Michael saw, the opening gambit of much of her conversation. A learnt trait, perhaps.

"It normally works better with me asking the questions," she said, then paused as if allowing her official tone to catch up.

"We're conducting," she continued, resting her pen, "house-to-house enquiries. In connection with an incident at your neighbour's house yesterday."

"An incident?" Michael said.

"Yes," she replied, taking up her pen again and returning to her notebook. "The Nelsons. A death."

Looking back over the years, Michael would come to see how his response at that moment, although formed in relation to his knowledge of what had happened, might still have replicated that of a neighbour genuinely hearing the news for the first time. It was something about hearing those words in the mouth of another. Of knowing for certain, through language not sight, that Lucy's fall had happened, that the fact of it was alive in the world. It was history, already causing action and reaction.

His intake of breath was involuntary, as if he'd touched a scalding plate. DS Slater looked back up at him.

"Who?" he asked.

"The youngest daughter," she said simply. "Lucy."

Michael brought his hand to his mouth. "Oh my God," he said, turning away. His words, his feelings were real. He didn't understand how, but it was like learning it anew. Hearing it, not just knowing it.

"How?" he said, turning back to her.

She met his eye. He half expected her to say, *You tell me, Mr. Turner,* or to pull his fingerprint from the back of her notebook. But she did not. She licked her lips, and he saw she was anxious. Was she meant to be telling him so much? Perhaps, for all her familiarity, she was a novice. Certainly her age would suggest as much.

"A fall," she said. "Most likely an accident, but . . ." She tailed off, then smiled again, brief and tense. "Well, you know. We have to be sure. So," she took up her pen again, "if I could just confirm your name?"

"Michael," he said quietly. "Michael James Turner."

"And your date of birth?"

The questions were standard. If she was a novice, then DS Slater acted her part well, reeling through them with a practiced rhythm. How long had he lived in the street? His occupation? For how long had he known the Nelsons? Michael answered them directly. None of them yet required him to deviate from the facts. But then, running into it as if it were as innocuous as any of her other questions, she asked him, "And what were your whereabouts between three and five p.m. yesterday afternoon?"

Michael began with the unaltered truth. "I had a fencing lesson," he told her. "At four. Over at the leisure centre in Highgate."

She wrote her notes. The silence unsettled him. The sound of her pen. "The one by the school," he added.

She looked up from the page. "Yes," she said, as if asking him to keep it simple. "I know." She looked back down. "And what time did you leave for your lesson?"

Michael paused. This had to be arrived at, not presented. Thought, not said. "Um," he said. "It must have been around three-fifteen, three-twenty at the latest."

Again, she brought her eyes up to meet his. "To get to Highgate?"

"Oh, sorry," Michael said. "I walk. I should have mentioned that. I always walk to my lessons."

"Right," Slater said, making another note in her pad. "And can anyone verify you were at the leisure centre?"

And that was it. Michael, with fewer than ten words, had spoken the course of his alternative day. And Detective Sergeant Slater had written it down. It was a statement. It existed. It could be questioned, challenged. Strangely calm, Michael went on to tell her about Istvan, looking for his number in his phone to give it to her. If she questioned Istvan would he mention Michael's being sick? And if he did, would she guess the cause? It couldn't be helped. It was a risk he had to take. Istvan was, after all, his alibi.

Was there, Slater asked him, anyone else who might have seen him at the lesson? A receptionist? A gardener? Michael didn't think so, as far as he knew. She nodded. When prompted he told her about his walk home, across the Heath. It was a beautiful evening, so he'd stopped, rested in the woods. He'd taken his time. Had he seen anything in the Nelsons' house when he'd left? Or when he'd returned? No, Michael said. No, nothing he could think of.

As he talked, Michael no longer felt as if he was hiding his actions from Slater, but rather pursuing a cause, beyond her detection. He knew he could help Samantha and Josh. That it was the right thing to do. As much as he wished he wasn't, he was a recent graduate of their breed of loss. It was the least he could do, to risk his own prosecution to remain in their lives.

Slater continued her questions: No, he hadn't seen the ambulance. And no he hadn't heard anything from next door once back inside his flat. Had he seen Josh? Not since . . . he paused to think of the night. Thursday night. It must have been Thursday. Yes, they'd had dinner.

"No," he corrected himself. She paused in her writing. "Sorry. It was the next morning."

"When you last saw him?" she asked.

"Yes," Michael said. Somehow he'd really forgotten. "I dropped round to lend him a screwdriver. For his glasses."

"A screwdriver? He didn't have one of his own?"

"Not of that size, no," Michael said. "It was from my fencing kit," he added, looking towards his fencing bag in the hallway.

"At what time was this?"

"It was early, before eight. Samantha," he said, remembering Lucy banging that spoon against the table. "She hadn't taken Rachel to school yet. So yes, it must have been early."

—

Minutes later Slater was leaving, putting her notebook and pen back into her jacket pocket and handing him her card—"In case you think of anything else."

"Yes, of course," Michael said, putting it on the kitchen counter.

He showed her to the door. "How are they doing?" he asked, as he opened it. "Samantha and Josh," he explained, although there was no need.

She frowned, then sighed, looking out into the stairwell. No, Michael thought, she hadn't done this many times before. "They're devastated," she said, still looking away and raising her eyebrows, as if there could be no other answer. She turned back to him. "It's been a terrible shock."

Extending a hand, she shook his. "Thank you for your help, Mr. Turner," she said. "I'm sorry to have disturbed your day."

"No, thank you," Michael found himself saying, "for letting me know."

She nodded, the flicker of a question passing through her expression. She let it go. "Not at all," she said, as she went to the stairs. "Have a good day, Mr. Turner."

And then she was gone, her small feet tapping down the staircase, carrying his false day in her notebook out of his front door and into the real one.

CHAPTER
FIFTEEN

THREE DAYS AFTER DS Slater's visit, Michael was sitting with Josh on their usual bench on Parliament Hill. It was early in the morning and the first time Michael had seen Josh since the night he'd watched him weep beside the fence. Samantha had called him the previous day. He'd been washing up at the sink in the kitchen when she'd rung. As the phone pulsed on the work surface, he'd stared at her name on the screen before answering it.

"Samantha." He hoped her name would be enough to carry all he wanted to say.

"Thank you for your card." Her voice was quiet, a whisper. She paused. When she spoke again her voice broke across his name. "Oh, Michael."

For a few minutes she cried. Michael listened, then asked if she wanted him to come round. No, she said, not yet. But could he, she wondered, go for a jog on the Heath? With Josh?

"He needs it," she said. "He needs to get out, to talk."

"It's very soon," Michael said.

"I know, but honestly, he needs to get out." She paused. "I need him to get out. Just for a bit."

"Yes," Michael said. "Of course."

"I think he'll talk to you," she went on. "Because. Well . . ."

"Yes," he said again. "I know."

After Samantha hung up, Michael stood for a while where he'd answered the phone, looking out at the street below. Then he'd gone into his study, selected a Beethoven string quartet on his iPod, and sat at his desk, letting the long, reverberating notes wash the room, and him.

Hearing her voice, he'd wanted, desperately, to tell her. On the wall above his desk was a postcard of a Grecian urn with Keats's lines written underneath—*Beauty is truth, truth beauty.* He was consigning himself to ugliness, to a single lie that would bleed through the years ahead of him. He would be a deceiver forever. Not as he was in his writing, in pursuit of a greater clarity, but in his life, in pursuit of an omission, a lie. He'd become a manifestation of his authorial technique, disappearing himself from those minutes in the Nelsons' house just as he'd always disappeared himself from the page.

But he was determined. And as the music moved on to the next movement, it seemed to confirm the rightness of his resolution. The sacrifice of it. So he'd resisted and said nothing. He hadn't called Samantha back. Instead, he'd done as she'd asked of him and woken early this morning, dressed in shorts, T-shirt, and trainers, and gone next door to call for Josh.

Michael found him already waiting outside their front door. He could tell he hadn't slept. The skin below his eyes was bruised with tiredness. As Michael had answered Samantha's call with her name, so as he approached Josh he met him with his.

"Josh."

He didn't reply, but just nodded and began walking down the street towards the Heath, as if they had a job to do that was best done, if at all, quickly. Turning onto the grass at the bottom of the street, they began their usual route, walking in silence up through the colonnade of London plane trees, through the worn fields of the fairground sites and on into the shaded path of the boundary road. As they crossed the South Meadow, Michael felt his calf begin to loosen, the knots of muscle opening like a rose. But Josh, pacing beside him, remained closed. Michael didn't want to be the first to talk. He knew, from those first days after Caroline had died, when Peter had been so often in the cottage—coming by, cooking him meals—that for Josh his silence would feel like the only part of himself he still owned, that he might still understand.

On reaching Highgate Gate they dropped down through the trees into the grounds of Kenwood, then rose again onto the gravel path that traversed the façade of the house. As they passed its shuttered windows they heard the attendants preparing for the day inside. Opening the shop, stocking the tills. Somewhere in the gardens a strimmer worked at a hedge. In the last window Michael caught a glimpse of them both—Josh walking with his head down, as if following a guideline just in front of his feet. Michael, tall beside him, his amputated stride arriving in his shoulder as an awkward jerk. At the end of the house they followed a stream down between the layers of Bagshot Sand and Clayton Beds, then crossed a footbridge over Wood Pond and on up into the South Woods itself. They began jogging without any communication, picking up their pace exactly where they always did, at the edge of the Duelling Ground, crossing its oval of scotched turf to join the path leading down towards Hampstead Gate. Their route remained unchanged, undisturbed. And everything else about their run, too, was the same as it always had been. Except for the air they bore with them, polluted as it was with the unspoken knowledge of Lucy's death, partly known in each man, but only completely between them both.

On reaching Parliament Hill they slowed up the slope, walking the last few metres to the scattering of benches on its summit sitting in salute to London below. Michael sat on their usual bench, then felt the wood beneath him give as Josh added his weight beside him.

The heat wave had broken. Armadas of high cumulus were patching the city's mosaic with shadow. A cool breeze spoke of rain, approaching from the north behind them. A flock of starlings rose and fell on the sports fields below, like a sheet shaken over a bed.

Michael looked across at Josh. Apart from his tiredness, he looked unchanged. Although his eyes, he saw, had lost the distance of their focus, as if they could no longer bear the promise of a horizon.

"I'm sorry," Michael said, and he meant it, in the full scope of the word, more than he'd ever meant it before.

Josh didn't look at him. "How did you hear?" he said.

"The policewoman. She came to the flat."

Josh was already shaking his head, biting his lower lip. A vein, like a sudden worm, appeared across his forehead.

"That bitch," he said. "Treating me like a fucking criminal. A suspect!"

Josh turned to face him, anger enlivening his eyes. Michael saw how deeply it was rooted, below his heart, his stomach. "I mean can you imagine if after Caroline . . . someone had come along and pointed a finger and—" He broke off. "I'm sorry," he said, looking away again. "It's just . . ."

"I know," Michael said. "It's okay. Really."

Josh leant back against the bench. "At least that's done with now, anyway. The DCI, or whatever he's called. Her boss. He said there was no case." He let out a breath in disbelief. "No case? Of course there's no fucking case!"

"I'm sure it was just procedure," Michael offered. "Standard stuff."

"Yeah?" Josh said more quietly. "Well, then they should take a hard look at their fucking procedures."

There was no case. Michael leant forward, resting his elbows on his knees as he took in what Josh had said. For the last two days he'd been sure he would see her again. Detective Sergeant Slater. He'd waited, each morning, for the intercom to buzz, to hear the taps of her footsteps in the stairwell. To watch as she drew out her notebook and pen once more. He was sure his false day would have been tested and found untrue, his deleted minutes resurrected.

"The coroner gives his judgement today," Josh said from beside him. "They did the autopsy—" His voice broke over the word, the images it conjured. The smallness of her body. Silently, he began to cry.

Michael reached out and laid a hand on his back. It was the first time the equation of their contact had been reversed. He felt the muscles of Josh's shoulder blades spasm under his palm; the physicality of his pain.

"Christ, Mike," Josh said, when he could speak again. "I'm telling you. When you have kids. No one tells you . . . I mean, they do, but . . ." He rubbed his hands roughly across his face, then looked at them, as if expecting to see a stain of his grief. "The love," he said. "It's . . . it's . . ." He couldn't find the word, and when he did it came in a whisper. "Cruel."

Michael took his hand away. To feel Josh's fragility, to touch it, was too much. "How's Sam?"

Josh took a breath, gathering himself. "Not good," he said, frowning at the constellation of cigarette butts at their feet.

"She's beating herself up over the gate. The child gate." He sighed and began shaking his head again. "We took it away. I don't understand. She was always fine. Careful, like we'd taught her." He shrugged. "I . . . I just didn't hear her. Nothing. Only when she . . ." He trailed off again, unable to say what had killed his daughter.

Michael looked towards the city, the dome of Saint Paul's dwarfed by cranes, shafts of sunlight bursting against glass towers. He didn't understand, either. Had Josh been there? Is that what he was saying? Did he know? Michael swallowed, trying to naturalise his voice. "You were downstairs?" he asked.

For a moment Josh said nothing. When he looked back at

Michael, his expression was defensive. "Of course I was downstairs." The vein was proud across his forehead again. "Where else would I be?"

"I just meant if you were in the garden," Michael said. "When it happened. Then you couldn't be . . ."

Josh looked away from him. "No," he said, as if this was an answer he'd given too many times before. "I wasn't in the garden."

A woman walking two pugs came and sat down on a bench to their left. Rummaging in her handbag, she took out a pack of cigarettes, drew one out and lit it, the lighter cupped in her palm. The pugs at her feet breathed short and heavy from the climb.

For a few minutes neither of them spoke. Josh stared at the ground again. Michael sat beside him, still processing what he'd said. Josh must have told Slater he'd been in the house. Sam, too. Without knowing it, the two of them had conspired to make each other's versions of those minutes true. Josh in the house, Michael not. So where had Josh been? He'd never know and he could never ask him.

Michael felt a flush of desperate anger. If only Josh hadn't left the house—but he had, so it no longer mattered. All that did, and all that would now, over the coming months and years, is whatever Michael might do to help heal the wound they'd both made. This is all he had left to place in the scales against what had happened on that landing, on those stairs. His actions would have to be many, countless. But it was all he had to offer.

"If there's anything," Michael said eventually, "I can do. To help."

Josh didn't seem to hear him, and Michael was about to repeat himself, when he finally spoke. "It's because I moved her," Josh said, more to himself than to Michael. He was nodding, as if he'd worked out the answer to a puzzle. "That's why they questioned me."

From nowhere Michael saw Lucy fall again. Slowly, a bare foot searching, her blonde hair, her hand opening. And he always would. He knew that now. She would always be with him. She would never leave him. Just as the sight of his daughter lying in that turn on the stairs would never leave Josh.

"But, who wouldn't?" Josh said. "I mean, for fuck's sake, she's my daughter . . ."

"It's more likely," Michael said softly. "They were just following procedure. Honestly Josh. Going by the book."

Josh nodded, but with less conviction. Suddenly, he stood up. "I need to go home," he said.

Michael rose from the bench, too. The woman with the pugs looked over at them, blowing smoke from the corner of her mouth.

"On my own, Mike," Josh said, holding up a hand.

He looked as if he might cry again. Like a man at odds with the world, a man who was losing. "Sure," Michael said. "Of course. Give my love to Sam," he added, as Josh turned from him. "And I meant what I said. If there's anything . . ."

But Josh was already walking away down the path. Michael watched him go, this man whose life, in less than a second, he'd torn apart. A man who, like him, had chosen to save himself, and who in making that choice had unknowingly brothered them, bonded as they now were by their lies and the false minutes they'd conjured.

CHAPTER
SIXTEEN

"THAT'S IT. NOW walk away. Slowly now. Just walk away. Take it easy."

Daniel lowered the lunging whip, turned from the horse, an old bay mare, and walked towards where Sally leant, against a fence at the far end of the scrubby field.

"Don't look back," she called to him. Her two dogs, lying at her feet, raised their heads at his approach. "That's it," she said. "Nice and steady. Keep coming."

After five months at West Valley this was the first time Daniel had let Sally give him a lesson. Up until now he'd preferred to stay away from the horses and occupy himself with his maintenance jobs instead. But this morning, when she'd offered again, he'd accepted. He couldn't say why, but he was glad he had. In the role of teacher Sally seemed more settled than usual. As if everything else in her life was a distraction or a disturbance. As she spoke to him now her voice was coaxing, more gentle than Daniel had ever heard it before. And she was smiling too. So it must be working, he thought, as he neared her. The horse must be following him.

—

When Daniel had first come to work for Sally he hadn't been sure what to make of her. She was gruff, short-tempered, fiercely independent. Years of living on her own had made her terse, as hard-worn as her sun-leathered skin. How she'd managed to run a guesthouse all these years he couldn't tell. But she had. And not just any guesthouse, but one of the most highly regarded in all Sonoma County.

At some point there'd been a husband, but he'd left her, years ago. Daniel still didn't know the circumstances, only that because of his leaving, Sally, now in her seventies, needed help through the high season—with the garden, the maintenance, and all the other jobs she'd rather leave to someone else while she worked with her horses.

"No, it ain't fucking horse whispering," she'd said to him when he'd first asked her about it. "Just common sense, that's all. Listening, looking. Just taking some goddamn time to stop thinking all human for once. Realise ours isn't the only way of being, of talking."

Daniel had driven down her track from the nearby town of Sebastopol just a few days before. A simple handwritten sign had prompted him to turn off the road. *HELP WANTED*, written in red-marker capitals. Above it was another sign, painted and faded—*West Valley Guesthouse & Equine Harmony Centre.* It was early in the season, February. Which is why, Sally had been quick to tell him, she'd taken him on. Because he'd been the first one to drive down that track. One mistake, she'd told him as she'd led him to his quarters—a spare room with a single bed and a hotplate—and he could drive right back up it again.

But Daniel hadn't made any mistakes. Not anymore. So now, five months later, in July, as Sally guided him through her techniques, he felt secure in his position. Over the months the two of them had got into a rhythm. He thought they understood each other. Maybe, even, that they were growing to like each other.

—

"Okay, that's far enough," Sally said, raising her hand. "Now turn back around. Nice and slow."

Daniel followed her instructions and turned to find the mare close behind him, her head low, her flanks shivering under the touch of morning flies.

"Now walk to your left," Sally said from the fence. "Still nice and steady, now. That's it."

Daniel did as she said, slowly walking up the slope of the field. The mare turned with him and walked on beside him as if tethered, nodding into the incline. He went to say something, but at his intake of breath Sally cut him off.

"Don't talk," she commanded. "Just walk. Walk and feel her beside you. That's it. She's with you now. She's with you."

As Daniel walked on with the mare he thought how much Sarah and Kayce would have loved to have seen this. And Cathy, too. But they were all still in Las Vegas. It was one of the things he'd found hardest to get used to. Not being able to turn to his wife or his daughters and share a sight, a thought. But for the last year, apart from one single day, that's how it had been, ever since he'd reversed out of their drive in Centennial Hills and driven west to leave them.

—

After those first few days on the Sonoma coastline Daniel had decided to stay. To keep the sea close. But at the same time he'd had to keep moving, too, so he'd carried on driving. He couldn't go any farther west so he'd travelled the coast road instead, as far north as Florence, Oregon, and as far south as San Diego. As he'd travelled he'd avoided newspaper stands, bars with TVs, radio stations with regular bulletins. He soon realised, however, there was no need to be so careful. In a matter of weeks the story that had so ruptured his life had already slipped from the media's interest, surfacing again only when the inquiry reached its conclusion.

"Accidental killing"—that's what they called what he'd done. It had been an accident. People had died. She had died. A couple of columns on page three or four. An item on the occasional news channel. Even in Australia and Britain the Pentagon statement had been little more than acknowledged. The world had moved on. To other stories, other deaths, feeding its hunger for now, not then.

Through it all they'd managed to keep his name out of the press. Whether Agent Munroe had deployed suppressing tactics or the juggernaut of military protocol had just taken over, in the eyes of the world the drone had remained unmanned.

But so had he. In those first months travelling the coast, tracing its cliffs and fishing towns, Daniel had been unable to settle. His nerves were raw and his sleep, unless he drank enough, was cursory and restless. He'd known he couldn't return to Las Vegas while he was like that. But he also couldn't bear stopping anywhere for long. He was still getting by on his discharge pay, so with no job to root him, he'd drifted the Californian coast like a sixties throwback, exiled from his vocation, in possession of a home, but unable to return there. That home was, though, still his final destination. He was sure of that. Not the house in Centennial Hills itself, but Cathy and the girls. They were his home, and why he was staying away from them now, so that one day in the future they might continue to be so.

Although part of Daniel's agreement with Cathy had been to give her space, they'd still kept in regular contact. Weekly phone calls, emails. He'd Skyped the girls regularly too, close-shaving in guesthouse bathrooms to maintain his previous military smoothness. As far as Sarah and Kayce were concerned, their father's work had taken him away again. Which in a manner of speaking, Daniel had convinced himself, was true. It wasn't a difficult story for them to accept. Over the years of his service his absence had become as familiar to them as his presence. But even when on tour he'd always got leave, so a few months ago with Cathy's consent, he'd travelled back to Las Vegas to see them.

He'd been with them for only a day. Cathy had said it would be too disruptive—for her and for the girls—if he'd stayed for any longer, or come to sleep at the house. So instead he'd arrived the night before, checking in to a serviced MGM apartment just off the strip. As usual, he hadn't been able to sleep, so he'd spent much of the night strolling the covered malls and the casinos, watching the gamblers feed the machines.

They met over breakfast at one of the Paris restaurants, a foot of the Eiffel Tower planted through the ceiling above them. Seeing the girls had almost been too much for Daniel. But he knew Cathy would be watching him, weighing his responses, his behaviour, so somehow he'd held himself together, suppressing his desire to just take them in his arms and hold them. As he'd paid the bill Cathy had thrown him a look, one in which the wife he'd known and the wife he was coming to know both seemed to be imploring him to understand how fragile this was, to understand what he held.

That evening Daniel took the girls to Disney on Ice, but before that they'd had a whole day together. They'd spent most of it walking the strip, Daniel pushing Sarah in her stroller, Kayce holding his hand. Between shopping in the malls and eating snacks they'd seen New York, Paris, Venice, Egypt; dwarf versions of the Empire State, the Arc de Triomphe, the Pyramids. Later, on their way to the show that evening they'd stopped to watch the choreographed fountains in the lake before the Bellagio, their towering plumes shooting from shadow into light.

After his months in the wine country and coast of Sonoma, the city felt heavily present to Daniel, and yet film-set ephemeral too. He'd never noticed before how there was music piped everywhere on the strip. From the lampposts, potted plants, all along the fake cobbled malls. Even the walkways above the highway felt like themed zones of homelessness, these being, as far as he could tell, the only places where the city's beggars were allowed to ply their trade.

As Daniel watched the Bellagio fountains, the girls shrieking and jumping at his sides, he realised he'd been wrong. For all the time he'd worked out at Creech he'd always seen what he did there as a strangely jarring disconnect from the rest of Las Vegas. Here, in the city's heart, fantasy, escape, and gambling were the dominant notes of its song. Out there, in the desert, they faced reality, war, death. The strip was about forgetting death. Creech was about dealing in it.

But it wasn't that simple, and as those fountains had danced in unison he'd seen that, with a sudden clarity. Creech wasn't a disconnect from the aspiration of the city, but a continuum. In Las Vegas, versions of the world were translated to America so America didn't have to go there. In doing so, other countries, other places, were simultaneously brought closer and pushed farther away. Just like they had been on those screens he'd watched out in Creech. Because isn't that what they'd done out there too, he and Maria with their coffees cooling on the shelf? Brought a version of the war to America. A close-up yet far away version, a safe equivalent, so they didn't have to go there themselves.

All through the show that evening, as the dancers at Cinderella's ball had spun and pirouetted over the ice, Daniel felt the city's culture of imitation bleeding through his previous life there. All of it, he saw now, had been simulacra, representation. The broad streets and ochre houses of Centennial Hills were communal, but no more than an image of community. The desert bushes and trees planted in the gravel were miniature models of the real desert spreading beyond the locked gates of the cul-de-sacs. Even the Charleston Mountains, he realised, looked like a shrunken version of those ranges through which he'd flown in Pakistan and Afghanistan, as if they'd been bought in the same job lot as the Eiffel Tower under which they'd had breakfast. And them, too, he had to admit. He, his daughters, Cathy, sitting to eat pancakes like a real vacationing family. They, too, were no more than an imitation. A pretend family, hollow at the centre, and all because of him.

When Daniel handed the girls back over to Cathy that night, strapping them into their car seats in the Thomas & Mack Center's parking lot, he'd made a silent promise to all of them that whatever it took, he'd fill that hollow. That they would not, one day, be just the image of a family, but the real thing, living a life together, not making one up.

As he'd driven back west the following day, taking his old route towards Creech, Daniel finally turned off the highway and drove up into the mountains he'd only ever seen from afar when he'd lived in the city. Pulling up beside the road at the crest of a high valley, he'd got out of the Camry and breathed in the scent of eucalyptus on the breeze. At that altitude snow was still patching the ground below the bushes. Bending to it, Daniel had brought a handful to his face and pressed it against his cheek, its sting gratefully real.

"Are you getting help?" That's what Cathy had asked him the previous night before she'd driven the girls away. "Because you should, Dan," she'd said, one hand on the open driver's door. "You really should."

"I am," he'd told her. "And it's working. I'm feeling much better, Cathy."

"That's great," she'd said, giving his arm a squeeze. "God, that's so good to hear." For the first time since they'd met at breakfast Daniel had believed the honesty of her emotion. So maybe she really did want him back? Maybe he could make his promise to them true, and sooner than he'd hoped?

It had been a lie, what he'd told Cathy. But also not a lie. He was feeling better, and he had been getting help, just not the kind she'd meant. But it was still help. The combed vineyards patching the hills. The river mists and sea fogs. A red-tailed hawk lifting from a tree. He'd got as far as finding out about the local veterans' charities, and he'd seen their bumper stickers too, advertising their work with "heroes." But Daniel didn't feel like a hero. And he didn't feel like a veteran either. That was the problem. The military was like a family, that's what they told you. Until you left. One minute you're on the inside, the next you're out. Ever since college it was all Daniel had known. He'd spent a third of his life flying, and now suddenly he'd found himself grounded. Like Colonel Ellis had said, he'd upheld the American Airman's Creed—*My Nation's Sword and Shield, Its Sentry and Avenger.* And what had they done in return? Pushed him out the door as fast as they could.

Without flying Daniel felt lumpen, clumsy, as if deprived of one of his senses. He felt stripped, too, of everything else it had brought: authority, identity, purpose. Even through his time at Creech when he'd flown from a ground control station, not a cockpit, he'd still thrived on the sensation. Which is why he'd kept the veterans' charities at bay. Because if he couldn't have his military life then Daniel wanted to forget it, and he knew those charities would mean talking, remembering. And remembering would mean seeing too. Which was also why he'd fashioned his own kind of help in Sonoma rather than seek it elsewhere. Because of what he might see again if forced to remember. He'd seen too much already, of that he was sure. He'd looked for too long, until he'd wanted his eyes to rot. So yes, he'd lied to Cathy, but it was for the right reasons. If he wanted to get back to her, to the girls, then he knew he'd have to find his own route. For now, that meant staying out west, Sonoma, working at Sally's. And it meant the letters too, the letters he'd been writing to Michael.

—

"Okay, reckon that'll do." Sally pushed herself off the fence and began walking back to the farmhouse, her two dogs lifting themselves from the dust to follow her. "There's some pellets in the feed bin," she called to Daniel over her shoulder. "Give her a handful. But not too much, now."

—

Daniel had picked up other jobs, other routines, during his time on the coast—working on the grape harvest, helping out in a fishing harbour—but it was only when he'd come to Sally's that he'd felt ready to write to Michael. When the words had finally come, they'd come quickly and he'd written that first letter in one sitting; *Dear Mr. Turner, I understand this is a letter you most probably do not want to receive . . .* When he'd finished it, he'd read it through, put it in an envelope, addressed it to Michael's publishers, then got in his car to mail it from San Francisco. He wanted to make contact. He wanted to be known. But that hadn't meant he'd wanted to be found.

The only address Daniel put on his letter was that of a mailbox in the Bay Area. Not that he expected Michael to reply, at least not in the form of a letter. Perhaps he'd publish Daniel's name online, or go to the papers. It would be a story, after all, his writing to him. But whatever he did Daniel found it hard to imagine Michael would write to him directly.

This uncertainty about Michael's response meant in the weeks after he'd written to him Daniel had woken each morning washed through with a nervous anticipation. What were the consequences if Michael went public? What would be the military's response? But at the same time he'd also woken feeling relieved. Because he had finally done it. He'd completed the circle, and it was the only way forward, he was sure, regardless of what it might bring.

When, eventually, Michael did write back, Daniel wasn't just surprised to receive the letter, but also to open it and read his asking him for more. There'd been no blame, no recriminations, no anger even. Just questions. In a list. About himself, his family, his work. And about the day he'd killed his wife.

At first Daniel hadn't understood. He had confessed, he'd stepped out of the shadows. Wasn't that enough? But as he'd worked at Sally's that day, clearing out the stables, restocking the kitchen, cutting back the ferns along the brook, he'd come to see that no, it wasn't enough. To confess and leave was easy. But to confess and stay, to remain circling over your deed, to hunger after the detail of it, that was something else. He of all people should know that. So perhaps it was a form of punishment, these questions? Michael's way of making him pay through recollection, through offering up his life for dissection? A way for him to reap some kind of a victory from his loss; a victory through knowledge.

—

Opening his fist to reveal a handful of pellets, Daniel flattened his fingers and let the mare nuzzle into them, working her lips against his palm. As she did he ran his other hand along the muscle under her mane. The sun was warm against the back of his neck. He could hear the sound of a shower through the open window of one of the guest rooms. For the first time in what seemed like years, he felt content, calm.

—

Today Daniel would send his third letter to Michael. Having replied to his first Michael had sent Daniel another set of questions. Some asked for clarification or more detail. Others, though, were entirely new. Daniel understood Michael was a writer, but at the same time he couldn't imagine what he might do with the answers he was giving him. But despite this uncertainty, or perhaps because of it, Daniel had still decided to reply. And now, in response to a third letter from Michael, he would reply again today. Partly to pay his dues to the husband of the woman he'd killed, but also for himself. Because that's who else Daniel was writing these letters for now, himself. As a form of focused remembering, of purposeful recollection, and as a way to trace, through his answers to Michael, the convoluted paths that had led to what happened.

—

"I said not too much!"

Daniel, his hand already digging in the bin for more pellets, turned to see Sally behind him.

"It ain't about reward, remember. You want her instinct to work for you, not her goddamn hunger."

She was leading another horse out of the yard into the field. "Feels good, though, eh?" she said, as she passed him. "To have that connection? Without even touching?"

Daniel held the mare's jaw as she nudged under his arm, searching for the pellets.

"Yeah," he said, although Sally was too far away to hear him. "It does."

CHAPTER
SEVENTEEN

IT WAS TWO months after Michael and Josh had gone jogging on the Heath that Samantha told Michael her husband had left. They were in a café in South End Green, its French windows drawn open to the pavement. An overcast day had broken, its vanilla sunlight suggestive of autumn. A couple of buses were parked up nearby, casting shadows over their table.

Josh, Samantha told Michael, had moved out the day before. They'd talked for several hours, Samantha said, and agreed that for the time being it was the right thing to do. She was going to come round and tell Michael at some point, but as she'd bumped into him now, well, he may as well know.

Michael didn't know what to say. He offered her his sympathies, asked if she was all right. He hadn't expected them to break. He'd thought, in these last quiet months, they'd been holding each other closer, not coming apart. "God, Sam," he said, "that must be tough." Samantha nodded, her jaw tight, holding back. Then, suddenly, she laughed. A short, manic burst that made Michael think she might cry, too.

"It's amazing, really," she said, through the tail of it, "that we've lasted this long."

—

Michael had seen hardly anything of either Samantha or Josh since Lucy's death. The funeral had been for close family only, conducted just two days after the coroner had returned a verdict of accidental death. In the week afterwards Michael had gone for a coffee with Samantha, in the same café in which they were sitting now. She'd cried through most of their time together and left while her coffee was still warm. He'd seen her only a couple of other times since then and usually like this, unplanned, crossing paths around the shops, the supermarket. He'd found it almost unbearable, this sudden distance between him and the Nelsons. Having decided upon his course of action and justified his choices, the only outlet for Michael's guilt—the possibility of his helping Josh and Samantha—had been denied him with their absence. In the wake of it he'd been left, distracted and hollow, with the hauntings of what he'd done, of what he'd seen.

Since that run on the Heath a couple of months earlier Michael had seen Josh just the once. Michael had been gardening at the time, working on the borders along the hedge that divided his building's strip of lawn from theirs. It was evening and Josh had come out to smoke a cigarette down by the willow. On his way to the pond he'd only nodded at Michael, but on his way back up to the house he'd come over to speak with him. He was sorry, he'd said, about the other day, on the Heath. He shouldn't have gone off like that. Michael told him it was fine, that he understood. Which is when Josh had looked at him as if he didn't know him, as if someone had just reminded him of how recently this stranger had entered their lives.

"See you around," Josh had said, as he'd turned to go. But Michael hadn't. Since then, Josh and Samantha had kept themselves closer than ever. The house, when he passed it, betrayed little sign of being lived in. Rather, it was as if they were held within it, the way a box filled with tissue paper holds a blown egg, or a single, almost weightless, filigreed gem. Their loss had become delicate, and it seemed to Michael this was why they'd stayed inside, fearing any exposure or disturbance that might further its fracture.

Rachel, too, he'd seen only once, in a bookshop in Hampstead with her mother. He hadn't approached them. There'd been something in Rachel's expression that had stopped him. She'd always been a serious girl, but this was different. As he'd watched her, she'd moved through the shop as if a trick had been played on her, one that no one had told her about. A truth the rest of the world had always been in on, but about which, until now, she'd been kept in the dark. With a sullen slowness, she'd picked a couple of books off the shelves, flicked through their pages, then put them back. She was disengaged, her curiosity defused. And yet Michael was sure, had he gone to her, she would have known. In the way that cats or horses know. She would have sensed his falseness, the ugliness of his endeavour.

For much of the summer Rachel had stayed at Martha's in Sussex, in the company of her cousins. This was where Samantha was going when Michael had seen her on the street. To pick up Rachel and bring her home. But she had some time, she'd told him, before her train. Would he join her for tea?

"I didn't want Rachel to be there," she explained to Michael, as she stirred in her sugar, "when Josh left."

"Does she know?" Michael asked. "That he's moved out?"

Samantha looked into her cup, as if she'd been caught stealing. "Not yet," she said. "But I'm going to tell her tonight. Explain."

"It would be best," Michael said. "Before she comes home."

"It's the right thing," she said, looking up at Michael. "You have to believe me. It's all been so much worse since . . . He's been so much worse."

One of the buses started up and pulled away from its stand. Samantha watched it edge into the road, dislodging a wedge of sunlight onto the pavement.

"Worse?" Michael said.

"He's been drinking." She was still watching the bus, as if Josh was on it. "All the time. In the morning, before bed. He's always had a temper, but . . ."

"Has he gone back to work?"

She raised her eyebrows and let out another little laugh. "Oh, yes," she exclaimed. "As soon as he bloody could."

"Isn't that good?" Michael said.

"Maybe." She took a deep breath, exhaling it as a sigh. "He stays out," she said, returning her attention to Michael. "Or in the office. I never know which. Until one, two in the morning." She took a sip of her tea. Michael could see this was no longer about discussing a decision. Samantha had come to her choice some time ago, and this was already the aftermath, the resolution.

"Everyone has their own way of coping," he offered. "That might just be his."

"I know, I know. But . . ." She paused. Then, with a small collapse of her shoulders. "To be honest, we've been heading this way for a while."

"Really?" Michael thought of the dinners they'd shared, the walks, the parties. He'd often sensed a strain about them, and he doubted Josh had ever been faithful for long. But at the same time he'd never thought they might split, and he'd always found it difficult to imagine them beyond their marriage.

"What happened," Samantha said, her face tensing with even this vague reference to Lucy's death. "It's just . . . accelerated." She took another drink of her tea. Michael did the same. He didn't speak. He could tell Samantha was weighing up whether to tell him something. When she put her cup down, she did so carefully, like placing the final piece of a jigsaw puzzle, then leant forward, bringing her face closer to his. "I can't be sure," she said, looking him in the eye. "But I think Josh has been having an affair."

"Josh?" Michael said.

"With Maddy." Samantha said her name as if admitting something herself. "I think he's been screwing Maddy."

Michael thought of that night in the lap-dancing club, Josh pointing his finger at him as the dancer, Bianca, led him towards the private rooms. It had been so brash, so immature. It felt a country away from Maddy's buttoned-down eroticism, her held reserve. But then there'd been that meeting at the wine bar in Belsize Park—Josh's air of discomfort when they'd gone for their run the day after.

Samantha sat back in her chair, her definitive point made. There'd been no anger in her voice, no jealousy. Just the certainty of her choice. The drink. Maddy. She'd weighed the accumulating factors, all, he knew, in the light of Lucy's death, and decided her course. Her life was changing, altering by the second. It was both terrifying and exciting to witness.

"Christ," Michael said. "Do you think Tony knows?"

"I don't know," Samantha said. "And I don't care." But as she said those words a softness in her voice betrayed her. "I want him to be okay, Michael," she said, leaning forward again. "I really do. But . . ." Her eyes began to well. "I've got to think of myself, Rachel."

Michael reached out and laid a hand over hers. "Of course," he said. "Of course."

—

Samantha was twenty-five when she'd met Josh, on a train pulling out of Wandsworth Station. She was six months back from New York and had just moved in with some old school friends down the road. It had been her first week in a new job, as a PA in an architect's office in Victoria. She was still getting used to the routine, the early starts. If she hadn't been, there's every chance they'd never have met.

They'd both been late. As they'd come up the stairs to the platform the train doors were already closing. Samantha was a little ahead of Josh, so it was she who made it onto the carriage first. As she did, he jumped on behind her, clipping the back of her heel as he landed.

Samantha turned to see her shoe falling from the carriage and onto the track. The doors slid shut, and as the train shunted forward she'd found herself standing two inches shorter than she'd been on the platform. The man she was facing was only an inch or so taller. "Shit," he said, looking horrified. "Holy shit. I'm so sorry."

There was something about the earnestness of his alarm that made Samantha laugh. And something comforting, too, about his accent, which spoke of the streets of her student days. His name was Joshua, and yes, he confirmed, as he took her to buy a new pair of shoes in Victoria, he'd been brought up in New York. "Well, New Jersey," he'd said, as they'd entered an outlet of L.K. Bennet. "But who's counting, right?"

She'd been impressed with his confidence in the store, giving his opinion as she'd tried on various pairs of court shoes. He, in turn, had been impressed by her calves when she stood to look at her selection in the mirror. And by her enjoyment, too, of what had happened. Before they'd parted, he'd given her his card and then watched as she'd walked through the doors of her office, hoping she'd look back. She'd waited as long as she could, then glanced over her shoulder as she'd passed reception. He was still there, smiling at her through the revolving doors, his hand raised in a wave.

Josh had always wanted to visit Europe. It was, as he liked to remind people, where he was from. His father had traced his great-great-grandfather to Lancashire. So after college he'd inter-railed around the continent. He'd visited Lancaster, walked in the Pennines, camped on archipelagos off Denmark, slept in train stations in Brussels and Bologna, and went surfing in Biarritz. When his ticket had expired, his enthusiasm for Europe hadn't. So he'd stayed, working where he could, before enrolling in an MBA in London.

Despite his job in the city, he'd managed to hold on to a visitor's enjoyment of the capital. After New York, and the nature of her return, Samantha had been able to see London only as second best, a concessionary place to live. But Josh changed that. On the weekends he took her on open-top bus tours, to the John Soane's Museum, boating on the Serpentine. He wanted to see Stonehenge, to visit Edinburgh during the festival, to catch the ferry to Ireland. He was expansive, just when it felt as if her life was contracting. She'd sworn no more bankers or moneymen. No more trading nights. But this felt different, that's what she'd told herself and her friends. And it was. He made her laugh. They had good sex. He made her come and then afterwards wanted to talk. To know who she was, and why.

They married at the town hall in Prague, with three friends as witnesses, and honeymooned on Ko Tao in Thailand. The first house they'd bought was in Clapham, and their next, when Rachel was born, in Kensal Rise. But Josh was good at what he did. He was ruthless in his work. At first Samantha had liked it: his competitive drive, his refusal to come out anywhere other than the top, his willingness to take a risk. He got promoted. He rose. Before she became pregnant with Lucy they moved again, this time into a four-storey house backing onto the ponds on Hampstead Heath. A Georgian town house of solidity and peace. They'd have preferred to have been flanked by the same, rather than have a fifties block of flats to their left. But it was still more than they'd hoped. A family home. Somewhere they would stay. When they'd moved in, Rachel, at just two years old, had been the first across the threshold, carrying her own box of crayons and toys. Her parents had followed behind her, Josh insisting on picking Samantha up and carrying her inside like a newlywed. Five years later, on an overcast day in August, he'd left through the same door, alone and carrying no more than a couple of suitcases.

—

Michael withdrew his hand from Samantha's. "How do you know?" he asked her. "About Maddy?"

"Oh," she said, "it's been brewing for years. From before Tony even married her, in a way. I suppose I don't know for sure. But I'd be surprised if I'm wrong." She lifted her teacup to drink. "She's probably just playing with him," she said, as she put it back on its saucer. "To alleviate her boredom. She's that kind of woman."

"But Tony," Michael said. "Josh adores him."

"No," Samantha said clearly. "He wants to *be* him. He aspires to him." She waved a hand in front of her face, as if clearing a spider's thread. She didn't want to talk of it anymore. She gave him one of her smiles; distancing, a polite mask. "I'm enrolling in an MA," she said by way of changing the conversation. "In September. Photography, at the Royal College of Art."

For the rest of their time in the café, Samantha talked about her future, not her past. However much Michael wanted to help her through her loss, so far she'd barely mentioned her grieving to him, or the circumstances of Lucy's death. He'd tried to broach it, gently, when they'd gone for a coffee in the week after the funeral. But Samantha had just shaken her head. "I'm sorry, Michael," she'd said, crying quietly. "I can't."

Since then, recalling his own weeks after Caroline's death, he'd come to understand why Samantha might be holding her loss close. It was as if her grief was a newborn, an infant with whom she, and she alone, was learning to communicate. He knew she'd talk about it when she was ready, but until then his just being there would have to be enough, however impatient he was to be of more tangible help. So as they finished their teas and another bus moved on, unlocking more of the sky above them, Michael had listened, aware that this, as much as anything, could be a form of contribution. The promises Samantha was making to herself were, he felt, as much to bolster her decision to split from Josh as they were promises to be kept. The MA, finding a job, to pick up her yoga classes again, to join a friend's book club. How many of these might come to fruition, Michael couldn't tell. He remembered making similar plans himself in the months after Caroline died—to move back to America, to stop writing and work for a charity or NGO instead, or even to try and use Caroline's insurance payout to set up a foundation for young journalists in her name. And yet he'd remained in Britain, moved to London, and had, in the end, even through the turmoil and sleepless nights of the past two months, eventually returned to the comfortable pastures of *The Man Who Broke the Mirror*. But he knew now that the keeping of his promises had not been the point. And it was the same with Samantha. For now, their potency was in their making rather than their practice. And so Michael listened, realising that if what Samantha had said about Josh was true, and they'd separated for good, then it was likely that it would be in her alone his atonement would be focused. That it was to her his attention and time must be devoted.

As they left the café, Samantha paused on the pavement outside. She had a small case with her, on wheels, as if she might stay away for longer than just the one night. Michael was about to ask if she wanted him to walk her to the Tube station, when he saw she still had something to say. Something she didn't want to leave unspoken.

"It hasn't been just Josh," she said, as she put her purse back in her handbag. "It wouldn't be fair to make you think that. It's been me, too."

Michael stepped aside to let a woman with a pram pass. Samantha watched her push it on down the pavement, a child's arm hanging from its seat. Out in the light Michael saw how Lucy's death had etched lines about Samantha's eyes, her mouth. She turned to him. "I haven't . . ." she began, her eyes welling again. "I haven't been able to forgive him, Michael." She took hold of his arm. "For what happened. I mean, he was there." As she said this she squeezed his arm, her fingers pressing into his flesh. "He was *there*," she said again, breaking down.

Michael held her as she cried, feeling the stabbing breaths of her sobs, just as he'd felt the spasms of Josh's back on the Heath. Over her shoulder he watched the child's arm hanging limp from the pram as its mother pushed it up the street. In reply he saw a flash, as he did all the time, of Lucy's arm, hanging off the edge of the stair, her other twisted behind her. No, he wanted to say to Samantha as he held her. No, Josh wasn't there. But I was. This is my fault, everything—your grief, Josh's leaving, Rachel's hurt. I watched her fall. I heard her die. Because I was there, in your house. I was there.

But what good would it do? How would his confession help this woman sobbing in his arms? It wouldn't. It would be for his sake, not for hers. This is what Michael told himself as he gently pulled back from Samantha and, gathering herself, she, too, pulled away from him.

"God," she said, wiping at her eyes. "I must look a state. I'm sorry." She took a breath. The storm had been sudden but had passed. "I *want* to forgive him," she said, frowning. "I really do."

"You will," Michael said. "In time."

"You think so?" Her eyes held a child's look of hopefulness, the willingness to be told an adult's untruth, a lie even, if it would just make it all better.

"Yes," Michael heard himself say. "Of course you will. It was an accident, Samantha. A terrible accident. No one wanted it to happen, and everyone wishes it hadn't. But you can't blame Josh." Again, he wanted desperately to say more, to tell her. But he had to protect her. "Josh wasn't able to stop it happening," he continued. "But he didn't make it happen, either."

"I know," she said. "I just keep thinking of everything we could have done. Everything we should have done."

"Don't," Michael said, holding her by both her shoulders. He bent his head to catch her eye. "You've got to look forward now. Think of Rachel, like you said. And yourself. And help Josh, if you can."

Samantha nodded. "Yes," she said quietly. "I know." She looked up at him. "That American pilot?" she said, weighing her words carefully. "Have you forgiven him?"

Michael wasn't expecting the question. *Of course not,* he wanted to say. *Why would I? Just because he broke cover and wrote to me?* He thought of Daniel's most recent letter. How willing he'd been to answer his questions. How he seemed to see himself as another victim of Caroline's death, not the perpetrator of it. But Michael had to be careful. Samantha was looking to him for a way forward. And yet he couldn't lie. Not about this. "It's very different," he said eventually. "He aimed at Caroline. He had intent to harm. If not her, then someone. So I'm not sure if I have, yet. But," he went on, seeing disappointment bleed into her expression, "I suppose I've come to understand. A bit. That he didn't mean to kill Caroline personally. That in that way, at least, it was an accident."

Samantha nodded again. She had no idea that Daniel and his missile had killed her daughter, too. "Thank you, Michael," she said, taking his hand in both of hers. "Thank you. You're a good man."

He didn't reply. He couldn't. He was sick with himself. He'd secured those false minutes again. For Josh this time, as much as for himself. Perhaps, he thought, this was also to be the breed of his atonement. His contribution to Josh's healing. A making of his lie into a truth, a blending of their shared lies into one.

Samantha looked at her watch. "I should go," she said. She extended the handle of her case. "I'll give you a ring when we're back," she said, flashing him another smile, warmer than before. "Bye, Michael," she said, walking away. "And thanks again."

"Bye," he said as she went, raising a hand to wave her off. Samantha waved back, calling over the heads of the crowded pavement between them. "I'll bring Rachel round," she said, standing on tiptoe. "I'm sure she'd like to see you."

CHAPTER
EIGHTEEN

ON THE MORNING of September 16, 2008, news channels across the world showed footage of Lehman Brothers employees leaving their offices in Canary Wharf, carrying boxes of files and belongings. The crisis had been building for weeks, and Josh had known they wouldn't escape it. His team, and the whole London office, had always remained profitable. But he knew the country of finance wouldn't be sensitive to such details, or to any concepts of national borders. The bonds bets in the U.S. had failed. Construction work across thousands of hectares of developments on the fringes of Las Vegas and Miami had come to a halt. A few days later Josh had stood on the trading floor along with hundreds of other Lehman's employees, all of them going silent as they'd watched their stock plummet. From then on the building in Canary Wharf had been coursing with the chatter of exit: heads of teams leaving rooms to make phone calls, younger traders calculating with whom they should align.

When the end came, it came swiftly. Within a week of a meeting with the U.S. Federal Reserve in New York, the bank no longer existed. Josh heard the news on the radio as he was making himself breakfast. He'd expected it to be bad, but not this bad. He hadn't thought the bank would die altogether. By the time he

got in to the office he'd found his colleagues were already vacating
the building, walking to cabs or the underground station carrying
Iron Mountain data boxes, bin liners, shopping bags, desk plants.

From his office on the thirtieth floor, Josh watched as a crescent
of camera crews covered his colleagues' departures, tracking them
like flowers following the sun. If he was going to find another position, he knew he should already be making phone calls, setting
up lunches. It wouldn't be difficult. He was good at what he did,
and people knew he was good. It was the bank that had failed, not
him. But instead he remained by the window, the phone on his
desk unplugged and his mobile turned off.

Eventually Josh turned from the scene below. Checking his
drawers one last time, he picked up his briefcase and left his office,
asking his secretary, who was clearing her own desk, to courier the
box of his personal items to his new flat in Hampstead. Taking a
service elevator, he descended through the floors, which just a few
days ago had hummed with activity, and left by a side entrance
of the building. He didn't want to give the cameras, or anyone
else, the satisfaction. But more important, beyond any professional
pride, Josh didn't want Rachel to turn on the TV and see her father
losing his job in the same way she'd already seen him lose her sister, his wife, and his home.

Stepping out into the light, Josh walked west, along Middle
Dock. The sun was catching the higher windows of the towers and
flexing in brilliant flashes on the water beside him. He thought
of the view from Parliament Hill, how from up there these towers, the facets of their pinnacles, sparked from the city like small
explosions. Maybe he would go there today. He hadn't been on the
Heath in months. But perhaps today he would. Suddenly he had
the time, the space. He loosened his tie as he walked, then took it
off altogether. Yes, he'd like to feel the wind up there again. To see
it shuffle the trees like a card dealer, to hear it bring the oceans to
the branches of an oak.

But first he'd go for a drink. Not here, but somewhere farther north. A pub up towards Mile End or Bow. A quiet, midday boozer, dark with close walls. Or perhaps one of the old all-day strip joints, its windows boarded over and its drinkers, from company director to delivery driver, levelled by the clink of their coins in the pint glass. Or maybe he'd just buy a bottle of Teacher's and take it to a bench by the canal. Somewhere he wouldn't have to look at the faces of others. Somewhere where nobody knew him; where he could forget, for an hour or so, who he was and who he'd been.

—

The flat to which a courier drove Josh's boxes later that day was in a Victorian terraced house on the east side of the Heath, set back two streets from its edge. An attic conversion of a bedroom, living room, bathroom, and kitchen with Velux skylights in its sloping roof through which Josh smoked at night, looking over the chimneys and eaves of his neighbours. It was the kind of flat one of his more affluent juniors might have rented, fresh from university. A first-timer's flat. Neat, minimal. A starting place. But for Josh, on moving in, it had felt like an end. A contraction of his hopes and everything for which he'd ever worked and loved to three cramped rooms with predictable furnishings and an air of bland expense.

He'd chosen it simply because it was available, and for its proximity to South Hill Drive. This was the only stipulation he'd given the letting agent. Nowhere more than ten minutes from his home. From Rachel and Sam. He'd agreed to leave the house, but that didn't have to mean leaving their lives. He understood why he had to go. It was becoming unbearable. The way Samantha looked at him each morning, her face thickened with blame. Having to see those stairs every day, to walk down them and see, in his mind's eye, Lucy caught in their turn like driftwood between rocks. That's why he'd stayed away so much, why he'd drunk so much. He wanted to be nowhere other than home, where he could keep

Rachel and Samantha close. But when he was there, he couldn't stand it. Every brick, every chair, every picture, was a part of the canvas of Lucy's death, and his contribution to it. And not just her death, but her short life, too. These were the rooms in which he had first held her, her newborn eyes still welled with the womb's darkness. Where he'd watched her infant sleep, hovering his open hand above her stomach to feel it rise and touch his palm with a breath. Where he had witnessed her growing delight in her childhood discovery of being alive. Loaded with these past visions, and more terrible recent ones, too, Josh's home, once his refuge, had become inhospitable, a wilderness of guilt, grief, and regret. So when Samantha had said she wanted him to leave, that she wanted time apart, he'd offered barely any resistance. It was, beyond the sadness of the action, of carrying those two suitcases out the door, a release. And, he'd thought, as he'd unpacked those cases in his new attic rooms, the only way, in the end, they might stay together.

But if Josh's moving out gave Samantha the space she needed, it did nothing by way of helping him find his own. He felt trapped between what he had done and what he hadn't, between what he'd said and what he hadn't said. A corrosive cocktail of self-loathing and grief continued to eat at him from within. And within was the only place it could be. There was nowhere else for it to go. No one else to whom he could explain or confess. He had left the house. He had not been there. And why? For his secret conquering of Tony's assured world. For the thrill of it. And just because he could. Because in letting him do so Maddy had intoxicated him, not with beauty or allure, but with the simple reveal of her ordinary self behind that impossible façade. But none of that mattered now. All that did was that Josh had left Lucy alone. The only other person who knew was Maddy herself, and she'd already gone, distancing herself as fast as she could the moment she heard what had happened.

She and Tony, like others, had sent them a card with a note

expressing their sympathies, offering to help. A week later Tony had taken him for a drink. They still had their place in Vermont, he'd told Josh. It was empty right now, so if he and Sam wanted to get away for a while? But Maddy Josh hadn't seen since Lucy's death. For all of August she and Tony had been away, in Italy on the Amalfi Coast. At the end of the month Tony had come back to work, but Maddy, he'd said, had flown straight to America. To see her sister, spend time with her nephews and nieces. Tony seemed strained when he'd told Josh this, and Josh wondered if he wasn't the only man from whom Maddy was distancing herself. She was a survivor, and always would be. It was what they'd first seen in each other. The ability to move through, to emerge the other side. But now he hadn't. Now he was left, and she was gone.

Josh didn't care. Maddy's absence, like Samantha's request for him to leave, was also a relief. It removed a low-grade anxiety that had haunted him below his grief ever since it had happened. What if, through Maddy, or through Tony via her, or through some confiding friend he didn't even know about, Samantha were to learn he hadn't been in the house? What then? No, he never wanted to see Maddy again. Not now that her scent, her touch, her submissiveness which had so surprised him, excited him, were all no more than markers of his guilt, reminders of those seconds in which his daughter had fallen through the air without her father there to catch her.

In the weeks after he moved out, as Samantha held her grief close within their house on South Hill Drive, so Josh cradled his guilt in those high rooms on the east side of the Heath. He ate badly: late-night pastas in the nearby Italian, take-out curries and pizzas, ready meals from the corner shop, all accompanied by drink. Wine, whisky, vodka. His work suffered, but he knew they were all going to suffer soon enough. He'd seen what was coming, like a rain cloud over a hill. At another time he might have tried to run for cover, to get out while he could. But as it was he was too apathetic to make the attempt, or to care. And in a way it felt apposite—the foreclosures sweeping the Midwest, the collapse of the markets—it all seemed in rhythm with the descent of his own domestic life. There were those who believed it would correct itself, who revered the system like a religion. Somehow, these people thought, it would all be allowed. But if this was a religion, then it was a creed that demanded sacrifice. And not just of individuals and families, the small people in small towns the young men of Wall Street and the City would never meet. They'd spent too much for it to end just there, imagined too much, wanted too much, and gambled too much. The money gods would need a greater sacrifice than that, a public sacrifice. The banks, they'd been told, were too big to fail. But not a single bank, not a lone bank, the collapse of which might just satisfy that ravenous system and trigger the rescue of others.

The first time Josh and Samantha met after he'd moved out she told him she'd started seeing a bereavement counsellor. She asked him to do the same. So he'd registered, but then missed the appointments. He was gaining weight, his secret heavy within him. He was often angry, always tired. Some mornings he didn't get out of bed but remained curled under the duvet, wishing himself a child again. The only commitments he ever kept were those to Rachel. Whether collecting her from school or taking her out on the weekends, he was always sure to be on time for her and sober. He was always, as much as he could be, the father she'd known before.

Samantha told him she'd explained everything to her: why her father was living in another house, why they weren't together at this time. But whenever Josh sat opposite her, at a café in Hampstead or riding the Tube into town, her hurt expression, the slow bruise of her being, told him Rachel understood nothing. And why should she? She was just eight years old. The world, which had always seemed so benevolent, had been proved malign. He wanted to tell her different, to reassure her there was so much to come that would give her pleasure, that she would love the world again one day. But it was an effort beyond his spirits, and so they'd end their time together in silence instead, the two of them in a park, a museum, a restaurant, joined and apart in the still presence of Lucy's going.

With Sam it was even harder. She needed him to be away from her. Her love for her dead daughter was fierce, and overrode any empathy she might have felt for her husband. And there was, too, the weight of all she did not know. All Josh had done which only now, too late, he wished undone. He was weak against her, depleted. She, however, although drained by Lucy's death, was not. Josh saw again, as he had done in the early years of their relationship, her strength. It wasn't obvious, or displayed as Maddy's was. And neither was it aggressive, competitive, as his own had always been. It was purer than that. Constant, sustained, like a slow wave building far out at sea, travelling its power towards an ever-receding shore. He felt distant from her, and not just because of his moving out or the unspoken blame that hung between them. But also because he saw that she was rising, with a mother's ancient will of survival, to meet the sad suddenness of her situation. She was rising and would take Rachel with her. Their strength would be in their solitude. He could see it happening. With Lucy's falling, Samantha's need of him had fallen away too.

He had hoped, in time, that Michael might be the person to bridge their distance. That just as his presence had once made their family motion smoother, so he might ease the journey of their grief. Josh liked Michael: his quiet talk, the way he listened to the girls, his interest, without any intention or demand, in his work at Lehman's. But Samantha had always liked him on another level. Josh had always known this. That for her, his arrival in their lives had introduced a thread into the fabric of her days she could follow back to her youth before marriage, to her student life of ideas and art, before Ryan McGinnis, money, and a shoe falling from a train had disturbed her trajectory. Because of this it was Josh's hope that with Michael alongside them, as a friend to them both, but a kindred spirit for Sam, they might draw closer again. That with him as a listener, as a reminder of their family, a sounding board for their grief, Samantha might be slowed on her course. That she might, once she felt secure in Rachel and herself, need him again.

But then, one evening before he'd moved out, Josh had spoken with Michael over the hedge dividing their garden from his building's next door. He'd left the house for a smoke. He'd wanted to be alone, so he hadn't talked to him when he'd first seen him. But by the time he'd finished his cigarette he'd been calmer. A week or so earlier, after their jog, he'd walked away from Michael on the Heath. He hadn't been able to abide company. He'd mentioned Caroline, aggressively. He'd been angry and hurt and had taken it out on Michael. So on his way back up to the house he'd gone over to apologise, to try and start again.

As Michael stood to meet him he'd cleaned some dirt from his hands, wiping his palms together to brush them free of soil. Which is when, with a sudden chill, the idea passed across Josh like a shadow. When Lucy had fallen he hadn't been in the house himself, but that didn't necessarily mean his daughter had died alone.

Within weeks of moving in next door, Michael had taken on the communal garden of his building. It was something, he told them over one of those early dinners, he'd inherited from Caroline. He'd never been green-fingered himself, but when they'd moved to Wales she'd introduced him to the pleasures of spending time with plants, of having his hands in the earth, being close to bark and leaf. Samantha and Josh had been grateful. For many years the garden of Michael's building had been left to no more than the occasional mowing by a contractor hired by the managing agent. Under Michael's hands it began to come alive again. He pruned back the trees by the pond. He cleared the beds of weeds and fed the acid soil with nutrients. And when the heat wave had come in June, he'd kept it watered, too.

In comparison, Josh had neglected their own garden over those same summer months. He'd wanted to hire someone in to take care of it, but Sam kept saying she'd prefer to do it herself one day. It was the same when Michael offered to help. She had a vision of her and the girls setting out with trowels and packets of seeds. But it never happened. So over that heat wave their flowerbeds and herbaceous borders suffered. The lawn yellowed, and its earth, whenever Josh picked it up, crumbled dry in his hands.

It was one of the first questions DS Slater had asked Josh the afternoon of Lucy's death. "The soil on the landing," she'd said, as they'd sat in that windowless room in the police station. "And on the floor in the bathroom. Had you been in the garden?"

He'd said no. Because he already had his story. He could already see, in his mind's eye, where he'd been. He'd already rehearsed it so that now, for him, it was real. He'd been reading the paper in the conservatory. He'd had the radio on. But not so loud that he didn't hear, when . . .

"Had anyone else been in the garden?" Slater asked. Her pursuit of the question frightened him. So he'd lied again. Rachel, maybe, he said. Yes, now that he thought of it, Rachel had been playing in the garden that morning. And he'd been out there himself, too, just the evening before. That, at least was true. So that's where it had probably come from. From him or from Rachel. DS Slater had nodded, written in her notebook, and then moved on to her next inquiry.

After he and Samantha returned to the house that evening Josh had gone into the bathroom to shower. As he did he'd examined the carpet on the landing to see what Slater had been talking about. He had to get down on his knees to see it; it was barely soil at all, just a few motes of earth. Brushing them away, he'd stood up and forgotten about it. Any of them could have brought it into the house, at any time over the last few days. The same was true of the marks on the bathroom floor. And right then, with Rachel still oblivious to her younger sister's death, with Samantha crying into her hands in the kitchen downstairs, and with Maddy bearing a knowledge that could sink him, Josh had put it out of his mind.

But on that evening when he'd spoken to Michael over the hedge, as he'd watched his neighbour stand from his freshly watered beds and brush his hands clean, Josh had remembered that soil again. Not just because it had been there, but because whenever it had fallen to the carpet it had been damp, not dry. By the time he'd returned from the police station it was like dust. But the marks it had made when first deposited—tiny smears across individual strands of fabric—suggested it hadn't always been. The earth in his own garden hadn't been watered for days. Which could mean only one thing. The soil on the landing had come from someone else's.

So this was the other reason Josh had asked the letting agent to find him a flat close to South Hill Drive. Because although he couldn't alert anyone, having claimed to have been in the house himself, and although he had no other proof than those crumbs of once-damp soil, he no longer trusted Michael. The man, Josh came to realise, as he smoked each night at his open Velux windows, as he looked over the rooftops, aerials, and satellite dishes of his neighbours, was a storyteller. By trade and by inclination. A loner when they'd first met him. A loner who, from what he could tell, had gathered few other friends since. A loner they'd welcomed into their home. But who was he, really? Beyond his books and his tales of other people's lives? Josh didn't know. After all the hours of their walks and their jogs on the Heath. After all their conversations sitting on that bench on Parliament Hill. He still didn't know. He'd been a chattering fool, he told himself. While he'd talked and talked, Michael had listened. It was what he did, he'd said so himself many times. An "immersion journalist," that's what he'd called himself, and it was what Tony had called him, too. "One of the best immersion journalists I've read." At the time, despite his nodding and agreeing, Josh hadn't understood what Tony was talking about. He'd been too wrapped up in his own life to notice, or to care. Tony seemed impressed by it, and Samantha excited by it. That had been enough. But now, unemployed, estranged from his wife, and grieving for his youngest daughter, Josh thought he did understand, and in a way that neither Tony nor Samantha ever had. Now he was living away from Rachel and Sam. Now that they were so vulnerable, and Michael, who'd arrived as their neighbour from nowhere, was still there, living beside them, Josh thought he understood all too well.

The idea of it, the wild possibilities spiralling in his mind, wouldn't let go of him. Yes, he was to blame for leaving the house. But was someone else to blame for his daughter's death? And was that someone Michael, their quiet, listening, watching neighbour? Because of these suspicions, Josh knew that for as long as Michael lived next door to his wife and daughter, then he must keep them close, too, also watching, also listening, waiting for when he might learn more about Michael's intentions and where he'd really been on that hot Saturday in June.

CHAPTER
NINETEEN

"IT WAS JUST experimenting at first," Samantha said, leafing through the prints in their box. "But after a while it became something else. A kind of meditation, I suppose. Certainly a routine." She paused at one of them. It was taken in autumn, the pond skinned with fallen leaves. A single child, a boy in red Wellingtons, apparently alone, was looking at his reflection in the water. "And then they became something else again," she said. "A kind of story."

"It's the accumulation," Michael said, picking up the print and looking at it more closely. "It builds a narrative, whether we want to or not."

It was an evening in January. Rachel had only just come home from school, but already the Heath beyond the kitchen windows was dark. A clear sky was discovering its stars, the lights of aeroplanes blinking above the city. The year was young, but London had already been covered by snow once since Christmas and, according to forecasts, would be again that night.

"I like that," Samantha said, picking up her wine. "*A narrative of accumulation.* I might steal that."

Michael had been wrong about Samantha. Her promises had been for the keeping, not just the making. And in their keeping she'd grown, become more herself. They hadn't, after all, been a vehicle of transition, but rather had become that transition, a change in her and her life.

"Why didn't you show me these before?" Michael said, placing the print of the boy in red Wellingtons back in the box.

Samantha took it out again, slipping it back in its chronological order. "I don't know," she said, looking at the photographs as if for the first time. "I suppose I wanted to keep them mine. To discover what it was. Get some distance." She looked up at him. "Isn't that what you're always saying? You need distance to see anything clearly? To become your own editor."

She'd recently cut her hair shorter. She wore jeans now, more than dresses. Michael remembered something his bereavement counsellor once said—about how after a death men tend to change their place, women their appearance.

"And now you've got that distance?" Michael asked.

"I want to share them," Samantha said proudly, with the assertiveness of a child. "I thought, fuck it, even if they aren't any good, I want them to be out there. I want them to be *looked* at, otherwise there's no point, is there? They'd only be half cooked."

"Not necessarily," Michael said, picking up another print. It was of the same pond as before, at the same time of day. Only this time it was winter, the trees bare above the water. A low mist clung to the ground.

He offered her more wine. She declined, putting a hand over her glass, so he filled his own instead. "Is a story half cooked," he asked her, "if it's only been written but not read?"

"Absolutely!"

He laughed, thinking she was joking, but then saw that she wasn't.

"Without the reader, it's just thoughts on a page," she said. "Imagination in ink. A printed tautology."

"Tautology? How?"

"Well, a repetition then. Of what was in the writer's mind when they wrote it. But when it's *read . . .*"

"Yes?"

"Well, then the words gather new imagery, don't they? The meaning gathers new association. It's like a chemical reaction. It all depends on how they react with the reader, their life, their mind."

"Let me guess," Michael said, narrowing his eyes in mock estimation. "Susan?"

Samantha laughed. "Yes, okay, but with some of me thrown in, too."

Susan was a member of Samantha's book club. When the group had learnt that Samantha knew Michael, they'd asked her to invite him to speak to them about *BrotherHoods.* The session had been far from an easy ride, but Susan, an ex–English professor, had been particularly dissective of his writing, and of what she'd called "creative nonfiction" as a whole.

"But she's right, isn't she?" Samantha said. "Surely you must have seen it with *BrotherHoods*? How it becomes other books in other people?"

"Yes, but as a book in itself, it was done," Michael replied. "Or at least done to the best of my ability. I'd probably change it now—actually, I'd certainly change it now, but at the time I finished it, it was finished. It wasn't the book itself that was half cooked," Michael said, warming to his theme. "So much as the experience."

Samantha shook her head. "Now you're just getting into semantics."

"No, no, I'm not." Michael put down his glass and picked up the top photograph, the pond beneath bare branches, the mist like cannon smoke. "All I'm saying is that these are far from half cooked. They're quite the opposite. They're bloody good, and they'd be that good, that true, whether people saw them or not."

He handed the print to Samantha. "The communication was

made when you took this, when you printed it. From then on it exists in the world, seen or not."

He took another drink of his wine, looking for the right phrase.

"Its weight has been added," he said eventually.

"Its weight?" Samantha looked doubtful, but she could tell Michael was being serious.

"Yes." He picked up another print, the same pond, at the same time of day again, a swan and her cygnets drifting across the foreground. "Its telling has happened. That's how I see it, anyway. The vision, your intention, your motivation, whatever you want to call it, is no longer purely internal. So regardless if I or anyone else looks at it, its story has still been told. Its purpose served."

—

Samantha started taking photos of the pond shortly after Josh moved out. It had begun as a way to get to know the new camera she'd bought for her MA. She still wasn't sleeping, so early one morning, a few hours after dawn, she'd set up a tripod next to the fence at the bottom of the garden. She stayed there for an hour, experimenting with exposures and timings as the Heath altered under the rising light. The next day she'd found herself awake at the same time. On coming into the kitchen, she'd noticed how different the Heath looked from the day before. It had rained overnight. The light, it seemed, had been washed, cleaned. The water of the pond, dark the previous morning, was metallic, polished. She took her camera to the fence again and, setting the tripod legs in the holes it had made the day before, began taking photos.

On the third morning, despite having fallen asleep in the small hours, she'd woken at the same time once more. She knew why. Those quiet, focused minutes. The slow reveal of the day, its light and weight, its texture and scent. Her body was expecting it, and her mind was asking for it. The exact same scene she'd stood before the previous mornings, but changed, altered. Never the same. Capturing it stirred in her a sense both of movement and of continuity. Of seeing afresh. How many times had she looked out her back door and seen that view? But never, not one of those times, as she'd seen it on those mornings, a unique recipe of light, weather, and season, framed in the lens of her camera.

Samantha's morning sessions became the foundation of what had now become her weekly routine. Every morning, regardless of the weather, and more often because of it, she could be seen out there, next to the willow, bending to her viewfinder. On three of those mornings, after taking her pond photographs and walking Rachel to school, she went to work as a PA for a film director in Hampstead village. The work wasn't taxing—organising his expenses, replying to emails, ordering prints and booking lunch meetings, screenings. But it was new to her, and sociable. While he worked in his office at the top of the house, Samantha worked on the kitchen table, making her party to the movements of the day. Not just the editors and writers who came to meet him, but also the comings and goings of his wife and two sons. It was a workplace, but also a family home. Martha, her sister, had feared it might make Samantha grieve for her own. But the variety and rhythms of the house invigorated her, inspired her even, reminding her of what she'd once wanted and of how much of it had somehow drifted from her over the years of her marriage.

On the other two days of the week she studied at the Royal College, going to lectures and seminars, spending hours in the computer and printing rooms. Again, despite her being ten years older than most of the students, the environment excited her. But it frustrated her, too. She was impatient to learn, to improve. She felt as if she had years to catch up on, a lost decade. Whereas the other students behaved as if time was an inexhaustible luxury, Samantha, knowing it to be a rare reserve, harried at her course and her tutors.

Over those first months after Josh moved out, Samantha gradually came to realise that just as she had autonomy over the hours of her days, so she could choose how to spend her evenings and nights. There was no mortgage on the house, and although Josh no longer had a job, he was still able to pay regular contributions for Rachel and the housekeeping. Whatever Samantha earned from the PA work was hers to spend how she wished. For so many years she'd allowed her socialising to be dictated by Josh's work, by his colleagues and their wives. There were few of them she'd liked on her own terms, so when after a few months she'd begun to contact friends again, to email them about cinema showings or phone someone for a drink, it was nearly always a case of reconnecting with a friend from years ago, rather than anyone, except for Michael, whom she'd seen regularly before Lucy's death.

In this way, between her hours at the director's house, her studies, caring for Rachel and a few old friends, Samantha occupied herself. But none of it did anything to appease her grieving for Lucy. Her daughter had been just four years old. But Samantha had known her for longer than that. Ever since her body had begun forming within hers, ever since the tides of its growing had driven her cravings, her sleep patterns, and mood swings. And yet, at the same time, she'd only recently felt as if she were becoming acquainted with who Lucy actually was, and with who she might become. In the last few months before her death, when Samantha watched her playing with Michael, or on her own, engrossed in a conversation with her dolls, she thought she'd begun to see the hints of the girl beyond the child. And then, within those hints, like a receding line of mirrors within mirrors, the teenager beyond the girl, the woman beyond the teenager and even, in certain fleeting expressions, the elderly woman beyond the adult.

But now Lucy's would be an imagined life, existing only in her mother's projections of who her daughter might have been. The ache of her loss became as familiar to Samantha as breathing, or opening her eyes to see. It was just there, and would always be there, a translucent presence behind the scenes of the day. A shadowing that hurt, but which Samantha would never want to live without, its essence now being all that was left of Lucy beyond the ephemera of memory, photographs, and film, all of which were too painful to ever look at for long.

Rachel, once she'd emerged from the numbing of her own shock, soon became sensitive to these depths of her mother's remembering. In the light of their altered relationship, she'd developed a breed of admiration for Samantha, which she felt but did not yet understand. From out of nowhere, death, like a meteor, had struck their home. There had been sadness, rupture. They were scattered by its impact. Her father was now a man who met her from school, or took her out on the weekends. He was no longer bound by the family walls. She, herself, had been sent far from her own knowledge, and her mother, too, had been on a long journey. But now, from all this disturbance, her mother was back and revealing a warmth Rachel had never previously known. Focused and strong, as if she was recklessly pouring love directly into her. She asked Rachel more questions, her opinion, as if she were eighteen, not eight. She allowed her to stay up late, to stay on the sofa with her, watching TV together. Sometimes Rachel became aware her mother wasn't watching the screen at all, but was watching her instead. Without intention or observation, but merely to witness her. Over breakfast, as Samantha asked her which blouse she should wear, or which skirt, it could seem as if they were impossible sisters, rather than a mother and daughter. And then there were those other times, too, when their roles felt reversed completely. When, on entering a room and discovering her mother to be there, Rachel would sense Samantha's darkness, and would come to her silently, folding her body into its contours in an attempt to at once absorb and soothe her pain.

For Michael, every minute spent with Samantha and Rachel was like torture. There had yet to be a moment, in all the seven months since he'd left their house that day, when, being in their presence, he hadn't felt acutely the sadness of the loss he'd caused, or that somehow Rachel cradled a secret knowledge of her sister's death. And yet at the same time being with them was the only salve his conscience knew. To be there, contributing to their recovery, their new lives. It was both his privilege and his punishment. In practice this often meant no more than giving his encouragement or advice to Samantha, or coming round for a drink or some food, or agreeing to look after Rachel on nights when she had to be out. It was as simple as being her friend. Someone who'd known them before, and with whom, now that she was ready, she could talk about her loss as an equal, as a colleague in grief. No one else Samantha knew had lost anyone other than their parents. No one else had had death enter, so suddenly, their lives. Michael, however, had been there before her, felt and thought his way through its aftermath. And so she'd found herself looking to him for markers, for acknowledgement and consent. He made her feel normal and, perhaps more important, possible, a woman shaped by her daughter's loss, not defined by it. A woman who would still extract joy from life, not despite her grief but because of it.

Alongside his involvement with Samantha in the wake of her grief, Michael's own life continued to expand and gain momentum in the diminishment of his. In December, just before he travelled to Sussex to join Samantha and Rachel at Martha's for Christmas, he completed the first draft of *The Man Who Broke the Mirror.* It was shorter than he'd expected, and not the book he'd set out to write. The exploration of Oliver's thesis had become no more than a subplot, a hinterland to the account of his life over those two years that Michael followed him. A portrait of a man in emotional and intellectual extremis, a thinker and a drinker burning brightly as he burnt out.

The book was imperfect, and Michael knew when he submitted it to his agent that unlike what he'd said to Samantha about *BrotherHoods,* it was far from "cooked." But that it had been written at all was a personal achievement for him. It had begun, in those early months in his new flat, as no more than a muscle memory of routine. As a way of tricking his mind and his body into living again. There'd been no financial imperative for Michael to write it. *BrotherHoods* was still selling well in the U.S., and although he'd sworn not to touch it, there'd also been the compensation money and the payout from Caroline's insurance, too. In the writing of the book, however, Michael had rediscovered a rare peace in the age-old formation of experience into words. Not necessarily always in service to the broader story, but just in honour of certain minutes, even seconds. Past moments he was able to bring into being in a way he often wished he could in real life, but which he knew was possible only like this, at his desk, on the page.

Such was the solace Michael found in his writing that on delivering *The Man Who Broke the Mirror* he'd immediately embarked on a new project, even before his agent had finished reading the draft. This was to be a book closer to home, in every sense of the phrase. With his silent promise to Samantha and Rachel he had bonded himself to London, to their street and to his flat beside their home. So this is where he went looking for his next book, one in which he would immerse himself not just in the life of an individual subject, but in the stories of four houses and the families who'd lived in them. The houses had once all formed part of South Hill Drive, each built on a plot of land where a modern block of flats much like Michael's own now stood. It was a map in a local museum that had first brought these buildings to his attention. The map, of the Heath and its surrounding streets, was marked with a pattern of black dots, each marking the site where a bomb had fallen during the air raids in the Second World War. Instinctively, Michael had looked for his own street on the map, and then his own flat within it. A single black dot marked its position exactly. He looked at the other three dots scattered around the loop of South Hill Drive. All of them marked other modern blocks, built after the war and slotted into the sweeping curves of the original houses.

The research that such a book would require—hours at the Public Record Office in Kew, or trawling the local archives in Hampstead—promised Michael the scope and structure of a regular routine. But beyond this he couldn't say exactly why this project had appealed to him above others. He knew there were probably reasons for his preference that at this stage in his planning he'd rather not look at directly—a historical study of death from the air, an exploration of the relationship between a family and its home. But he knew, too, that the project's attraction was in some way associated with his penance, a private accumulation of gestures on the other side of those scales. And that it was about the nature of ghosted existence as well, the way Caroline had appeared to him in that bath. Or the way every time he passed the Nelsons' staircase he still saw, with such clarity, the detail of Lucy's falling. Every house in the street was layered with such existence, the spaces within them thick with lived human lives. But the four modern blocks of flats were haunted by entire buildings, not just people. Homes that had gone in a matter of seconds. And it was this, Michael sensed, that was drawing him. The prospect of re-creating the houses themselves as well as their inhabitants. Of rebuilding the very vessels and witnesses of the living that had occurred within them. As if, in having seen one ghost and created another, Michael was leaving himself no other choice than to immerse himself in an endeavour of multiple resurrection.

Beyond his writing, Michael's life was beginning to move on in other areas, too. He'd begun going for drinks with a group of other fencers after club nights in Highgate. There was a woman among them about whom Samantha often teased him. A divorcée in her early thirties who'd already made it known among her friends that if Michael was interested, she'd love to see more of him. Michael took Samantha's teasing and probing in good nature, but her comments were an effective sounding of his emotional state. The thought of what she suggested in her jokes still felt impossible to him. Caroline was too present, and perhaps, he sometimes wondered, always would be.

"I suppose," Samantha had said one night in the pub, as they'd waited for Rachel to finish at her drama group, "you lost her early, didn't you?"

"Early?" Michael said, although he already knew what she meant.

"Oh, I don't know," Samantha said, playing with her half-eaten salad. "I mean before you had a chance to ever feel bored with each other. Or pissed off."

"Maybe," Michael said.

"Oh, God, I'm sorry." She leant forward and laid a hand on his arm. "None of my business. It's just . . ."

"No, no," Michael reassured her. "You're probably right. It was all just starting, really."

Samantha sat back in her chair. "It's what she'd have wanted, you know. Eventually."

"What? For me to start sleeping with other women?" Michael couldn't keep the distaste from his voice.

"Yes," Samantha said. "Or, at least, to have someone. To not be on your own. Unless, of course, that's what makes you happy. Being on your own." She smiled and reached forward to give his arm a squeeze again. "But you mustn't be afraid of it, Michael. Or feel guilty."

They'd had that conversation more than a month ago, but nothing had changed since, and Michael was yet to make any attempt to find that person, or even begin a journey towards them. But he knew Samantha was right. Caroline would have wanted him to be with someone else. If he was honest, it was possible this might even have been true if she'd lived. He'd often wondered, if never aloud, for how long they'd have been together. He'd hoped forever, of course, but he'd never known for certain. Not for sure. Caroline had found solidity in him, in their marriage. She'd found a peace. But she wasn't naturally of an exclusive nature, and had always been more multiple than singular of character.

Despite his reluctance to enter another relationship, Michael still missed women physically. Recently, late at night after a day's work, he'd found himself typing "Hampstead + Escorts" into his search engine more than once, browsing the posed thumbnails of "Erika," "Giselle," and "Cindy," the lists of their services and rates in bold below each of them. But his desire had never taken him as far as the contact email or phone number, and although he'd told himself that hiring one of these girls would be preferable to risking the feelings of a longer-term partner, he'd always ended up closing his laptop and walking away from his desk.

Instinctively, Michael felt that if he were ever to start again with another woman, then it would have to happen elsewhere, beyond London. Already, despite his resolve to be governed by the lives of Samantha and Rachel, the prospect of a move was increasingly seductive. Once the new book was done. Once he knew Samantha and Rachel were further along their recovery. The thought of it, when he allowed it to, excited him. He was grateful to Peter for his flat, but it had always been intended as a holding pattern. And soon, he could feel it, he'd be ready to leave. The guilt, the pain of what had happened here, he would always own. But a move, he knew, would alter the texture of that pain, the nature of its ache. Perhaps to somewhere on the continent, or back to New York. There was something about the fabric of the city that would suit his situation. Its streets, breathing with single lives, were fed by their hungers. Once there, having changed the geography of his living, then Michael could imagine perhaps finding someone: a woman from elsewhere who, having altered her own landscape, might be ready to accept someone like him with whom to share it.

CHAPTER
TWENTY

THE GALLERY WAS crowded, so Michael saw Josh only when he'd already been at Samantha's private view for more than an hour. He was standing in a far corner, talking animatedly to a younger couple, occasionally pointing at the framed print beside them. He was tanned and had lost weight, but still looked much older than when Michael had last seen him at close quarters. The grey that had always seeded his hair had spread, and his face was more lined than Michael remembered. The collar of his shirt was worn on one side, its sleeves rolled. His forearms, Michael noticed, were crosshatched with cuts and scratches.

—

The gallery was owned by a friend of Sebastian's, the director for whom Samantha worked as a PA. It was a small, two-roomed space on a mostly residential street beyond Flask Walk. Originally a florist's, it now housed four or five temporary exhibitions a year. It was Michael who'd persuaded Samantha to show her employer some of her prints, but Sebastian who'd done the rest. A week later the gallery owner, Emmanuel, had written to her. Could he exhibit

Samantha's work? Only for a couple of weeks at first, but if it sold, then maybe longer.

With the arrival of Emmanuel's email, Samantha's previous confidence in her work evaporated. She told Michael it was too soon, that she still had over a year to go with her MA. That the work wasn't good enough.

"What happened to the only-half-cooked idea?" Michael asked her.

"Very funny," she'd said, a spread of her prints covering the dining table. Their family portrait still hung above it, and as she slid the photographs over one another her younger self looked over her shoulder, Lucy on her knee, Rachel sitting on Josh's lap beside her.

"Seriously, though," she'd said, running a hand through her hair. "How am I meant to choose? He said he could hang twenty-five at most. Maybe thirty at a push."

She'd been taking her pond photos for over eight months by then. Over 240 images, all from the same position, at the same time of day.

Michael, who'd been leaning against the kitchen island, came to sit opposite her. "I'll help," he said, spreading the prints and turning them round so he could see them.

"Really?" she said. "God, that would be amazing."

"I wouldn't get too excited," Michael said. "I'm no expert."

"Yes, you are," she countered, as Michael placed a winter scene next to a morning in March. "It's meant to be what you're good at, isn't it? Finding the story?"

Since that evening, Michael had assisted Samantha with other elements of the exhibition, too. Bringing the framed prints back to her house, choosing their positions in the gallery, suggesting a title for the show: *And Again.* Earlier that evening, forgoing his fencing-club night, he'd shared a cab over to the gallery with her and Rachel, its floor filled with boxes of wine, glasses, and fruit juice. Samantha had been quiet on the journey, her nerves drying up her talk. "Don't worry, Mummy," Rachel had said as they'd driven up alongside the Heath, the boxed glasses chattering at their feet. "They'll like you, I know they will."

—

Moving away from the drinks table where he'd been serving, Michael began edging through the crowd towards Josh. He'd barely seen him since the night they'd spoken over the hedge. After moving out, Josh had remained on the periphery of Samantha and Rachel's lives. He saw his daughter regularly, and he kept in touch with Samantha. But it was one of Michael's most persistent regrets that Josh had chosen to keep him at a greater distance. Twice now, Michael had seen him on the Heath as he'd walked back from his fencing lesson. Too far away to call, but close enough to make each other out. Neither time had Josh made any attempt to approach him. And somehow Michael had known Josh hadn't wanted him to go towards him, either. So he'd walked on instead, along his usual route, aware of Josh's eyes following him.

Samantha, when Michael asked her, couldn't say why Josh had retreated from him. "Who knows?" she'd said, when he pressed her on it one night. "It's his way, I guess, of coping." She was stacking plates into a cupboard, reaching on tiptoe to complete the pile. "But it isn't just you, you know? He's become more solitary in general. He hardly ever sees anyone." She turned round to rest against the counter. "I don't know," she said and sighed. "He'll come round. He just needs time, I suppose." She picked up another stack of plates. "We all do."

If Samantha had surprised Michael with the keeping of her promises, with her growth after Lucy's death, then she, in turn, had been wrong-footed by Josh's reaction to losing his job. At first, he'd done nothing; rarely leaving his flat as if he'd given himself completely to inertia. The only times Samantha had seen him was when he'd come to take Rachel for the day. Michael would occasionally glimpse him coming up the street for these appointments, unshaven, wearing tracksuit bottoms or creased jeans, like the forgotten father of the man Michael had first met when he'd moved in. Samantha became worried about his state of mind. She began to wonder if she should let Rachel go with him alone.

But then, within a few weeks, he'd changed. He'd asked to meet Samantha for a coffee. When they did, he'd told her he'd decided not to reenter banking for a while, but to take a break and do something different. "The whole thing's going downhill fast, anyway," he'd said. "And it's only going to carry on, too, before it ever picks up. There's enough money, for a while, at least. So don't worry, nothing will change on that front. But, yeah, I thought I'd stay out of it for a bit. Get some space." He'd looked down at his cup, then spread his hands, palms up. "I just wanted you to know," he'd said, as if admitting a new relationship.

Before they left the café, he'd asked Samantha not to file for a divorce. The subject had crossed her mind, but only in the abstract. It was all too soon. She was still processing so much of what had happened. She was still grieving. "Of course not, Josh," she'd said. "What makes you think I would?"

"I don't know. Moving out. Everything that's . . ."

She'd taken his hand. "You know what we said. Let's give it time. All of it."

He'd looked her in the eye, and she'd seen he was scared. Either of what she might do or of what he might say. "Just get yourself together," she'd said, squeezing his fingers. "For Rachel, at least."

Josh had seen the advert in the local newsagents, between the rooms for rent and the mother and baby yoga sessions. Three mornings a week, volunteering with a National Trust gardener at two of their properties in Hampstead: Number Two Willow Road, a 1930s modernist home, and Fenton House, a seventeenth-century merchant's house crowning the hill above Hampstead Village.

For a couple of months, as autumn gave way to winter, those three mornings came to define Josh's weeks. Clearing bamboo, weeds, and rubble at Willow Road, or pruning the apple trees, their branches furred with frost, at Fenton House. He was unskilled but took to the work well. His mind, he realised, had been looking for this: hours outdoors in which it could wander beyond the repetition of his jobs. Nathan, the National Trust gardener, was a quiet man and was content, once he knew Josh could be trusted, to set him going, then leave him alone. The other volunteers tended to come and go frequently. They were actors between jobs, gap-year students, or just people fulfilling the hours demanded by another organisation—the Duke of Edinburgh Award, community service. Once these were completed, Nathan never saw them again. But Josh proved to be constant, a regular. Often, on finishing a shift he'd stay on, especially in Fenton House, sitting on one of the benches in the walled garden, breathing in the iron scent of freshly turned soil, or listening to the birdsong. Which was why, when Josh applied for a vacancy with one of the conservation teams on the Heath, Nathan had supported him so enthusiastically. Because in all his years of gardening, never before had he met a man who so clearly needed to feel the earth again, in whom the exertion of physical work had so plainly brought peace, and with it, pleasure.

"I know, ironic, isn't it?" Samantha had said when she'd told Michael. They'd been in her garden, weeding and dividing clumps of perennials. "He's working for the City again. It's like he can't bloody escape them."

"The City?" Michael said. "How do you mean?"

"Well, they own it, don't they?" Samantha cleared a strand of hair from her face and sat back on her heels. "The Heath," she'd said, wiping her forehead with the top of her wrist. "Or at least the Corporation of London does, which in my book is pretty much the same thing." She threw a handful of weeds onto the pile between them. "So, yeah," she'd said, returning to her work. "He's on the payroll again."

For a moment neither of them had spoken. There was just

the tearing sound of the weeds being uprooted, the barking of dogs from the Heath.

"But it's working for him," Samantha had said after a while. Michael's mind had drifted and at first he didn't know what she was talking about. He'd looked over at her, but she was focused on her work, pulling at the weeds with short, steady tugs. "I even think it makes him happy," she said, throwing another clump onto the pile.

—

As Michael parted the bodies in the gallery before him, gently touching backs and shoulders as he pressed forward, Josh, looking up from his conversation, saw him approaching. Michael managed to free a hand and raise it, nodding over the expansive hair of a blonde woman between them. Josh didn't acknowledge the greeting, but just looked back at him, a disturbance in his eyes. His expression stopped Michael in the middle of the crowd. Not because it had been so unexpected, but because it was a look of such long-held animosity, not a sudden aversion. A look of knowledge, not question.

Michael was about to continue towards him when a whine of feedback punctuated Emmanuel's stepping up to a microphone to ask the crowd for quiet. The heads around Michael all turned in the direction of his amplified voice. As Michael did the same, he glanced over at Josh again. He, too, was looking towards the microphone now. He looked calm, smiling at Emmanuel's opening jokes. So perhaps Michael had been wrong. Perhaps his guilt was making him see things and fear things that weren't to be seen or to be feared. He took a drink from his glass and, as Samantha stepped up to speak, tried to focus on what she had to say.

The speeches were short. Samantha thanked her course tutors, Sebastian, the owner of the gallery. And she thanked Michael, too, for his help, and Rachel as well, for hers, raising her glass to each of them in the crowd. She spoke briefly about how the photos on these walls had been found as the result of a loss. But she said nothing else about Lucy or the specifics of her own journey towards those early minutes of the day, waiting to discover what its light would deliver. When she finished speaking and backed away from the microphone there was applause, a few whoops from her fellow students, and then Emmanuel stepped up again to encourage everyone to drink and, if they could, buy one of Samantha's prints.

Over a final smattering of applause, the crowd began to move again, towards the drinks or to view the work. Michael looked for Josh where he'd last seen him. But he wasn't there. He glanced over the rest of the room, then pushed his way through to the second space. Josh was nowhere to be seen in there, either. Michael was aware of his heart racing. He realised he had to talk to him. He had to know why he'd been keeping his distance. Why he'd looked at him that way across the gallery.

Squeezing himself back through the crowd, he made his way outside into the cool of the night. There were three smokers on the pavement, but none of them was Josh. He looked up the lamp-lit street, a spring mist gathering about the rooftops. It was empty. Josh had gone.

Michael thought about walking up Flask Walk, trying to catch up with him. But it was no good. He could just have easily turned the other way and could already be walking across the Heath, or along any one of the surrounding streets.

Michael turned back to the windows of the gallery, fogged by the crowded bodies inside. Someone wiped a sleeve across a pane, swiping an arc of clear glass. Michael peered through it, just in case he'd missed him in there. But there was only the drinking and talking crowd, and at its centre Samantha, flushed with her success, her images of the pond hung around her, its stilled waters a silent witness to everything Michael had done.

CHAPTER
TWENTY-ONE

"I SOLD SIX! Can you believe it? Six!"

The private view had rolled on to a nearby pub, and then again for a nightcap at Sebastian's house. Now Michael and Samantha were back in her kitchen in South Hill Drive. Samantha was drunk. But she was also elated. The exhibition had opened well. There had been praise, attention. She looked years younger.

"Sebastian said that hardly ever happens," she said, pouring another shot of whisky into her glass. "Not on the first night."

"It's great," Michael said. "But I'm not surprised. Of course people want them. They're . . ." He picked up one of the unselected prints, still on the dining table. "Well, they're calming, aren't they?" he said. "And they reveal more with each looking."

"Oh, shut up!" Samantha said, dropping into one of the armchairs in the conservatory. "You're always so bloody nice to me. Last drop?" She held the whisky bottle towards him.

"You're right," Michael said, sitting down opposite and holding out his glass. "They're pretty ordinary, really, and most people there couldn't tell the difference between a decent image and crap, anyway."

"Steady," Samantha said, mocking a hurt expression as she poured out the last of the whisky. "Don't go too far."

Michael raised his glass. "Congratulations," he said. "You deserve it."

They both drank, Samantha releasing a deep breath on swallowing. Tipping her head back against the chair, she closed her eyes.

Michael wanted to ask her about Josh. Had she spoken with him? What had he said? Why had he left? But now wasn't the time. She was infused with her present and her future. She didn't want to talk of the past. Not now, when this was all so fragile, so passing.

"I've been thinking," she said, her eyes still closed. Her speech was slow, liquid. "This house. It's way too big for just Rachel and me. We rattle around in here. We don't even ever go up to the top floor." She opened her eyes and stared at the ceiling for a moment, then brought her head forward to look at him. Her expression was serious, but then a slow smile spread across her lips, followed by a girlish shake of her head. She looked down, away from him.

"I don't know, you might not want to," she said. "But it's crazy. I mean, you renting that place next door and us with all this space. I just wanted you to know." She got up, suddenly more business-like, nervous. "If you wanted to," she said, taking their glasses over to the sink, "you could rent here instead." She turned and leant against the counter, looking back at him. "The top floor. There's a study, a bedroom."

Michael stood and went over to her. "Thank you," he said, taking her by both shoulders. She looked vulnerable, exposed. "That's such a kind offer. But . . ."

She broke away from him, turning to the sink and running a tap to wash the glasses. "Christ, Michael," she said, sounding cross. "I didn't mean like that. I just thought it would make sense, that's all."

"I know," he said. "And I mean it. It is a kind offer. And good to know, too. Really, thank you."

"Well, it's there if you want it. That's all." As she took off her watch, Samantha looked at its face. "Jesus," she said. "Is that the time?"

Michael looked at his own. It was nearly two o'clock. "Sign of a good night, I guess," he said.

Samantha turned from the sink to face him again. She was frowning, as if trying to work out how they'd got here, to this late hour, this position. Michael could see she was coming down from the night's excitement. A brief cloud of longing passed through her expression. For what? he wondered. For before all this? For her previous life, however imperfect, before she'd had to create this one in the wake of her daughter's death?

"I should get to bed," she said eventually, crossing the kitchen to turn off the lamps in the conservatory. "Rachel's got a hockey match tomorrow. Christ, no, today. All the way over in bloody Ealing."

"Well," Michael said, picking his jacket off the back of a chair. "Congratulations again. You did really well tonight."

"Thanks," Samantha said, looking out at the darkness beyond the glass. When she turned back to him, her expression had softened. "And for all your help, too," she said, smiling. "Really. Thank you, Michael."

—

As Michael got undressed for bed that night, he knew he had to tell Samantha. At some point, she would have to know. It couldn't be avoided. For her as well as for him. Walking down her hallway to the front door, after her offer, passing Lucy's portrait of him, it had almost crushed Michael completely. As if he'd been walking, with every step, into a deeper and deeper depth. Whatever the damage it would do, to the opening of her new life, to his, to Rachel, he had to tell Samantha the truth. If he didn't, his knowledge of those minutes he'd spent in her house before Lucy died would continue to suck the goodness from every second they spent together.

But then, once she knew, there would be no more seconds together. This he also had to acknowledge. Another plank of Samantha's life would have been swept from under her. Once the true minutes of that Saturday afternoon were exposed, she'd never want to see him again. He would have perverted the course of justice. She would tell the police. He would have to leave. But still, as he got into bed, the lamplight from the Heath thrown faint against the walls of his bedroom, Michael knew it was only a matter of time. He couldn't keep those minutes to himself much longer. He had to cut them out, like a tumour, and the only way to do that was in their telling.

CHAPTER
TWENTY-TWO

THE VIDEOCASSETTE WAS on a high shelf in the groundsman's office, wedged with a pile of others between a stack of *Top Gear* magazines and a tool box filled with screws, nuts, and bolts. A manual for a power drill was resting on top of it. With all the other boxes and tools in the room it was unlikely Josh would have found it so easily, had it not been for a date on its spine written in black marker. **07/06/08.** Seeing those numbers, in that order, was like hearing his name rise clear above the hum of a bar for Josh, or seeing your child's face in a crowded station. Even among the clutter of that small office, it was a date that sang out to him. A date he'd never forget, branded as it was within him as the date of Lucy's death. The date on which, for all of them, everything had changed.

Josh had been working with the Heath conservation and maintenance team since the start of the year. There were usually just three of them, sometimes more on the bigger jobs, coasting their pickup along the Heath's paths, its hazard lights blinking and its wire cage filled with branches, off-cuts and sacks of leaves. When he could, Josh started as early as possible, and it was often he who'd unlock their storage shed, or who could be seen, an hour before the shift, drinking a coffee on one of the benches on Parliament Hill. The work had opened him up. He'd come to learn the touch of different winds and breezes, to see oncoming rain in a texture of light. Standing from his bench to start his day, Josh would glance over at the distant city towers as he dropped his empty coffee cup into a bin and feel like he'd escaped. As if he were a survivor who'd been thrown a lifeline on which he was only just now gaining a firmer grip.

During his working week on the Heath, Josh was able to observe his family from afar. And then again at closer quarters when he saw them on the weekends. He'd become more comfortable with the silences he shared with Rachel, and calmer, too, about the woman he was witnessing Samantha become. But hanging over it all was still the question of Michael. The question of who he was and of what he wanted; of the soil on the landing and of where he'd been during those few minutes on the Seventh of June 2008.

More than once Josh had considered telling Samantha the truth, confessing to her that he hadn't been in the house when Lucy fell. But if he ever hoped to get her and his daughter back, then he knew this was impossible. And, he told himself, that person had been another Josh, anyway, another man, and he couldn't let him ruin the chances of who he was now, of who he wanted to become.

But Josh couldn't let Michael ruin his chances either. As long as he was close to Samantha and Rachel, as long as he was there, living next to them, Josh knew there'd never be space to make them his again, and him theirs. Not while there was still so much he didn't know about Michael and what had happened that day. He'd told Slater he'd been at his fencing lesson. That's what she'd told Josh when she'd talked him through all his neighbours' statements. At the time he'd listened with only his own self-interest in mind. Had any of them seen him leave the house? Had any of them seen him return? But none, according to Slater, had. So Josh just felt relief when Michael's statement had been added to those of the others on the street.

But now he felt only suspicion. How did Slater know Michael was at his lesson when Lucy fell? Had she checked with his instructor? Had he been seen walking there across the Heath? Josh had wanted to find the card she'd left him and call her and ask her. But he knew he couldn't. The way she'd questioned him, the manner in which they'd all treated him. He knew she suspected him, sensed his lies at the edges of his story. So he couldn't provoke her to look any closer than she already had.

No, if Josh wanted to corroborate Michael's story, then he would have to do so himself. If it was true, then he could let go of his suspicion. But if it was not, then—then he didn't know what he would do. But at least he would know. At least he'd be able to extinguish the agonies of his uncertainty, defuse some of the unforgiving questions that still haunted him about what had happened to his daughter.

After that evening they'd spoken over the hedge, Josh, whenever he could, began watching Michael. He wanted to understand him, to discover what he wanted. Was it Samantha? Is that why he was spending so much time with her? Was she what this was all about? Josh couldn't be sure, not without knowing more about Michael. So he watched him. He became familiar with the times his bathroom light came on in the morning, and his study light turned off at night. He followed him, at a distance, to his favourite cafés, or to the archives of the local museum. Just the other week he'd watched from up the street as Michael had helped Samantha carry her prints from the framer's, loading them into the back of his old Volvo. And he'd watched, too, as Michael had walked to his fencing club on a Thursday, then taken the same route across the Heath for his lessons on a Saturday. Which is when Josh had first seen the Heath's conservation team unloading tools from a storage shed at the school.

It was a shed they shared, it seemed, with the school's caretaker, in whose office they also took their breaks when working on the Highgate side of the Heath. On that same afternoon Josh had seen them at the school he'd also noticed the security camera angled above the entrance to its sports hall. Had Slater viewed the tape from this camera on the day Lucy fell? Had she seen, for sure, Michael enter the building? But, more important, Josh had wanted to know as he'd walked back across the Heath to his flat, how might he find a way to see the tape himself? How might he witness, with his own eyes but without raising the suspicions of Slater, the truth of Michael's story?

Josh had told Samantha it was Nathan, the gardener at Willow Road, who'd put him forward for the job with the Hampstead Heath team. But that had been a lie. Instead, he'd applied directly, using Nathan as a reference and an old City connection on the corporation's board to push it through. Josh began working with them the following month, but he'd known he'd have to be patient, that there were no guarantees. He was acting purely on speculation. But then wasn't that what he'd always done, and what he'd always been so good at with Lehman's? Speculating, betting on outcomes, playing a waiting game, then striking when the opportunity came.

In time, his patience won out. It was early in April when Josh and his team were sent to cut back the rhododendrons on the Highgate side of the Heath. The area they were working edged the grounds of the school, and as Josh had seen the year before, to save themselves the daily trip across the Heath, they borrowed one of the school caretaker's storage sheds while they were there.

Jim, the caretaker, was a widower in his early sixties, talkative and sociable. As well as caretaking the school, he performed groundsman duties for the leisure centre. It was the Easter holidays, and the school was empty. So Jim was more than pleased to offer the team the use of his office again. To make teas and coffees, get out of the rain, or just to take the weight off their feet for a few minutes in one of his broken-down armchairs.

—

Josh was sitting in one of these armchairs, slung back in its spongy springs, when he'd first seen the videocassette. Once he had, he'd been unable to take his eyes off it. He'd assumed, having first got to know Jim, he'd then have had to find a way to steer him onto the subject of the school's security cameras, and then again on to where their footage might be kept. Beyond that he'd had no other plan about how to get hold of the footage for himself. So to see a tape above him, written with that date, it almost seemed like a bait, as if someone was setting him a trap.

He looked around the rest of the room, on the other shelves, for other cassettes. But there were none. Just this crooked pile on the shelf above him, each spine written with a date. While Jim talked on—about his time as a semi-pro footballer, his grandkids—that top tape seemed to gather a luminescence at the edges of Josh's vision, its black numbers burning into his mind.

As Josh and his colleagues finished up, the three of them putting their mugs in the sink, Josh nodded at the shelf. "Those tapes," he'd asked Jim. "What are they?"

Jim looked up at the shelf, squinting, as if he hadn't considered that part of his office for a while. Josh swallowed. He was nervous. He felt he should have given some kind of explanation for his question. The other members of his team had already left the room. "The date on that top one," he'd said, taking off his glasses to clean them on his shirt. "Seventh of June. It's my daughter's birthday."

"Oh!" Jim nodded, seeing them. "Those. Yeah, they're old security tapes. CCTV. The police had them for a while. Can't remember why. We'd switched the whole system by the time they came back." He looked back at Josh. "All digital now, see? More cameras, too. Isn't a metre of this bloody place that isn't covered."

Josh nodded. "Right. Well, better safe than sorry, I guess." He went towards the door. "Thanks for the tea, Jim," he said as he left.

"How old is she?" Jim called from inside. Josh looked back into the room. "Your daughter," Jim said. "How old is she?"

"Four," Josh replied, his knuckles white on the door frame. "She's four."

"Lovely age," Jim said, smiling from his desk. "Lovely age."

—

Josh waited until their last day working alongside the school before he took the cassette. Jim wasn't going anywhere, so he'd had to ask him about the settings on one of the mowers he had parked up outside to get him to leave. Once they were at the mower, Josh patted at his pockets. "Shit," he said. "My phone. Won't be a sec."

Jogging back to the office, he'd pulled out Jim's chair, stood on it, and reached up for the cassette, slipping it into the back of his shorts. Its spine, he saw, as he took it off the shelf, was thick with other dates, layered-on stickers reaching back through weeks and months.

Josh was back with Jim in less than a minute. As Jim talked him through the mower's operation he'd tried to listen, but his mind was already rushing through possibilities. It could be nothing. There was no reason, other than the date, that the police hadn't requested the tape for another investigation entirely. But then, he'd told himself, what were the chances of that? This was, after all, where Michael had said he'd been. That must be why they took it. But surely if there'd been anything in it, then wouldn't Slater have noticed? Wouldn't she have pulled Michael in? But still, Josh had been waiting for months, for something more than just a sense or a few crumbs of once-damp soil. So he had to see it. He had to know.

He bought the TV the following day, from a Cash Converters on the Finchley Road. It was an old silver portable with a VHS player embedded under the screen. "I've got loads of films for that, too," the checkout clerk told him as he paid. "There's some great eighties porn. Classic hairstyles." Josh told him he was good, thanks. He just wanted the TV. That was all he needed.

The image quality was poor. Black-and-white, with the occasional jump and shiver in the image. But it was clear enough. An elevated view of the sliding doors at the entrance to the sports hall. At first Josh began viewing it in real time, watching as a shard of sunlight slid across the floor, stretching the shadows of the door's lettering. But then, remembering the time of Michael's lessons, he'd pressed fast-forward, sending the counter in the corner of the screen climbing through the hours of the day. In jerky speed, a cleaner mopped the tiles, a pigeon hopped in, got trapped, then flew out. Every hour or so Jim would appear, carrying a different tool each time. Then, for several accelerated hours, the view remained empty. Just the municipal floor, the edge of a notice board and the encroaching shadow of a branch beyond the glass doors.

As the counter reached three o'clock, then three-fifteen, Josh slowed the tape to real time again. He didn't care how long it would take. He just didn't want to miss anything. He wanted to be sure. Michael's lesson had been at four o'clock. It always was. But if he didn't arrive, or if he was late, then maybe, just maybe that would be enough. So with the TV propped on the coffee table, his elbows on his knees and his fists under his chin, Josh watched the empty entrance, glued to the filmed minutes in front of him. As the counter reached three-twenty he felt a stab of guilt. It must have been around then, in the world on the screen, that he'd left his house by the front door. He tried to focus, to forget, as the minutes continued their steady climb, the moment he'd abandoned his daughter, and what else had followed.

All through the next half-hour, there was nothing. Three-fifty-nine. Four o'clock. The view remained unchanged, empty except for than the shadow of the branch edging closer to the door. Josh could feel his pulse quickening. With every second of Michael's absence from the screen the prospect of proof was closer to hand. Perhaps Slater had taken the tapes but then never watched them. Perhaps, once the DCI had declared there was no case, they'd just sat in a storage cupboard for months before eventually being returned to the school.

But then, at the edge of the frame, another shadow began encroaching fast upon the shadow of the branch. Within a few seconds it had happened. The doors slid open and Michael, wearing shorts and a T-shirt, his fencing bag slung over his shoulder, entered the building and walked across the screen, clearing its frame in just four strides.

Josh paused the tape, Michael's exiting right foot still frozen on the far left of the screen. He pressed the rewind button, sending him back across the entrance and out the doors. Then he pressed play again, watching as closely as he could. Michael repeated his entrance. Josh's breath was shortening. Once Michael had cleared the frame he immediately rewound the tape and pressed play again, but this time with his finger hovering over the pause button too. In this way, switching between play and pause, Josh watched as Michael walked across the screen in slow motion. Which is when he knew there was no doubt. It was the jerk in his shoulder that betrayed him, the shortened stride as if his right leg was weighted. Michael was limping. There were only four of his strides in frame, but they were enough. Josh had walked beside that limp across the Heath many times. But only ever at the beginning of their jogs, when Michael's right calf was still cramped.

He paused the tape again. Leaning in to the screen, he tried to make out Michael's expression. But he couldn't. His face was a grey blur. It didn't matter. Josh knew. That was all that mattered. He finally knew. However Michael had got to the school that day, he hadn't, as he'd claimed in his statement to Slater, walked there.

CHAPTER
TWENTY-THREE

"MICHAEL."

Michael was at the edge of the clearing when he heard Josh call his name. It was a warm evening towards the end of April, two days after they'd seen each other at Samantha's private view. Just minutes earlier, pausing on his way home from a fencing lesson, Michael had been standing alone at the clearing's centre, looking up at a flight of house martins darting for insects in the fading light. The trees of the South Wood were coming into leaf all around him. The white candles of the horse chestnuts already shone bright against the darker shades of foliage and bark.

The only time Josh had ever called Michael by his full name was when he'd introduced him to other guests at that first party. Otherwise he'd always been "Mike" to Josh. At times, even "Mikey." But never Michael.

He turned, slowly. Josh was standing at the far end of the clearing. He wore his Corporation of London uniform: a pair of dark combat trousers and a dark green polo shirt bearing the corporation's crest on his chest. Michael was relieved to see he held nothing in his hands. He wondered how long Josh had been watching him.

"Josh," he said. "I didn't hear you."

"You were in my house," Josh said, not moving. "That day. You were in my house."

Michael felt the air leave his lungs as if he'd been plunged underwater. He'd known as soon as he'd seen Josh standing there. As soon as he'd heard him say his name. But it was still a shock, to hear the words, to hear him state them so baldly. He thought for a moment about trying to pretend he didn't know what Josh was talking about. But he knew it was no use. His expression would have already told Josh all he needed to know. So, instead, Michael completed the dismantling of their false minutes.

"And you weren't," he said.

Josh remained motionless. His hands were balled into fists. He said nothing, leaving Michael's words to fall in the air between them. Michael was about to speak again when Josh started walking towards him. "Why?" he said, his jaw tense, the tendons showing on his neck. His voice was hoarse, a strained whisper. "Why? That's all I want to know. Why did you do it, you fucking bastard?"

Michael backed away a couple of paces, his hands held out to appease Josh. "I didn't," he said. "I was there, but I didn't do anything."

Josh stopped advancing. "I should kill you," he said. His eyes were welling. Michael could see the mix of rage and grief swelling through his body. "I should kill you now."

"Josh, please," Michael said. "You've got to listen to me. You're right, I was in your house. I was there." He paused. He had to say it. "I saw her fall."

Josh's face began to twitch with suppressed tears.

"But it was an accident." Michael continued. "I swear. An accident."

Josh was upon him before Michael had time to move. Somehow he breached the distance between them in a single stride and, grabbing at Michael's T-shirt, pushed him backwards towards the fence. Michael gripped his wrists and wrenched them away, pushing Josh off him at the same time. "Josh!" he shouted, backing farther off, his fencing bag falling to the ground. "For Christ's sake, just listen. Please!"

Josh was breathing heavily. He looked as if he might come at him again, but then, as quickly as he'd launched his attack, his body softened. "Just tell me why," he said again, quietly.

So Michael did.

He described how he'd come round that day, looking for his screwdriver. He hated saying the word. It sounded so trivial, so insignificant, to have caused such pain. But that, he told Josh, was why he'd been there. Then Michael tried, as best he could, to explain about his concerns. He'd found the back door open. He'd wanted to make sure they hadn't been burgled. And then he tried to tell him about Caroline too. But it was too much for Josh. Or too little.

"A ghost? A fucking ghost?" he shouted at Michael. "Is that what you're fucking telling me? You killed my daughter because you thought you saw a ghost?"

"No!" Michael shouted back. He could feel his own anger rising. If Josh had been there, if he'd just stayed at home instead of going to screw Maddy. If he'd just been there, then none of this would have happened. "Not a ghost," Michael said. "Just her. You have to understand. It was all so soon. I'd had those fucking letters . . . It was all—" He broke off and looked at Josh. As if to say, *We've both done this, both of us.* We are both to blame.

"Then what?" Josh said.

There was a bench to the side of the clearing. Michael went and sat on it. With his head in his hands, he told Josh how Lucy had appeared from nowhere, how he'd tried to catch her but he'd failed, and had watched her fall instead.

"And then," Josh said, pacing in front of Michael, "you left. You fucking left."

"Yes," Michael said, staring at the ground. "I left. And I wish with all my life I hadn't." He paused, looking up at Josh. "But then so did you." Josh turned and looked down at him. "You left, too," Michael said. "You left. And if you hadn't . . ."

"All right!" Josh said, cutting his hand through the air. He walked away from Michael. The ground within the clearing's fence was bare and tired, patches of short grass between the earth. But beyond it, beyond Josh, Michael could see swathes of bluebells carpeting the woodland floor. Beyond the fence there was life. Michael wanted to be out there, among those bluebells. He wanted for all of this to be over.

Josh turned back to him. He looked exhausted. There was so much Michael wanted to ask him. Why had he left the house? Was it really for Maddy? And why then, leaving Lucy alone? But he saw Josh was not to be pressed. He was like a charged mine, sensitive to the slightest of pressures. But he had to keep him talking. Michael knew that, too. So he asked him, instead, how he knew. How had he found out he'd been in the house?

Josh's answer was short, staccato, his mind engaged elsewhere, battling competing impulses of revenge and survival. Michael stayed on the bench while he talked, nodding as Josh told him about the soil, the tape, his betraying limp. When he'd finished, Michael knew there was only one question left for them to answer.

"What do you want to do?" Michael said. "Now you know."

Josh was frowning at him, staring. He nodded, slowly. "You have to leave," he said. "Samantha and Rachel. You have to leave them. The street, London. You have to go. Now."

"Go?" Michael said. But he knew Josh was right. They couldn't continue like this. "And what do I tell them?" he said. "I can't just disappear. They'll be suspicious. They'll call the police."

Josh laughed. "The police? Yeah, as if they'd be of any fucking use!"

"It's lucky for you they weren't," Michael snapped. Josh stepped towards him. "And me," Michael said, raising a conciliatory hand. "And for me."

"Tell them whatever you want," Josh said, turning away again. He was pacing back and forth, back and forth, as if trying to recall some lost instinctive movement. "You're the fucking writer, aren't you?"

Michael got off the bench and went to pick up his fencing bag. "If I go," he said, "will you tell Samantha?"

Josh looked at him as if he'd spoken in a foreign language. "And tell her I wasn't there?" He shook his head. "No. But," he said, pointing at Michael, "if you come back. If you write to them, or call them. I will. I swear. I'd rather bring us both down than have you fucking anywhere near them."

Michael looked at Josh. He was a new man. A man transfigured by loss, by anger. His cheeks were sunken, his eyes both alive and dead. A man with nothing and everything left to lose.

"Tonight," Josh said, dropping his hand. "You have to leave tonight."

CHAPTER
TWENTY-FOUR

IT IS EARLY evening in Manhattan, at the beginning of the Easter weekend. The sun is just an hour from setting over the New Jersey skyline. In a few minutes the red Colgate sign will light up over the Hudson and Statue of Liberty tourist boats will unfurl their sails to steer by the wind towards the mouth of the estuary.

Michael is sitting on a bench beside the river, on a pier across the highway from West Twenty-Sixth. He is at the pier's end, beside a large steel waterwheel that is turning, water and light falling from its paddles. On one side of him a young woman in shorts, vest, and trainers is stretching her hamstrings, a low fizz leaking from her headphones. On the other, a Mexican couple is sitting on a bench, rocking their baby in its buggy. From farther down the river, at the next pier, Michael can hear music playing from The Frying Pan, a floating bar on a decommissioned fireboat. Together with the pulse of the traffic behind him and the sound of the water falling from the wheel, its faint beat completes a soundscape he's come to think of as calming. Manhattan is never quiet, but this, whenever he has needed to find space, to think, to remember, to capture a sense of quiet if not quiet itself, is where he comes.

It's been almost a year since Michael left London. The note he wrote to Samantha on returning from the Heath that day was short and to the point. He told her that leaving was simply something he had to do. That he knew he should say good-bye to her, to Rachel, but he couldn't bring himself to say those words with them standing before him. The note had made him seem weak and selfish. He knew Samantha would think it a reaction to her offer for him to move into the house. It would anger her. She would think herself a bad judge of character. One day, when Rachel was old enough, she'd tell her to forget him or, at best, forgive him for being so damaged and for passing on that damage in hurting them.

His own hurt is gradually healing. The last letter he received from Daniel, like all of them sent via his publishers, had made it clear it would be just that. The last letter. He had given Michael everything he could. They both needed to move on, he'd said, so he would not be writing to him again. In the same letter he'd told Michael he'd recently moved back east, that Cathy had returned with the girls to upstate New York and he'd decided to follow them. He hoped, he'd written, that one day he might move back in with them. Until then he'd found a cabin to rent outside Hudson and a job at a local organic distributor. Twice a week he drove into Manhattan, delivering local farmers' produce to downtown delis and restaurants.

Michael often thought how strange this was, that twice a week the two of them were in the same city, on the same streets. That over these past months, unknown to either of them, maybe they'd already shared a sidewalk, or a bench like this. Although Michael had searched for Daniel more than once online, he'd never found an image, so he'd never know if they had. Even now, Daniel might be driving down the highway behind him in his truck, leaning his elbow out the window. If, while stopped at a red light perhaps, he were to glance to his right, then he'd see Michael sitting at the end of the pier. A tall man silhouetted beside the turning wheel, looking over the glimmering waters as he presses play on a Dictaphone to listen to the voice of his dead wife, killed by a "fire and forget" missile on a mountain in Pakistan.

Guess who's upstairs? Caroline whispers to Michael from across the years. *Want to come and join me?*

But then Daniel wouldn't know either. So as the lights changed to green he'd look away from the pier and drive on into the city, unaware he'd just seen the man to whose life he'd brought death, and who in turn had brought death to the lives of others.

—

Michael listened to Caroline twice more, then removed his headphones and put the Dictaphone back in his pocket. He rationed himself such listening now. Just as he rationed his looking: at photographs, her news reports on YouTube, a video they'd taken on their first night together beside the fire in Coed y Bryn.

Rising from the bench he turns from the river and begins his walk home. It is a short walk, down along the Hudson then turning left into the streets of the Village. His apartment is on the top floor of a five-storey walk-up. It has a fire escape that looks onto trees, a desk beside a window, a bedroom in which he has hung one of Samantha's prints of the pond. So he might remember, he supposes, or never forget.

It is beside that pond that Michael always imagines Josh when he thinks of him. Sitting at dusk on a bench facing the backs of all those houses, their rear walls and rooms more window than brick, the ponds, the trees, the willows, the Heath. He imagines Josh sitting there after a day's work, his arms tired and cut, perhaps sipping on a coffee, watching as those windows light up in the evening. Watching, as in a few of them, his wife and then maybe his daughter appear and disappear, going about their lives, inhabiting the place he'd once called home and which he hopes, one day, he might again.

Michael crosses the highway and enters the city at Christopher Street, passing gay and lesbian clubs, sex stores and psychics. He watches the people walking towards him, the young women, and tries to picture what Samantha might have been like when she'd been here as a student. When all her world was still possible, and only just beginning.

Michael has never heard from Samantha. He knows this is for the best—that the note he left must have provoked the hurt and annoyance he'd intended. He'd wanted his leaving to be complete. It was, in a way, his final offering to her. Which is why, telling his agent he wanted to work on it some more, he'd withdrawn *The Man Who Broke the Mirror* from publication. And why he'd taken up a teaching job here in New York rather than embark on any more books. So that Samantha and Rachel wouldn't ever have to see his name again in a shop window or in a magazine. But even though Michael knew this was how it had to be, for several months after he'd moved back to New York he'd still often found himself scrolling to Samantha's number, or hovering his cursor above her email. For a long time he hadn't been sure why he did this. Any contact from him would only be painful for her and he had, after all, made a promise to Josh. But then, as the months passed, he'd come to understand.

It was because he'd never told her the truth. He'd never let the true story of what had happened in her house, to her daughter, exist in the world, and in not doing so it had remained unfinished within him. It was like Caroline had told him back in Coed y Bryn—an untold story, it was like landfill, unseen but still there, seeping into the soil. Which is why, six months ago, Michael decided to find a way he might keep his promise to Josh, but still also release those true minutes and finally tell the true story.

All he had to do, he'd realised, was what he'd always done best, and turn the authorial technique he'd practiced throughout his adult life upon himself. Rediscover the alchemy of experience formed into words and disappear himself from the page again, although this time in a different way to how he'd ever done so before. Not by removing himself from the story, but by putting himself into it. If he forced himself to do this, every day and every night, then eventually, regardless of whether what he wrote would ever be seen, it would at least be over.

——

Michael leant back in his chair and looked at his screen, its white page printed with the black of all he'd done, all he'd remembered. Reaching forward he scrolled back to the first page of the document, centred the cursor, and wrote a dedication:

For Samantha

Which it was, even if she'd never see it. Although of course he knew it was for himself too. And for Caroline, perhaps, who'd always, regardless of the consequences, so badly needed a story to be told— and who'd also have understood why he'd had to tell it like this. Not with just the facts, as she'd quoted to him in the Frontline on that first night they'd met, but with everything else, too.

Whether it would be enough, Michael would know only in time. He'd once told Samantha a story didn't need a reader to be complete. But now, as he printed off the pages he'd just written and added them to the pile beside his desk, he was no longer so sure. Perhaps Samantha had been right and this would only be a temporary solution. Perhaps one day he would, after all, have to follow the example of the man who'd killed his wife, and slip these printed pages into an envelope addressed to the house where this had all begun: *32 South Hill Drive, Hampstead, London, NW3 6JP.* But until that happened, if it ever did, then this pile of pages beside his desk would have to suffice. At least in them Michael had finally told their story. He'd offered what he could. He had brought it into the world. As a confession, yes, but also as an attempt to bring it to a close for all of them—for Samantha, Caroline, even Josh. To bring it to a close, their truths told, with this last sentence, these last words, and this full stop.

ACKNOWLEDGEMENTS

This novel is written in memory of Deborah Rogers, literary agent and exuberant champion of readers and reading.

Several books were particularly helpful in my research, including *Drone Warfare* by Medea Benjamin and Barbara Ehrenreich, *Wired for War* by P. W. Singer, *Mirroring People* by Marco Iacoboni, and *The Hunters* by James Salter. NBC's interview with Brandon Bryant was an invaluable insight into the life of a UAV operator.

I am grateful to Alan Little, Derek Gregory, and Giles Hannah for sharing their specialist knowledge, and to the staff and administrators of the London Library, Burgh House and Hampstead Museum, Fenton House and 2 Willow Road. I would also like to thank the following institutions and individuals for providing me with space, time or both to write this novel: The Dorothy and Lewis B. Cullman Center for Scholars and Writers at the New York Public Library, the University of Falmouth, the Pavilion café in Victoria Park, David Harrower, and Francesca Simon.

My thanks and gratitude to my editor Sarah Savitt and all at Faber & Faber, to my agent Zoe Waldie for her unfailing guidance and support, and to Nan Talese for her graceful faith and patience.

Lastly, and firstly, thank you and more to Katherine and Anwyn, for making sense of it all.